BOLD ENCOUNTER

Bold
Encounter

A Novel Based on the Life of
ST. JOHN OF THE CROSS

FATHER PETER-THOMAS ROHRBACH, O.C.D.

THE BRUCE PUBLISHING COMPANY
MILWAUKEE

IMPRIMI POTEST:

    FATHER DENIS READ, O.C.D.

NIHIL OBSTAT:

    FATHER ALBERT BOURKE, O.C.D.
    Provincial

NIHIL OBSTAT:

    JOHN F. MURPHY, S.T.D.
    Censor librorum

IMPRIMATUR:

    ✠ WILLIAM E. COUSINS
    Archbishop of Milwaukee
    July 31, 1959

J
ROb
fix

Library of Congress Catalog Card Number: 60–8292

© 1960 THE BRUCE PUBLISHING COMPANY
MADE IN THE UNITED STATES OF AMERICA

*Dedicated, with appreciation and
respect, to my confreres in the
Carmelite Monastery, Washington, D.C.*

$\cdot\Big[$ Contents $\Big]\cdot$

PROLOGUE

BOLD ENCOUNTER

$\left[\text{ Prologue }\right]$

(Incident at Medina del Campo, Spain: July 28, 1563)

THE young Spaniard in the faded green shirt strode rapidly up the walk and, glancing along the length of the stucco-walled Carmelite monastery, tugged resolutely at the bronze knocker hanging on the door. He stood there, waiting somewhat apprehensively, gazing intently at the stolid door, as if trying to pierce it with his eyes, to ascertain visibly what reaction his knock had caused within. Then suddenly, with a sharp pang of dismay, he realized that his knock had produced no reaction at all, that no one had apparently heard it; and this increased his nervousness.

John Yepez, standing before the formidable oaken door, wiped away some of the perspiration that had formed upon his broad forehead. It was warm, that summer of 1563 in Medina del Campo. John pursed his lips grimly; surely someone would be at home. After all, the superior of the monastery, Father Ildefonse, had asked him in his note to meet him here this very Friday after the daily siesta period. The young man turned and looked quickly down the cobbled street: the afternoon siesta period was over; the shops were open, their owners standing outside, vociferously inviting potential customers to enter; the townspeople were moving slowly over the rough Castilian streets once again. Yes, this was to be the hour of their meeting.

John lifted the knocker again and let it slam noisily against the massive door. He nervously fingered the prior's note, which protruded from the pocket of his patched brown trousers, as he recalled some of the phrases etched in the small, meticulous

1

script . . . "most happy to learn of your desire to become a
Carmelite friar . . . many applicants for the Order . . . would be
pleased to have you visit me at the monastery." Yes, John thought,
this would be a vitally important interview, one upon which focused
all the hopes and the dreams of the difficult years that lay behind.

He fully realized that there was no shortage of vocations in
Spain, that religious houses were overcrowded, that the monastery
had no real need of him, but yet he would make his bid. He
would attempt to convince the prior of the intensity of his desire
to enter the Order, of his willingness to perform any task, any
occupation in the monastery, however trivial. And then came the
panic-driven thought that perhaps Father Ildefonse had invited
him there today only to inform him of the unacceptability of his
application. He tried not to think of that . . . however, what would
he do if he was refused admission to the Order? Nothing else
appealed to him, not even the excitement and the romance which
bristled through Spain in these years following Columbus' dis-
covery of a whole new world; only the monastery, with its un-
paralleled opportunity of a life for God alone, afforded him any
real attraction.

With growing anxiety and increasing dread, he grasped the
knocker for the third time and was about to let it fall when the
door jerked suddenly open, and a tall, gaunt figure in brown peered
querulously at the short intruder, who smiled back uncomfortably.

"What are you trying to do," grunted the friar, "wake the souls
of the friars out in the cemetery?" His amused smile belied the
severity of his voice.

"I'm sorry, Brother, I thought you didn't hear my knock."

"I daresay they heard it all the way to Barcelona," the brother
answered dryly. "But come in."

John stepped cautiously across the threshold into the darkened
lobby. He looked slowly around the large circular room, at the
cold, unattractive stone walls, the poorly executed sacred pictures,
the few uninviting wooden chairs which stood awkwardly on the
uneven stone floor.

"Now what can I do for our impetuous young visitor?" the brother asked pleasantly, closing the door firmly behind John.

"Father Ildefonse asked me to visit him here this afternoon. He sent me this note." John took the stiff parchment out of his pocket and flashed it significantly at the tall man in the billowing, ankle-length brown robe.

The brother cast an indifferent glance at the paper, then looked back into John's face. "All right, my friend, I'll get him for you. That is, if you promise not to break down any more doors."

John laughed. "I promise: no more broken doors."

"Good! At least you're not incorrigible. . . . Have a seat in that first office there, and the prior will be down in a minute."

John went into the small office, and sat down on one of the two taut chairs. Then he bowed his head, and began to pray in a soft, audible voice:

"Mother of God, please let me become a friar in this Order dedicated to you. You've always been so good to me; please don't fail me now —"

"So, we're getting applicants for the Order now who talk to themselves," a voice said from the doorway.

John looked up and saw a stocky, middle-aged friar smiling down at him. The friar laughed and moved toward the vacant chair as John jumped quickly to his feet.

A crimson flush swelled up over John's face and neck. "No, Father, I was just praying to the Blessed Virgin, asking her to allow me to join your Order."

"Well, that's a good start: at least we know that you pray. . . . So, you're John Yepez."

"Yes Father."

"And I'm Father Ildefonse, the prior."

Father Ildefonse studied the young man who sat opposite him in the narrow monastic office. He saw an almost dwarflike little man of not more than twenty or twenty-one — perhaps slightly over five feet — with large brownish eyes set in an oval face. The boy's head, he thought, reminded him of an inverted triangle. The en-

gaging feature, though, of this little man was his eyes, soft understanding eyes, but eyes which burned with a fierce determination
of purpose.

As the prior of the monastery continued to scrutinize his visitor,
John groaned within himself. I'm through, he thought, they'll never
accept a midget like me in the Order. Why should they? There's
no urgent need of any more candidates. Didn't someone tell him
recently that almost one fourth of Spain's population lived in
monasteries or convents? What would this overstaffed institution
want with him? His immediate impulse was to bolt for the door
and rush off down the winding Camino de Santa Ana; instead, he
breathed deeply, and braced himself for the barrage of questions
the prior was sure to hurl at him.

The prior — a ruddy-faced man with a smile that played at the
corners of his mouth — shifted his weight on the stiff chair and
spoke softly:

"You want to become a Carmelite friar, John. I presume that
you know something about our life and what we do. We don't
want our new candidates taking a step in the dark when they
enter the Order."

John wet his lips. "I think, Father, that I have an understanding
of the Carmelite life . . . and I'd like to enter the Order."

"That's fine. But before I can arrive at any decision on this,
I'd like to know a little more about you. I've been in contact with
Father Boniface at the *Collegio* — incidentally, he's very impressed
with your scholastic ability — and I've picked up some references
from people who work with you at the hospital; beyond this,
though, I know precious little about you, your family, and your
background. Suppose you sketch in the rest of the picture for me."

John proceeded to give a full résumé of his background, beginning with his birth in Fontiveros, twenty-one years before. He explained that his father, Gonzales Yepez, had been a weaver by
trade, who married Catalina Alvarez, having three children by her.
Unfortunately, both father and the eldest child died in one of the
fever epidemics, leaving a widow and two small children. After

the death of her husband, Catalina supported her family by weaving rugs and blankets at home, selling them for a meager profit to local merchants.

When John was ten, the Yepez family, mother and two sons, moved north to Medina del Campo, so as to be situated on the main trade route between Valladolid and Salamanca, where they would have better opportunities for selling their woven products. In Medina, where the family fared better financially, John attended school at the *Escuela de los Ninos de Doctrina Christiana,* and later at the *Collegio de la Sociedad de Jesus;* during this time he also worked at a small, private hospital, caring for the patients and doing all the work that could be handled by a nonprofessional. His recent schedule, he explained, had been a full, exacting one: school; work at the hospital and at his mother's weaving shop.

"Yes," Father Ildefonse mused aloud, "you've really had a time of it, haven't you? Tell me, though — there's one more thing — is your mother dependent upon you for financial support?"

John smiled wryly. "She could use any extra *ducats* I might bring home, of course; but — no — I wouldn't say she's dependent upon me. The weaving shop is doing nicely now. Francis, my older brother, has learned the trade, and he's really running the business."

"Good, good," Father Ildefonse said. He sat immobile for a few moments, then as if suddenly awakening from sleep looked quickly back at John. "I think that's all I need to know about your background. . . . Now, tell me about yourself: what's your basic reason for wanting to become a Carmelite?"

John sucked in his breath uncomfortably. Was it possible to explain, to formulate in words his reason for seeking admission to the Order? Could he adequately convey to this Carmelite his desire to belong totally to God, to leave everything for Him, to dedicate his entire life to Him? . . . And what would he give as a reason for joining this Order, the Carmelites, in preference to the white-robed Dominicans, or the sandaled Franciscans, or even the Jesuits, who conducted the *Collegio?* Well, *that* could be explained. His motive for selecting the Carmelite Order revolved around one person, the Blessed Virgin; this was the Order dedicated to her, the Order to which she had given such unmistakable signs of her affection. It was almost inevitable that he, who professed such a tender devotion to the Mother of God, should choose this Order consecrated to her.

Thinking over his conversation with Father Ildefonse later, he was unable to recall the exact phrases he had used to answer the prior's question; he vaguely remembered mumbling something about wanting to live completely for God in the Order of the Blessed Virgin. But whatever his answer was, it apparently satisfied Father Ildefonse.

"And your health, John, John — how are you physically?"

"I'm certainly no Goliath — you'd only need a little bit of cloth to make a Carmelite habit for me — but what there is of me is in good shape."

The prior chuckled softly. "The physical stature of a man is of no importance, John; it's only his spiritual stature that counts."

John was feeling better now, less nervous, more relaxed: he had become somewhat confident in parrying the prior's questions. However, he was completely unprepared for the middle-aged friar's next interrogation.

Father Ildefonse's eyes twinkled slightly as he gazed impishly over John's head. "Don't you think, John, that someday you might like to marry one of the pretty señoritas of Medina?"

"Why, no, Father, I want to serve God," John gasped.

"But you can serve God with a wife, you know."

John grimaced, feeling that the prior was toying with him. "I know that married people can serve God. . . . I mean that they *must* serve God."

The prior laughed outright; he was enjoying John's confusion.

"But, Father," John continued plaintively, "didn't St. Paul say than an unmarried person can serve God better because he has only God to think about?"

Father Ildefonse stretched out his legs, and then drew them

back again. "That's right, John: St. Paul advises virginity as a
state of life because it gives a man more freedom to love Christ
and work for Him. And if that weren't enough, we'd be happy to
choose celibacy just to imitate the unwed Christ. Right?"

"Yes," John grunted.

"However," the prior said gravely, abandoning his frolicsome
mood of a few moments ago, "do you feel that *you* can live a
celibate life?"

John returned the prior's steady gaze, saying with the utmost
sincerity he could muster:

"Yes, I know I can."

Father Ildefonse kept his eyes fastened on John, slowly nodding
his head. Then he broke the somber spell, scraping his chair
shrilly along the stone floor while he pulled himself to his feet.
"I guess we're finished then with the inquisition of John Yepez.
You're going to be all right, I think. . . . When do you want to
come live with us?"

He *was* accepted, he *was* going to enter the monastery, John
thought. He felt as if a whole new world were opening for him.
He looked gratefully at the prior.

"I'd like to enter as soon as possible," he said. "Would next
Monday be all right?"

"Indeed it would," the prior said, smiling.

"I'll be here first thing Monday morning then."

"Fine! I'll tell our brother tailor to prepare some cloth for a
new novice's habit — not too much cloth, though."

John laughed amiably as they walked out through the corridor
toward the main door. "But please, Father, pray for me that I
may do well in the Order."

The prior pulled open the door, then turned to the small man
beside him. "I began to pray for you, John, when I first learned
of your interest in the Order. I know now that my prayers were
for a good cause — you'll do well as a Carmelite."

"I hope so," John said brightly, as he shook the prior's hand.

The prior stood at the open door, watching the small figure

walk rapidly down the gravel path, his eyes squinted in a curious, reflective gaze. "I'm going to keep my eyes on you, John Yepez," he whispered softly to himself, "and I have an odd feeling that some day the whole of Spain may have its eyes on you."

PART I

The Land of Carmel

⌠ Chapter 1 ⌡

THE bell in the tower tolled languidly, sending its rich tones down into the Carmelite church at Medina del Campo.

Inside the narrow structure, a short friar knelt alone on the polished stone floor of the sanctuary.

The congregation hushed and grew quiet. They all had their eyes fastened on the tiny figure in the brown and white robes of the Carmelite habit; all of them — Spanish gentlemen in their ruffled collars and pleated short trousers; ladies in their lace *mantillas* and sweeping gowns; visiting clergy in black and brown robes; and hundreds of the ordinary Medina citizens. They watched, fascinated and awed.

John Yepez — known for the past year as Brother John — rose from his kneeling position, stepped quickly to the bottom of the altar, and began to mount its marble steps. He dropped to his knees before the prior, Father Ildefonse, who was seated on a stiff chair arranged on the predella. John placed his thin hands into the great, bony hands of the priest, and in a firm voice recited the formula of his perpetual profession in the Carmelite Order:

"*Ego, frater Joannes, promitto Deo, Virginique . . .*"

In melodic Latin phrases, he promised God that he would serve Him faithfully under the three solemn vows of poverty, chastity, and obedience. As the result of this simple ceremony, he would be irrevocably bound to those three radical promises: the vow of poverty would destroy his right to possess material property; chastity would forbid him the human satisfactions of wife or family; and obedience would place his life, his work, and his talents under the direct supervision of his religious superiors. It was a mad, adventuresome series of promises, but he had thought it out

11

carefully during his year and a half in the monastery. After all, what better thing could a man do with his life than offer it back, completely and unreservedly, to God?

There were some people, John supposed, who must think life in a monastery was utterly insane — especially today, in sixteenth-century Spain. This was the age of Spain's greatest glory, the age in which the sun never set on the Spanish empire, and surely every young Spaniard would want to be part of it. And as a layman, what prosperity he could have looked forward to, despite his earlier hardships! Cortez had conquered the Aztecs in Mexico, and the loot of gold and jewels that was pouring back into Spain was fantastic; Pizarro had occupied Peru, and Spanish colonists were sending home more than a hundred thousand pounds of silver a year. The Spain of Philip II — rich in faith, rich in resources, rich in power — was the country to live in during the sixteenth century. And yet John was, for all practical purposes, withdrawing from it by the three vows he was now taking. But the loss of all these things didn't bother him. His only thought was of what he would be gaining: the friendship of Christ, and a life of complete dedication to Him.

John came to the end of his profession formula, and then descended the steps, returning to his position in the middle of the sanctuary. He lowered himself gently to the floor, stretching his body out lengthwise on the cold stones. He lay prostrate, motionless, as the huge reed organ in the rear of the church thundered out the first few notes of the ancient profession hymn, *Te Deum*.

Father Ildefonse, intoning the hymn, selected a note quite at variance with that offered by the organist, and in his tremulous voice sang out the opening words. The organist, now long accustomed to Father Ildefonse's discordant singing, struck the keys of the organ fiercely as if in a musical rebuke to the prior. The Carmelite friars, who lined the sides of the sanctuary, joined in the hymn, letting their throaty voices rise and fall over the simple Latin words.

John remained prostrate on the floor, his forehead pressed into the hard stones, while the music ebbed gently over him. It seemed incredible, he thought, that he had been in the monastery for over eighteen months, that he was now making his final profession. His mind flashed back over the events that had transpired since his admission to the monastery. He reviewed them rapidly, placing them in orderly fashion, one beside the other. . . .

His new life had been, from the very beginning, an absorbing one, absolutely precluding any reminiscences about the past, or — what would have been even worse — any pangs of homesickness. It was a new world of brown robes, hushed voices, rattling rosary beads, incessant processions, interminable community acts, and — above all — bells, bells, and more bells. There was a bell to prod the friars out of bed in the morning, a bell to move them into chapel, a bell to move them out — there was a bell for every conceivable monastic activity. The harsh metallic clanging at first annoyed John, but he soon came to accept it as a practical necessity for monastic efficiency.

And the incessant activity! John had imagined that a monastery was an oasis of silence where the friars hid themselves away in their rooms, meeting only for prayers and meals. But no! — the friars were in continual motion throughout the corridors all day long. They shuffled from classroom to choir, to instruction period, to — well, almost anything. It was a new world, indeed; but it was a new world vitally alive with cheerful, spirited men of God.

John was given a room on the top floor of the monastery and told that a friar's room is euphemistically called a "cell." He liked his cell — a strange word which caused the new men to smile — a small room containing a bed, a desk, a stool, a washbasin, and a bookrack.

A short while after his entrance into the monastery, John had been invested with the brown Carmelite habit, a garment of voluminous folds and many parts. Each morning he had to work his way through the intricate procedure of dressing himself in the complicated garment. As a basic piece of clothing, he wore the *mutandi,* the white woolen undergarment composed of a shirt-like section, with long sleeves, and tight-fitting breeches, reaching down to the knees. Over this he placed a long brown tunic, and then the thin scapular, and finally the cowl. Sometimes John had to add the sweeping white choir cape, a garment worn by the friars on more formal occasions.

He discovered a confusion at first in investing himself each morning, and it was some time before he obtained any dexterity in handling the monastic garments. He noted, with some amusement, that the newer men in the community invariably made a later appearance in the chapel each morning than their older companions. The neophytes had to lay out each piece of the habit carefully, study its position, and lift it hesitatingly over their shoulders; the veterans, however, could throw on each piece with a facility that was almost irreverent.

As a novice, John lived in the secluded corridor occupied by those newcomers in the religious life. In the novitiate section, he was under the immediate jurisdiction of the novice master, Father George, a middle-aged friar, with a drawn ascetic face. Father George was a quiet, soft-spoken man, who kept his eyes continually half closed; only on rare occasions did he permit himself the gratification of a full sweeping look at his surroundings — but during those rare occasions, he saw everything, or at least so the novices thought.

John liked his novice master, finding in him an adept student of the spiritual life, a sometimes stern disciplinarian, but an always warm friend. There was only one condition for success in Father George's novitiate: rigid obedience of the rules. If a novice conformed completely to the rules of the Order and Father George's directions, he could expect no difficulties from the man, but if a novice began to cut corners here or there, he would find that the kindly novice master could become a very thorough disciplinarian. John had no such problem.

John's fellow novices constituted a composite group of all sizes, shapes, backgrounds, and — most important — temperaments. He was fond of them all, collectively and individually, but, although he knew that the masters of the spiritual life demanded an equal affection for all members of the community, he could not help being especially fond of Brother Peter, a robust, handsome friar, whose family name was Orozco. Peter Orozco was the son of a wealthy *hidalgo*, the owner of a vast cattle ranch on the outskirts of Medina, who had lamented his son's passing up the opportunity of inheriting the opulent estate. If Señor Orozco was displeased at Peter's entrance into the Order, even more displeased — John learned from some of the other novices — were a considerable number of young ladies who had fallen under the spell of the handsome ranch owner's son with the flashing eyes and dancing feet.

Peter, when asked one day why he had abandoned so favorable a career in the world, responded truculently:

"Because I wanted to!"

Brother Peter had a penchant, John was forced to admit, for embroiling himself in a constant series of skirmishes with the novice master. Peter was a carefree young man who lived above precision and detail; as far as he was concerned, the only requisite for sanctity was largess of heart — all the rest was pettiness. Unfortunately, the novice master took a rather dim view of Peter's philosophy and spent considerable effort attempting to remind the novice of the many details contained in the Carmelite life. But John liked the loud, dashing friar — and he felt that, deep in his soul, Father George liked him, too.

Peter was a constant jester, but he found in John a ready, if sometimes, subtle match for his wit.

"Brother John," he said drily one day, "if you don't get some more height the Bishop will refuse to ordain you — you'll be so small that he won't be able to reach down to place his hands on your head."

John feigned a pose of mock perplexity, then answered:

"If it comes to that, I'll just have to be ordained riding on your shoulders."

During the year John spent in the novitiate, there was a constant shifting of population because new men were being admitted and older men, after making their profession, were advancing on. However, John remembered three friars who left, but did not make their profession: they returned home. One of the friars was a pensive, frowning youngster who seemed to be on the constant verge of tears; it caused no surprise in the novitiate when his departure was announced.

The second departure caused more of a stir, for the boy was an earnest, likable friar, who had appeared, to John at least, as a well-adjusted religious. Peter's comment on the affair was indicative of the general mood in the novitiate.

"You just never know" he said laconically.

The third departure was cloaked in more mysterious circumstances. The novice in question — a listless boy who hid behind an immobile façade of a face — was an enigma to John, a friar no one ever seemed really to know. The irrepressible Peter appeared furtively at the entrance to John's cell one day, whispering:

"The Fathers have just had a meeting, and they voted to send our friend home."

Peter never revealed the source of his information, and as much as John pressured him, he remained adamant in his secrecy. However, Peter's whispered information proved to be perfectly correct, and the listless friar was seen shortly afterward rapidly pushing his belongings together with more energy than he had shown in all his time in the novitiate.

It was only last month that John's own time arrived, and he, himself, was being considered by the Fathers for religious profession. He had no real fear that the Fathers would expel him or postpone his profession; nevertheless, he was definitely relieved when he was informed of his acceptability by Father George. He had been summoned to the novice master's cell and stood there awkwardly, while the novice master spoke rapidly to him:

"I want you to prepare yourself for the three vows which you will make on the first of May. This is something you do only once in your life; so do it well. Bring the greatest amount of generosity to your vows, hold nothing back. Do you understand?"

"Yes, Father."

"Now, after your profession, we've decided to send you to our monastery in Salamanca, where you'll attend the university. Classes don't begin for you until the fall, so you'll have a few months here in which you can review your Latin grammar."

A dark frown passed over John's face. "That means you want me to begin studies for the . . . priesthood?"

Father George looked at him exasperated, as if John had heard nothing he had said to him. "Naturally," he said icily.

John studied the tops of his leather shoes. "I hadn't planned to study for the priesthood in the Order. I just wanted to be a Carmelite. I think, Father, if you don't mind, I'd prefer to remain a brother in the Order."

"And why, pray tell?"

"Because I feel that I could serve God better in the hidden, prayerful life of a Carmelite brother."

"Nonsense!" the novice master said peevishly, "you've got all the necessary qualities for the priesthood: virtue, intelligence, health, personality. It would be sinful to refuse ordination."

John shook his head slowly. "I appreciate your confidence in me; but I still feel that I could serve Christ better as a brother."

Father George scratched the side of his thin face, and his tone became more conciliatory. "You want to render obedience to your superiors in the Order, don't you?"

"Of course, Father."

"Well, it is the express wish of your superiors that you study for the priesthood," Father George said triumphantly.

John nodded his head slowly three or four times. "If that's what my superiors want, then all right. I'll accept it as the will of God."

"It *is* the will of God. He wants you to be a priest . . . and a good one, too."

Lying on the floor as the hymn continued, John marshaled all these thoughts in his mind: his introduction into the novitiate, his new friendship with Peter, the command to study for the priesthood. They made a pleasant prelude to this epochal moment of his life, his final profession. And then, deftly, but surely, he pushed these thoughts out of his mind, concentrating on the joy of the present moment. The past lay irrevocably behind him; he had no connection with it any more. It was not, to be sure, a purple past, one speckled with sin, but it was, he reasoned, one that was less holy, less perfect than the road that lay before him.

John fastened his attention to the Christ in the tabernacle before him and renewed the oblation he had pronounced just a few minutes before. He spoke directly to Christ, simply and earnestly. This was, perhaps, the most significant thing that had happened to him since entering the monastery: his new conviction of the nearness of God. Christ had suddenly become vividly alive to him, a real person he could know and love and serve. In the past, so much of his praying was lip service to a distant, obscure God, but in the Order, he had learned to treat Christ as an intimate friend.

His request to remain a brother had been a sincere one, prompted by a firm conviction that he could better serve God as a humble religious in a monastery, rather than as a priest administering sacraments or preaching. After all, he had reasoned, were not more souls saved by prayer and by penance, than by all the preaching or pulpit-thumping in the world? Furthermore, it was his implacable belief that the sacrifice entailed in selecting the hidden, often misunderstood life of a brother in preference to the more glamorous career of the priesthood would, in itself, be eminently pleasing to God. He had thought it all out carefully, turning the matter over and over in his mind, and had come to what he felt was the proper decision, the one God wished him to choose. But the novice master had changed all that in a matter of minutes. Father George had said it was the will of God that he be a priest, and as far as John was concerned, that settled the issue. This, however, was not an unpleasant decision for John to accept: he was strongly attracted to the priesthood, and to the fantastic amount of good he could accomplish as an anointed minister of Christ. His diffidence in accepting the priesthood had been in the nature of a personal sacrifice, a denial of something to which he felt himself drawn. He would be a priest, then; but only because it was the will of God — and of that he was now certain.

With a thundering crescendo, the organ pounded through the final verse of the hymn, dragging the monks' voices to their maximum volume; and then, in a crash of music, drowning out their exhausted "Amen."

John, still lying prostrate on the sanctuary floor, felt a soft tap on his shoulder. He drew himself to his feet, made some futile attempts to rearrange his habit, and marched resolutely over to the choir stall, where he resumed his usual place in the line of friars.

Father Ildefonse, surveying the scene from his position on the predella, followed John with his eyes until the newly professed Carmelite had settled himself in the ranks of the brown-and-white-robed friars. Then he snapped his fingers softly. Immediately, as if goaded by invisible spurs, the friars began to file rapidly out of the stalls, reciting a psalm in muffled, almost inaudible voices, while they walked in procession. Father Ildefonse watched the uneven procession as it moved out through the sacristy door, and then attached himself to the end of the straggling line; his was the last brown and white figure to be seen by the congregation.

The sanctuary was empty; the ceremony was at an end.

⌈ Chapter 2 ⌉

JOHN usually experienced no formidable difficulty in keeping his attention on the subject matter of the lectures at the University of Salamanca, but today he found his mind playing truant, his thoughts diverted from the lessons he should be learning. Perhaps it was due to the stifling heat in the crowded lecture hall on this first really warm day in early May; or perhaps Father Navarro, the swarthy Dominican priest on the lecture platform, was even more uninspired than usual; at any rate, John was totally unable to follow the careful logic of the professor as he droned out the Latin words of the scholastic philosophy he was teaching. Only a few moments of classroom time remained, and John decided to admit defeat by devoting the concluding minutes of the lecture to a survey of his notes piled neatly on the small wooden desk at which he was seated.

His notes themselves were written testimony of the fact that this particular class had been wasted time for him: the Latin sentences scratched in the careless script of a student contained no continuity or plan; they were mere snatches of statements wrenched uselessly from the lecture.

In all honesty, John could console himself that during his year at the university, he had not squandered many classes as he was doing now; he had been able to follow the lectures reasonably well, copying down in his notes the general outline of the matter presented by the professors. In the evenings, back at the Carmelite monastery outside the walls of Salamanca, he had studied his notes, revising them when necessary, and at times checking them against the thick tomes of philosophy in the monastic library. He had done well, he thought, in his studies, and lapses such as the present one were excusable for any young student who attended so many lectures at the university each week.

The lecture on ontology, to which he was now unsuccessfully listening, was a particularly difficult one to follow; it was entitled, euphemistically, "the Vesper lecture," because of the fact that it was the final lecture of the day delivered late in the afternoon. When John and his fellow students had finally shuffled into the hall to attend the Vesper lecture each afternoon, they had already endured a rather long, tiring day. They had risen early in the morning, spent almost an hour in choir chanting the Office and praying, bolted down a quick breakfast, hiked through the city to the university, attended the morning lectures, returned home for lunch and siesta, and walked back to the university for the Vesper lecture. No wonder that a number of heads nodded during the final lecture of the university day.

John glanced up from his scrambled notes and noticed that Father Navarro was now closing his book, the unmistakable sign that the lecture was almost completed. Accordingly, John pushed his notes into a small pile, produced a short length of brown cord from the pocket of his habit, and proceeded to tie his jottings into a tight roll. Father Navarro scraped his chair behind the desk on the lecture platform while uttering his invariable closing phrase:

"*Sufficit hodie.*"

The silence of the hall which previously had been violated only by the drone of Father Navarro's voice was instantly shattered by the pleasant sound of sixty young clerics breaking out in conversation after their period of enforced silence.

Peter, who was seated on John's right, shook his head sleepily and said:

"Brilliant lecture, eh? That man actually retards education; he's a menace to intellectual development."

"I'll grant you," John said amusedly, "that he's not the most stimulating lecturer at the university."

"The understatement of the day! Come on, let's leave so I can get the taste of Father Navarro and his ontology out of my mouth."

"Judging from your remarks, I wouldn't say that you'd taken a very big taste."

"All right, you win; let's go."

The lecture hall was rapidly emptied, the students pushing and heaving their way through the slim door of the classroom out into the corridor, and finally into the spacious quadrangle of the university.

The wide quadrangle, paved with broad stones polished smooth by the thousands of students who treaded over them each year, was enclosed on three sides by the university building itself; the fourth side was open, leading into the Calle de Collegio, which ran north, farther into the city, and south out to the city wall beyond which the Carmelite monastery of St. Andrew lay. In the middle of the great square stood a squat, weather-chastened stone fountain surmounted by a statue of St. Michael, the Archangel, brandishing his sword against some unseen enemy.

The students, now free of the oppressive atmosphere of the lecture hall, milled around the quadrangle and then slowly began to assemble in small groups all over the wide surface of the university square; these tiny knots of students were forming to participate in a traditional custom of university life: the postlecture discussion. The groups were of varying sizes, depending upon the popularity of the particular professor who formed the nucleus of each gathering of students.

These informal, and often unpredictable, discussions were of a practical necessity in student life, since questions from the floor during the course of the formal lectures were absolutely forbidden; thus, the postlecture discussion was the sole opportunity afforded the student for proposing questions, or even objections, to the professors.

John and Peter were among the last to emerge through the ornate metal door of the university; they strode leisurely out into the square, surveying the eighteen or twenty groups which were already engaged in discussion.

"Do you have any preference as to which one of these brilliant men you want to hear today?" Peter said sarcastically.

"Let's listen to Father Navarro," John said mischievously, his brown eyes set in a bland stare.

"Ugh," Peter groaned. "I'd rather listen to the statue of St. Michael." He gestured indifferently at the stone statue.

"If you don't have any objections, though," John said, "I really would like to hear Father Gomez."

"Fine," Peter said enthusiastically.

Father Simon Gomez, the mentor of the largest discussion group on the quadrangle, was the professor of Church history at the university; he prided himself on being a critical historian, never conceding any point of history until it had been logically and conclusively proved by documentation. His lectures were thoroughly enjoyed by the young students. Father Gomez' particular delight lay in attacking some of the ancient traditions of the different religious orders, whose members attended his classes; but however violent may have been his criticisms of these traditions, he was sincerely liked and appreciated by his students. This could be ascribed, doubtlessly, to the fact that the religious were convinced that his objections rose from a true sense of historical critique rather than any basic animosity toward religious orders.

Father Gomez — the typical, lean, spare scholar — was engaged in one of these very discussions as John and Peter drew near the wide circle of clerics which ebbed around him. A confused Franciscan was the uncomfortable object of Father Gomez' remarks.

"So you say, my good Franciscan friend, that Pope Honorius had a dream in which he saw a strange man holding up the walls of St. Peter's in Rome? And because of this dream he gave approbation to Francis for the foundation of your Order, although he had previously made up his mind to forbid it?"

"Yes," answered the brown-robed friar warily.

"But — here is the important point — can you prove it? Are there any documents which corroborate it?"

"Not that I know of."

"Not that you know of — or anyone else knows of! There *are* no documents, of course. It's merely a pious tradition of your Order."

Father Gomez turned his attention away from the perplexed friar, addressing himself to the group at large. "You men who belong to religious orders possess a number of revered and cherished traditions about your own organizations. Some of them are true and historical; and some of them, unfortunately, are mere fables. But please, my young scholars, don't try to pass them off as historical facts unless you can substantiate them by documentation."

He paused momentarily as his eyes fell upon John and Peter, who stood at the edge of the crowd peering in at the scene; then he smiled slyly. "Here's another good example of what I mean. We have with us today two Carmelite friars; and I'll let them demonstrate to you, by their own words, a shoddy bit of religious history." He stretched out his arm in a beckoning gesture. "Would you, my good Carmelite friends, have the kindness — and the humility — to step in here and answer some of my questions about your Order?"

John looked intently at the historian. "Certainly, I'll be delighted to answer your questions."

As the crowd parted to allow the two men to advance closer to Father Gomez, Peter whispered frantically to John:

"Don't do it; he's too clever for you!"

John, pretending not to hear his confrere worked his way through the crowd, while Peter followed skeptically behind.

"This is very good of you, Brother . . . eh, what is your name?"

"Brother John."

"Ah, Brother John," Father Gomez announced with aplomb. "Tell us then, Brother John: who is the founder of your magnificent Order?"

"St. Elias."

"St. Elias, the prophet of the Old Testament?" Father Gomez asked in mock surprise, arching his eyebrows.

"Yes, that's right."

"The prophet who lived nine centuries before Christ?"

"Yes."

Father Gomez smiled triumphantly. "You've just heard this bright young man state one of the venerable traditions of the Carmelite Order: that Elias, the Old Testament prophet, is the founder of their organization." He turned to John again. "But now, Brother John, can you offer any proof, any documentary evidence for that contention?"

John started to respond, but Father Gomez cut him off sharply.

"Excuse me a minute, Brother. I know that the Old Testament — the Book of Kings, to be exact — mentions that a group of Jewish hermits gathered in the caves on Mount Carmel about the time of Elias. But this, of course, is not historical proof that Elias founded the religious order whose habit you now wear. I just mention this to warn you of the historical invalidity of that argument which your men sometimes employ."

John nodded his head as though in agreement to the terms of combat.

Father Gomez stretched out his arms to their full length in a dramatic gesture. "Now, Brother, tell us if you can offer any acceptable proof that Elias is the founder of the Carmelite Order."

"I think I can offer excellent proof, Father." The calm poise of his voice was in definite contrast to the excited phrases of the priest.

"Well, let's hear your proof then," Gomez said.

"You see," John said. "the Scriptures give us a clear description of the eremitical life led by Elias on Mount Carmel — and no one, of course, can dispute the historicity of the Scriptures. Now, our argument is this: there have been hermits dwelling on Mount Carmel — and now here in Europe — from the time of Elias down to our own days; and they have imitated and perpetuated the form of life inaugurated by Elias."

Gomez raised a finger in objection, but John pursued his argument, permitting the scholar no opportunity for interruption. "But let's prescind from all that. Let's suppose that we have no historical proof of the existence of the Carmelites before . . . let's say, five years ago. Even then we would still maintain — and rightly so — that

Elias is the founder of this Order which began just five years ago."

"Why?" Gomez asked, puzzled.

"Because these men would be following the same type of life as did Elias. He would be their model, their inspiration, and — if you will allow me to use the word — their founder. These new Carmelites would not, of course, be able to claim Elias as their physical founder, one who sat down and composed a set of rules and instructions for them to follow; but they could maintain that Elias was their *moral* founder, that he gave them a pattern of life to follow. And in the foundation of a religious order, the moral founder is definitely more important than a physical founder."

John looked directly at Gomez, who appeared rather stunned by his calm, incisive logic, and then lowered his eyes to the pavement. The group turned to Gomez for some rebuttal.

Father Gomez sighed heavily. "That's good clear thinking, Brother. I must admit, in all fairness, that you've demonstrated your point. . . . I've been lecturing at Salamanca for eighteen years, and you're the first cleric ever to give a rational answer to my objections. Brother, I salute you!" He smiled pleasantly at John. "Having been confuted by the logic of my young Carmelite, I think I'll terminate this discussion right here."

The large circle of clerics listening to the debate between the young friar and the now vanquished historian immediately splintered into small groups which proceeded to shuffle away toward the Calle de Collegio. Peter drew alongside John, and together they walked slowly across the quadrangle, their black shoes clicking sharply against the paved stones.

"I thought old Gomez had you when he started baiting you with questions," Peter said, still astonished at John's victory. "Where did you pick up that business about a 'moral founder'?"

John shrugged his shoulders. "I don't know — I guess I read it someplace."

"Well, it sure did the trick, anyway. Did you see the expression on Gomez' face when you started giving him your stuff? It was magnificent: he looked like he'd just been kicked by a donkey. . . .

But, say, Gomez was right: you did handle yourself smartly. I liked the way you answered him so calmly, without losing your temper."

"But that's the only way to argue anything out, Peter; if you lose your temper, you can't do any thinking."

Peter shook his head gently from side to side. "That's the only way *you* can argue. If I'd been arguing with Gomez, I'm afraid I'd have wound up by calling him a cynical jackass."

John laughed. "Ah, well, star differeth from star."

Striding with his confrere along the winding Calle de Collegio, John analyzed the emotions that had oddly spawned themselves within him during the debate with Gomez; he found that they were, for him, novel emotions, ones that he had not previously experienced.

His discussion with Gomez had been in the nature of an encounter, a battle; and, while he had neither desired nor sought the conflict, he had responded to the challenge hurled at him with an excitement and a thrill that charged recklessly through his body.

The pungent smell of battle, of encounter had beset him; and he discovered, to his own surprise, that he enjoyed it. . . .

⌠ Chapter 3 ⌡

THE following day, Thursday, was the feast of the Ascension, and classes at the university were suspended. John, therefore, was not obliged to make the rapid double hike to the university to attend morning and afternoon sessions; for him, as well as for the other Carmelite students, it meant a day at home in the monastery of St. Andrew.

John rather liked the monastery of St. Andrew, although it was vastly different from the monastery at Medina where he had spent his novitiate year: the building at Medina was a spacious structure, containing what seemed to be endless miles of corridors, while St. Andrew's was a compact, efficient little dwelling, constructed solely to house the young men who attended the university. John felt, though, that the smaller building encompassed a warmth and atmosphere that was lacking in the rather somber institution at Medina.

However, despite his predilection for the house, he had precious little time to spend in it, or so it seemed to him; it was almost as if the university were his home, and the monastery a place where he studied and slept. Therefore, John appreciated the feast days on which he could spend extra time in the chapel, or visit the library, or — what especially appealed to him — visit the subprior of the monastery for an informal chat.

The subprior was technically charged with the instruction, direction, and guidance of the students preparing for the priesthood; it was to him that the young men reported, and from him they received their permissions to do anything not covered by the general rules of the Order. The present subprior at St. Andrew's was Father Alphonse.

On that Ascension Thursday in 1565, John knocked on the door of the subprior's cell. A clipped, precise voice invited him in and bade him sit on the small stool, which the young Carmelites occupied during these interviews with their subprior.

Father Alphonse had been reading, and he still held the book open in his lap, waiting to discern whether the visit would be a short one, or if he would be compelled to close the book in order to devote some time to his visitor.

John cleared his throat.

"I have something I'd like to talk to you about which has been bothering me a bit lately," he said.

Father Alphonse wearily closed his book and placed it on a table beside his chair. "What's on your mind, Brother John?"

"Father, I've been doing some reading about the history of our Order —"

"I heard about your fracas at the university yesterday with Father Gomez," interrupted the priest.

John winced in embarrassment. "Well, no, it's not so much about the ancient history of the Order that I've been concerned, but rather with the more modern period."

"Yes?"

"Specifically," John said, "I've been interested in the period since the mitigation."

Father Alphonse stirred uneasily in his chair. He had never cared much for the word "mitigation." Not only was Father Alphonse unhappy about the word itself, but he was not altogether pleased with the fact. Certainly there had been just reasons for the superiors in the fifteenth century to request a mitigation — he preferred to call it a "readjustment" — of the rule and constitutions. It had been the era of the black death in Europe, that strange plague which ravaged the continent; the Carmelites had been unable to observe the strict fasts and abstinences of the Order, and their rigid rules of cloister made it difficult for them to assist those who needed the help and consolation of priests. Vocations had decreased alarmingly, and the Order's legislation cried for some readjustment in those critical times. The Pope was readily convinced of the crisis, and accordingly permitted some modifications to be written into the Carmelite rule. Instead of abstaining entirely from meat, the Carmelites were obliged to abstain only on Wednesdays and Saturdays; the long fast of the Order, lasting from September to Easter, was radically shortened; and, most important of all, the rules of cloister and retirement were relaxed so that the friars might more expeditiously engage in work for souls. Father Alphonse was convinced that what had been done was correct; but he, nevertheless, experienced some vague displeasure when he thought of the changes made in the original rule.

"What about the period since the mitigation?" Father Alphonse asked uncomfortably.

"I know," John said, "that the mitigation was necessary two hundred years ago, and perhaps it's still necessary today — but I wonder if the mitigation is necessary for me."

"What do you mean by that?" Father Alphonse asked.

"What I mean is this: I feel that I could, and I should, in my private life attempt to follow the original Carmelite rule."

"Oh, so that's it!" Father Alphonse said.

"Yes, that's it," John said, smiling.

"I don't know about this, Brother John. How would we ever run a monastery here if some of the friars were to follow one version of the rule and others were to follow another version? It might become a bit awkward, to say the least."

"That isn't exactly what I planned, Father."

Father Alphonse smiled pleasantly. "I know it's not what you planned — I was teasing you. What did you plan, though?"

"I thought, Father, that I could observe the original rule in an unobtrusive and inconspicuous way, especially in regards to the fasting and extra prayer time."

"No one can say that's a bad thing." Father Alphonse turned his head away to gaze briefly out of the window, fastening his eyes on the gray walls of Salamanca, and then on the taller buildings and churches of the city above them. The office of a subprior in a monastery adjacent to a university was certainly never dull; he never knew what questions or permissions one of the young students might request. And here, this Brother John wanted to skip back two centuries and live like the Carmelites of old. He was amused, but, as he honestly had to admit, he was impressed, too.

"All right, Brother John, I'll give you your permission to live the original rule . . . with one restriction."

"Yes?"

"That you don't make a nuisance out of yourself."

John's face lighted up. "I'll be careful, I won't become a pest."

"You'd better not," Father Alphonse said, half seriously, "or I'll yank you right out of the primitive rule."

John laughed comfortably.

"Now, if you're going to live like a hermit, you'd better stop talking with me and get out of here."

"Thank you very much, Father," John said, as he rose to go. "You don't know how important this is to me!"

When the door had closed behind his visitor, Father Alphonse ruffled through the pages of his book to find the place where he had discontinued his reading. But when he found the place he did not begin reading immediately; instead, his thoughts lingered on John and his unusual request.

$$\left[\text{ Chapter 4 }\right]$$

THE road from Salamanca to Medina del Campo stretched resolutely for some eighteen leagues across the red, parched plain of León. It was a broad, heavily traveled road, conveying an almost endless stream of carts, wagons, ornate coaches, and foot travelers who kicked up billowing clouds of red clay dust, which swirled about oppressively in the air. The first request made by a traveler completing a journey across the plain was for a bath and change of clothing. Even the *hidalgos,* who bounced along uncomfortably in their enclosed carriages, were powerless to escape the choking dust which filtered through the cracks and openings of their wooden vehicles. Gentlemen discovered that white linen shirts and ruffled collars were quickly tinted a gritty, muddy brown; ladies were advised to wear dark gowns on the journey, and to carry extra petticoats. It was only when the thin Castilian snow blanketed the ground that the traveler was immune from the dust, but then the icy road and the glazed rocks made the journey even more unattractive.

The late summer of 1567 found two young Carmelite priests striding along that road in the direction of Medina del Campo. The travelers in the brown habits wore ludicrous wide-brimmed straw sombreros to protect themselves from the fierce sun, and in their hands they carried a bundle of clothes, neatly tied in a canvas sack. Their black shoes were covered with the red dust of the road, and perspiration glistened on their foreheads. The taller of the two priests was handsome, stocky, and marched along with effortless, giant strides; his companion was a stunted man with an oval head who seemed obliged to take twice as many steps to remain abreast of his clerical co-traveler. The taller priest gesticulated with his

32

free hand as he talked, while his associate listened attentively in an attitude of interest and sometimes suppressed amusement.

"Two nights ago," Peter chatted along, "when I sat down on my bed I had to pinch myself — I could hardly believe it."

John smiled, nodding his head slightly; Peter's present remarks required no comment from him, only his attention.

"Imagine, I thought to myself, I'm a priest; it was almost unbelievable. Even now, two days after the ordination, it still seems like a dream." They walked a few paces in silence, then Peter became aware of John's presence again. "How does it feel to have people call you 'Father'?"

"It's strange," John answered. "It takes me a moment or so to realize that I'm the one to whom they're talking."

"Yes, *Father*," Peter said, "it's strange . . . but wonderful."

"Do you think we'll be in Medina by nightfall?" John asked.

"We will if your short legs don't give out," Peter said.

John quickened his stride a bit. "The way I feel I could hike all the way to Barcelona today."

Peter raised his hand above his head in a mock salute. "Hail, the marathon champion!"

John ignored the jest, saying:

"If we get to Medina tonight, we can offer our first Masses in the morning; but if we don't make it by nightfall, we'll have to wait another whole day."

John lapsed into silence again, thinking of the satisfaction that would be his when he offered Mass by himself for the first time. Two days ago, at the ordination ceremony, he had co-offered Mass with the bishop and the other newly ordained priests. Technically, that was his first Mass, the first time he had consecrated the bread and the wine; but he had not yet held the Host in his own hands, he had not yet stood at the altar as the sole minister of the Divine Sacrifice. It had been arranged that the new priests would offer their first Masses at their home monasteries, not at the college in Salamanca; and, for John and Peter, this necessitated the long foot journey back to the monastery of St. Anne in Medina del Campo.

The anticipation of this prospect forced the two friars along the road at a pace that was imprudent in the summer sun.

"Don't you think it's time we had something to eat? Even marathon runners have to eat, you know," Peter said.

"Yes, yes; you're quite right. I'd lost track of the time." He glanced up at Peter. "What time is it, by the way?"

Peter craned his neck, turning his face up to the sky, and squinted his eyes. "It's some time around noon; the sun is in the middle of the sky."

Under the meager shade afforded by a clump of trees, Peter untied his sack, producing a small package, which contained a loaf of bread, some cheese, and a slender bottle of wine. He thrust his hand back into the bundle once again, proudly drawing out a knife and two earthenware cups.

"Shall I serve, Your Majesty?" he asked, bowing deferentially to John.

Without waiting for a reply, Peter squatted on the parched grass and began to cut the bread into thick hunks. John uncorked the wine bottle. A few minutes later they were both munching bread and cheese and sipping wine from their cups.

After their meal, the two priests resumed their march toward Medina; they had agreed to foresake the traditional midday siesta so as to lose no time in the journey; and, therefore, they hiked along in the early afternoon, on an almost deserted road. Carts and wagons had been pulled off to the side where their owners had crawled under the vehicles to escape the more torrid part of the day; under almost every group of trees men were stretched out, their straw sombreros drawn over their faces. John and Peter plodded along doggedly.

"What do you think the superiors will do with us now we're ordained?" Peter asked.

"The first thing they'll do is send us back to Salamanca for another year of study," John answered. "We haven't finished our course in theology yet, you know."

"Of course. But after the year of study — what then?"

"That's something only the superiors know, Peter. But you can be sure they'll assign us wherever they feel we'll do the most good for the Order."

"It'll be wonderful to work for souls," Peter said. "It will certainly be a different life than the one we've been leading as students."

"Yes, it will," John said, his brow knitted in a reflective frown.

The significance of John's simple statement had not escaped Peter. "How are you going to fit all this primitive rule business into an active Carmelite life?"

"I don't know."

"You do know, don't you, that it'll be almost impossible to harmonize modern Carmelite life with a private observance of the primitive rule?"

John breathed heavily. "Yes, I'm afraid that's true."

"What are you going to do about it then?"

"I must confess, I'm in a bit of a quandary about the whole thing. I've come to love the life of prayer and solitude that I've been leading the past few years, and I'd hate to give it up now." He stared straight ahead. "In fact, I've been toying with the idea of transferring to the Carthusians. . . ."

"What!" Peter exploded, coming to a complete stop. "A Carthusian? Don't be foolish. You were meant to be a Carmelite."

"I know it must sound odd. . . . I love the Order of Carmel, but I feel compelled to live this life of more intense personal union with Christ. I don't think I can do it as a Carmelite priest."

"But you'd like to work for souls, wouldn't you?"

"Yes; but not in such a way that I would be forced to give up the life of prayer."

"Well, if you transfer to the Carthusians, you'll have no apostolic work at all, and you're going to be a terrific preacher and director of souls. That's what everyone at Salamanca says."

John laughed at Peter, who was now gesticulating wildly. "I'm just toying with the idea, I said. I haven't made up my mind yet one way or the other."

"Stop toying with the idea then," Peter insisted. "You were made to be a Carmelite, and you should remain a Carmelite."

Peter strode along angrily, muttering to himself. John was amused, and then touched by his friend's insistence that he remain in the Order. But it was such a problem — more of a problem than Peter could ever imagine. It was true that John had entered the Order to dedicate his whole life to God, and the Order certainly had given him that opportunity. But there was something more that he wanted now. The contemplative life — and its essential requirements: solitude, poverty, and silence — had become for him, over the years, a desperate need. He had begun to see and experience the pure beauty of God, and he now wanted, more than anything else, to continue and deepen that experience. Unfortunately, the modern-day Carmelite Order, with its activity and vigorous apostolate, seemed to preclude that, or at least make it very difficult.

During the past few years the problem had been solved by the permission he received to follow the primitive rule privately. But Peter was right in saying that he couldn't harmonize that rule with the life of a sixteenth-century Carmelite priest. A student for the priesthood could do it, all right, but a priest couldn't. As a Carmelite priest, he would be drawn, irretrievably, into the active apostolate. All his time would be given to the apostolate. And that would be the end of his contemplative life.

That was why he was now thinking of transferring to the Carthusian Order. It was the Carthusian monastery at El Paular, near Segovia, that he had in mind. And how often he thought, somewhat enviously, of those white-robed hermits at El Paular, of their life of solitude in their tiny hermitages, of the full contemplative vocation that was theirs.

But, he wondered, would a transfer to the Carthusians be the right thing? First, there was the sense of loyalty he felt to the Order of the Blessed Virgin. And then, strangely enough, he did want to do *some* active work for souls — but not at the expense of contemplation. The problem was, he admitted to himself, a complex one.

Suddenly, Peter, who had been walking silently beside John,

stopped short in the road. He clamped his hand on John's forearm, peering down into his face, and said:

"Didn't you always say that you entered the Order because of the Blessed Virgin, that you wanted to join her Order?"

"Yes."

"Fine! Pray to Our Lady of Mount Carmel, then, and ask her to work out this problem for you."

"I have prayed to her," John said quietly, "and I'll continue to pray to her. I know that the Blessed Virgin will resolve this dilemma for me."

As the two young priests continued their journey they could not know that the Blessed Virgin had already heard John's prayer, that she had already solved his dilemma. The solution to John's problem lay at the end of his journey in Medina del Campo; and each weary step he took brought him nearer to the unsuspected solution — and to the great adventure of his life.

Medina del Campo, John observed, had not changed much since he last saw the Spanish city some three years ago. The cobbled streets were as busy and crowded as ever; the merchants still hawked their wares in front of their shops; the housewives, with shawls drawn tightly over their heads, still carried sacks of vegetables triumphantly back to their homes.

John and Peter picked their way along the *Calle Santiago*, unnoticed. A cumbersome, mule-drawn cart rattled along in front of them, its driver unaware that he was being followed by two friars. The driver, a cadaverous man with craggy features, directed a steady stream of profanity at his beast. When some obstruction in the road forced the cart to a halt, John and Peter circled it, thereby drawing into the driver's view.

A perplexed frown creased the face of the driver, who was hunched impatiently on the seat of his cart; he was not altogether certain that the brown-robed friars had heard the epithets he was hurling at his mule. Nonetheless, he smiled broadly, displaying a blackened set of teeth.

"Good afternoon, Fathers."

"Good afternoon," John and Peter responded in unison.

"You know," Peter said impishly, looking up at the driver, "it's a fortunate thing that mules can't understand our human speech."

The driver leaned forward quizzically. "What's that, Father?"

"I said," Peter repeated slowly, "that it is fortunate that mules don't understand human speech."

"Oh . . . oh," exclaimed the driver. Then he laughed in a grated, artificial tone: "Heh, heh."

"Heh, heh," Peter mocked back.

"You shouldn't have been so unkind to him," John whispered as they walked off, leaving a bewildered driver behind them.

"Somebody has to speak up for the mules once in a while," Peter said tonelessly.

The church and monastery of St. Anne loomed into view at the end of the street. John felt a twinge of the same excitement he had experienced four and a half years ago when he came to arrange his entrance with Father Ildefonse. He would be ushered into the presence of the prior today as he had been then — only now he was a Carmelite priest greeting his superior instead of a prospective candidate applying for admission. Then, too, Father Ildefonse had been transferred; there was a new prior of St. Anne's, Father Anthony Heredia, a man whom he had never met, but about whom he had heard enthusiastic reports.

The new priests walked up the graveled path to the monastery and paused at the doorway.

"Do you think we should stay here?" Peter asked with a sly smile, "or should we put up at one of the inns of town?"

John, accepting his cue, replied:

"Let's try it for one night. If the prices are too high, or the food isn't satisfactory, we can switch lodgings tomorrow."

Peter laughed, reaching for the knocker on the door. "Let's get in there before they come out and drag us in."

Their knock was answered by the same brother who had admitted John four years ago when he visited the monastery as a nervous applicant. The brother greeted them warmly, and ushered them up to the prior's cell on the second floor. A soft rap on the prior's door brought a quick response in a deep, stentorian voice.

"Come in."

The brother padded into the cell, and John, still standing in the corridor with Peter, could hear the loud voice exclaim again:

"They're here? Well, bring them in, man."

John stepped over the threshold and saw the new prior of St. Anne's, Father Anthony, the man who was to be so much a part of his future career. He was, John observed immediately, a striking figure, a majestic, erect man, standing some six feet five inches tall. However, unlike so many tall men, he was neither too spare, nor too portly; his weight seemed evenly distributed over his long frame. The prior was an elderly man, now about fifty-seven years old, and the added years had splashed his hair gray and furrowed sharp lines into his firm, magnificent face. His sallow complexion, accenting his chiseled features, made him resemble more a Norse chieftain than a Spanish priest.

Father Anthony stepped briskly from behind his desk to greet the new priests.

"Fathers, it's so nice to have you with us, and my heartiest congratulations on your ordination! Now, won't you give me your priestly blessings?"

He dropped to his knees before the two new priests and reverently blessed himself as they traced the sign of the cross over their prior. Pulling himself to his feet, he beamed at his two new subjects.

"We've been waiting for you, and we're all prepared for your first Masses. Father Peter, we've made preparations for you to offer yours at the main altar at seven o'clock in the morning; and, Father John, yours will be at eight o'clock."

He stood there with them for a while, chatting about the recent events in Medina and inquiring about people and happenings in

Salamanca. But while he talked amiably to both of them, he seemed preoccupied with John, glancing frequently at him, attempting to measure his reaction to statements that were made.

Finally, Father Anthony slapped his hands together, exclaiming:

"But here I am clucking away with you like an old *señora*. You must be exhausted from your journey."

He turned to the brother who had been standing patiently a few steps behind the two new priests. "Brother, will you please show the Fathers to the cells we prepared for them."

Father Anthony escorted the two priests to his door and silently watched them as they followed the brother down the monastic corridor. He stood, leaning against the doorway, his gray eyes following John, and softly murmured to himself:

"Yes, I think he'll do. . . . I think he'll do very nicely."

⌐ Chapter 5 ⌐

ON THE following afternoon, the afternoon of the day on which John celebrated his first Mass, Father Anthony knocked softly on the door of John's cell.

"How's our new priest?" he asked after being invited in. He stood leaning against the wall, his arms folded comfortably in front of him.

"A little weary — but happy," John answered.

"You must be tired," Anthony said. "Rest up this afternoon, then, because I want you to accompany me on a little visit tomorrow."

"Visit?"

"I'd like you to meet Mother Teresa."

Anthony paused, allowing the effect of the name he had carefully inserted in the conversation to make its impression upon John; but he suddenly realized, from the puzzled frown on John's face, that the name held no particular significance for the young priest.

"Don't you know who Mother Teresa is?"

"I'm afraid I don't," John answered.

"Haven't you ever heard," Anthony continued, undaunted, "of the Carmelite nun who's been founding all those cloistered convents?"

John bit his lip, then brightened as he said:

"Oh, yes. . . . I think I remember something about a cloistered Carmelite convent; but wasn't it just a single convent at Avila?"

"It was originally; but that first convent has developed into a number of convents. And the nun who started it all — Mother

Teresa — is here in Medina right now, founding yet another cloistered convent."

John nodded his head. "You'll have to excuse my ignorance about all this; we didn't get too much news at the university about events outside Salamanca."

"Well, the important thing now is that Mother Teresa is in Medina — and she wants to see you!"

"See me?" John asked. "Why does she want to see me?"

Anthony had his hand on the latch of the door. "I think that I'll let her tell you herself what it's all about."

The tall prior of St. Anne's had the door of the cell open, but as he started to leave, he turned back to John for one final remark. "But this I will tell you: the matter she's going to discuss with you may well change your entire life."

The following morning, Anthony led John on a brisk walk through the streets of Medina, past the business area, and out to the suburbs, where the stately mansions of the more opulent citizens were situated. Anthony paused at the stone archway leading into one of these lavish buildings, gesturing to John that this was the end of their journey. The two friars crunched along the gravel path up to the house. John darted a rapid glance up and down the length of the impressive stucco building, which was decorated with graceful arches and a series of small balconies.

"Is this where Mother Teresa lives?" he asked.

Anthony smiled. He had sedulously avoided any further discussion of Mother Teresa during their half-hour walk. "She, and four of her nuns, are living here temporarily, while awaiting the completion of their convent down on the *Calle Santiago*. This is the house of Blas Medina, one of her benefactors."

John nodded his head slowly.

The front door of the mansion was of a sturdy dark wood, laced with thick iron hinges; a small bronze bell, fastened to the wall, hung a few inches from the door. Anthony jerked at the leather strip hanging from the bell's tongue. After a few minutes a slot in the door clicked open revealing a squinting pair of eyes.

"Can I help you?" asked a rasping female voice.

"I'm Father Anthony, and I've come to see Mother Teresa."

"Oh, yes, Father." The door swung open to admit the visitors.

The bent old woman who stood with one hand grasping the iron rung of the door was obviously a servant; she smiled a swift, toothless grin and pointed to her right.

"The Carmelites occupy the east wing of the house. You'll have to knock on their door to explain your business."

"Of course," Anthony said perfunctorily.

John smiled at the old woman as he followed Anthony. The prior was again obliged to seek admission through a closed door; but this time he was forced to rap on it with his large hand.

A thin, cultured voice from within asked:

"Who is it?"

Slightly perturbed at the delays he was encountering, Anthony answered somewhat testily:

"Father Anthony! I'd like to see Mother Teresa, please."

"Just a moment," said the voice sweetly.

Soon the bolt slid back, the door opened, and a smiling, middle-aged Carmelite nun stood in the doorway.

"Come in, won't you?" she said. "You'll have to excuse our quarters — we're a little cramped here."

The nun had been looking directly at John, and the statement was apparently made for his benefit. John and Anthony stepped over the threshold into a room which, as the nun had noted, was definitely overcrowded. The table had been placed in the middle of the room, around which were drawn six straight chairs. The rest of the room was piled with wooden boxes, bundles tied in different kinds of cloth, and religious pictures and statuary. John felt that some of the nuns had, undoubtedly, just fled the room, for three books lay open on the table.

"Father John," said the prior graciously sweeping his hands through the air in a wide arc, "I'd like you to meet Mother Teresa."

The nun bowed her head, as John said:

"I'm very happy to meet you, Mother."

Mother Teresa, John noted, was a woman about fifty years of age, but one to whom the years had been kind. She had full, attractive features, set in an oval face; her eyes were dark, expressive, and underlined with shallow black lines. A pert brown mole on her cheek added a touch of piquancy to her appearance. John thought that Mother Teresa must have been strikingly beautiful as a younger woman.

When the three had seated themselves Mother Teresa turned her probing eyes on John, examining him with unfeigned interest. John blinked under her scrutiny, letting his gaze fall upon his folded hands.

"I'm very happy that Father Anthony could bring you to see us," she said to John.

"And I'm very happy to come," John replied.

Mother Teresa shifted her eyes to Father Anthony. "Have you told Father John anything of our little plan?" she asked.

"No," Anthony answered, watching John out of the corner of his eye. "I thought I'd let you explain the whole thing to him."

John was slightly vexed; he felt like a small boy to whom some unpleasant news had to be tactfully and carefully communicated by two of his elders.

"Look!" Mother Teresa pointed at John. "Poor Father doesn't know what this mystery is all about." She spoke with an engaging lilt in her voice.

John was thinking how well the word "vivacious" would epitomize the personality of Mother Teresa.

As Mother Teresa talked, John felt himself being drawn — irretrievably, but pleasantly — under the spell of her melodious voice and her warm eyes.

"I'll explain why Father Anthony tricked you into coming out here today — "

"He didn't trick me," John said; "he ordered me to come." He hoped that his half jest would not be misunderstood.

But both Anthony and Mother Teresa laughed effortlessly.

"All right then," Teresa smiled, "he commanded you. But I'll have you know that I had my finger in it."

Anthony settled himself back in his chair comfortably, a mute signal to Teresa that the burden of the conversation would now fall on her.

"Let me tell you something about my wicked life, because it has an influence on what I want to say to you."

John bowed his head imperceptibly, in a reflex action of interest in what the nun was saying.

"I entered the Carmelite convent at Avila thirty years ago," she continued. "I led a rather indifferent religious life for almost twenty years of that period — "

"Oh, Mother, you can't say — " Anthony interrupted.

Teresa silenced him with a rapier glance. "A rather indifferent life for almost twenty years," she repeated emphatically. "Then, thanks to the mercy of our Lord, I was given the grace and courage to strive after a greater holiness in the religious state. Eventually, I began to consider how I could do more for Christ. Gradually the desire grew in me to live the primitive rule of our Order in a small convent with a few good nuns who might be interested in the project."

John had been following her words intently, but his interest quickened immeasurably on hearing the primitive rule mentioned. Teresa probably sensed his reaction, for she flashed a quick smile at him as she continued her narrative.

"I felt that the restoration of the primitive observance would be the most important thing I could do for our good Master. But," she said, "I'm only a woman, and my hopes of launching a convent following the primitive rule would, I am sure, have remained only a vague dream if it hadn't been for our Lord, Himself. The good Master appeared to me — in fact, He appeared several times — insisting that He wanted a convent of the primitive observance established. I won't bore you with all the details, but I can assure you that we had many, many difficulties in founding the convent. We had opposition from both the civil and ecclesiastical authorities. I thought for a while that we would never accomplish it; but our Lord had His way, and on August 24, 1562 — I'll never forget that date — four nuns and myself moved into a small building in Avila, which we named St. Joseph's Convent of *Discalced* Carmelite Nuns."

"Discalced?" John questioned.

"Yes," she answered, her eyes twinkling mischievously. "I thought it would be good to have some symbol that would typify the notion of the austere life we were embracing. The history of religious orders has been filled with various reforms, which called themselves barefoot. You've heard of Peter of Alcantra and his Discalced Franciscans, haven't you?"

"Yes, I have," John said.

"Look," she exclaimed, pointing a finger at her feet, which she slid forward from under the hem of her habit. John looked down at her feet, and for the first time noticed that she was not wearing shoes, but instead a rough sandal composed of what appeared to be woven hemp. The sole was constructed of several layers of this hemp, which wound over the arch of her foot, exposing her toes and heel.

"So," she declared, "we are discalced in name and in fact."

There was a slight pause as Mother Teresa drew her foot back under the edge of her brown habit, and John took advantage of the pause to ask a question.

"Could I ask you if you have the permission of the Holy See for this new . . . reform?"

She laughed. "Oh, gracious, yes. I did forget to mention that, didn't I? Here I am, showing you our footwear, and I forget all about the more important things. That's the feminine mentality, Father."

John felt his face flushing at her frank disparagement of her own sex.

"We've obtained," she said, "full permission from the Order and from Rome. I consulted the provincial of our Province, who gave a somewhat reluctant consent to my request; and then we obtained a brief from Pope Pius IV to found the convent and draw up the statutes and ordinances we'd need to follow the primitive rule. In fact, just this last spring the superior-general of the Order paid us a visit from Rome. We had quite a long discussion about the Reform, its purposes and ideals. He was delighted with the whole thing, and he nicely consented to the foundation of a number of other convents of the Reform in Spain — that's why I'm here now."

She slanted her head, regarding John from that crooked angle. "The superior-general granted me one more request, something which has been on my mind and in my prayers for the past few years. This permission, Father, is the reason why I wanted to see you today."

"Yes?" John asked warily.

"First of all," Teresa said, "let me tell you that I know a lot about you. Father Anthony has been my informant."

Anthony moved uneasily in his chair. He said:

"My information about you, Father, is, I must admit, second-hand. Most everything I've learned about you has been communicated to me by the Carmelites in Salamanca. But their reports are always exact . . . and complete."

"The thing that interested me most about you," Teresa said, almost ignoring Anthony's interruption, "was the report that you're now attempting to live the primitive rule. That's correct, isn't it?"

"It is, Mother," John answered, somewhat annoyed that this nun should know so much about him.

"Well, then, the permission I've obtained from the general should prove most interesting to you. He's given me permission to arrange for the foundation of two houses of Carmelite *friars* who will follow the primitive rule. We'll call them 'Discalced Carmelite Friars.' "

John remained silent, but the whole reason for this interview with Teresa was revolving into sharp focus. A welter of thoughts whirled around in his head, and he would like to have had time to arrange them, but he felt that he was expected to make some comment.

Reviewing his first visit with Teresa later, he thought that perhaps he should have taken some indirect form of response, but at that time the idea which charged into his head was the one to which he gave expression. "You want me to join the Reform of the friars, is that it?"

"That's precisely it," she answered, a broad smile breaking over her face.

"What will be the general make-up of the Reform?" John asked.

"As we envision it," Teresa answered, "the friars will follow the primitive rule as it was originally approved in the thirteenth century. That means they'll be primarily contemplatives, men of prayer and penance, leading a life of close union with Christ. However, unlike the monks who remain in their monasteries constantly, our friars will leave their monasteries to enter the apostolate in a limited way."

"In a limited way?"

"They won't undertake the more active works of the priesthood; they will, however, conduct retreats for religious and lay people, give spiritual direction, administer the sacraments — and, especially, hear confessions."

John nodded his head thoughtfully.

"You see," Teresa said, "our friars will be contemplatives and men of penance who will have the opportunity of giving the fruits of their contemplative life to the world." She moved to the edge of her chair in her excitement. "It's a wonderful ideal: friars combining the contemplative life with the apostolic life."

She looked inquisitively at John. "Does the idea appeal to *you?*"

John had been intrigued and fascinated at her description of a Reform for the friars, but, even more, he had been surprised, stunned by the way all this appeared to be a solution to the vocational problem he had discussed a few days ago with Peter. Teresa's Reform would, in one deft stroke, solve the conflict that had raged within him for the past year: the conflict between his love for the Order, and his persistent desire for a more austere mode of life.

"It does appeal to me, more than you can imagine," John answered.

Teresa wet her lips. "Does it appeal to you enough to join the Reform of the friars?"

John was amused at this Mother Teresa. Despite her religious vocation and her lofty ambitions, she now resembled any woman in the world placing a request hesitatingly before a man. She sat, he observed, with a shy, almost coy look on her face, her eyes wide open in a questioning gaze. He had already decided to agree to her request, but he wondered what her next move would have been had he refused.

"I don't often make hasty decisions like this," he said deliberately, "but the whole project is so attractive that I don't think I want to delay another minute before enlisting in it."

"Oh, that's marvelous!" cried Mother Teresa, clapping her hands together and glancing at Anthony.

"Could I ask you a few questions about the mechanics of the project, though?" John asked.

"Certainly."

"First of all, how will the Reform of the friars be arranged? Will it be governed directly by the general — or what?"

"No," she answered, "it will be placed under the immediate jurisdiction of the provincial of the Castilian province. The superior-general, of course, will be the ultimate authority. You see, the permission I received from the superior-general limits us to only two foundations — and these two must be made in the province of Castile. As far as the actual legislation and regulations of the Reform are concerned, we haven't made any definite arrangements about them. I've drawn up a tentative set of constitutions modeled on those followed by my Discalced Carmelite nuns. After the first monastery has been founded, you'll be able to discover how these work out in practice and then revise them as needed."

"How many Carmelites have you enlisted for the Reform?" John asked.

Teresa smiled. "Just two."

"Only two friars thus far?" John exclaimed. "And one of them myself? Who is the other?"

For the first time in many minutes Anthony broke into the conversation, saying:

"I am the other, Father."

"You! The prior of St. Anne's!"

Anthony laughed outright. "I guess we've been pretty clandestine about the whole affair. We didn't want to publish the news of the Reform and its members until we're just about ready to launch it. In fact, we wouldn't have told you about my enlisting if you hadn't agreed to join us."

"Hmm," John murmured. "How many do we need to begin?"

"I feel, as a start, we should begin with just two or three men," Anthony said. "If we begin with a large number, it'll be difficult to mold the Reform the way we want it — and also, the less noise we make getting this thing under way, the better it will be. The numbers will come after we get started."

"The whole thing sounds wonderful," John said. "Now, when do we begin?"

"Not so fast," Anthony said. "There're a number of details to be worked out before we can establish the first monastery, not the least of which is your final year of study back at Salamanca."

"Oh," John sighed unhappily. "I'd almost forgotten about that. I guess I do have to return for that last year of study, don't I?"

"You certainly do," Anthony answered, assuming the role of superior again.

"I'll need about a year, anyway, Father," Teresa said, "to make all the final arrangements. You don't have a house, or a location for the new monastery, yet. But, by the time you complete your course in theology, I'll have the house and the site."

"You will?" John said, a tone of uncertainty in his voice.

"Indeed, I will. The Reform has attracted many friends and benefactors from whom, I'm sure, we can obtain a suitable dwelling."

The prospect of embarking upon a life of prayer and solitude which would still be contained within the Order of Carmel surpassed John's boldest desires. In this one conversation with Teresa, the entire problem of his vocation in the Order and the possibility of his transferring to the Carthusians had been resolved; it would now be unnecessary to relinquish the brown and white habit of Carmel to find solitude with Christ.

"I'm leaving Medina shortly," Teresa was saying, "but I'll return here around the time you arrive back from Salamanca. I'd like to have some long talks with you about the spirit and legislation of the Reform."

She had spoken these words directly to John, as though she had already fully briefed Anthony on the spirit of the Reform; but the fact of the matter was that she had not discussed the intimate spirit of the Reform at any length with Anthony, nor did she intend to do so. With her shrewd evaluation of character, she now knew that John, the new priest, would be the hope, the promise of the Reform. Just as John had seen in her proposal the solution to his own vocational problems, so she had seen in him the answer to one of her most pressing needs for the Reform of the friars — a solid, inflexible character upon whom she could build. John, then, and not Anthony, would be the main object of her interest and concern; if she could indoctrinate him with the principles of the reformed Carmel, she had every hope that her dream would become a reality. She had, therefore, definitely concluded in that first interview with Father John that the success or failure of the Reform depended upon him.

Anthony, she reasoned, would lend his dignity, his authority, and his gifts to the movement; he would be an invaluable administrator, a more than competent superior. But John would be the inner strength of the project. He was the one, she felt, who could study and assimilate the doctrines of the Reform she had worked out with the nuns, and who could transmit them faithfully and completely to the friars; she frankly admitted that she was afraid Anthony could not do it, that it was beyond his talents. For this reason, she had been postponing the inauguration of the Reform until she discovered a man who she thought possessed the necessary inner strength and spiritual structure. She knew now, beyond any doubt, that she had found that man, and that she need not hesitate further.

Teresa ran her hand along the length of her brown sleeve, flicking off a tiny particle of lint. "But, Father John," she said, "there's one more point about which I think you should be advised before we begin. We're starting something new in the Church; we're making a break with the past. And a new venture that breaks with the past is always plagued with problems, difficulties, and suffering. The Reform of the Carmelite friars will be, I'm sure, no exception to that general rule."

"I'm prepared to expend myself completely for the Reform," he said firmly, an impenetrable mask settling over his face.

"I know you are," she replied, "but I don't think you have any idea of the opposition that you'll have. I've had painful experience with these difficulties in launching the Reform of the nuns. I was opposed by bishops and nuns, by civil authorities, by lay people — by almost everybody, it seemed. In addition to this, I had to undergo poverty, fatigue, and pressing physical hardships."

"And you're trying to tell me that these same things will happen to me in the Reform of the friars?" John asked.

"I'm trying to tell you," she replied firmly, "that they could very well happen to you, Father. This undertaking will be a glorious venture for Christ, but it will also be a struggle, an encounter."

An encounter. . . . Once again he discovered himself buffeted by that strange excitement which quivered within him as he responded to a challenge. And he knew then — with a grim certainty — that this sometime emotion would not remain sterile in his being, that his life was destined for conflict.

"All right, Mother, it will be an encounter," he said slowly. "But when we work for Christ, we must expect to fight, to live boldly and daringly. If it is to be an encounter, then we'll make it a bold encounter."

Teresa's face brightened. "Yes . . . a *bold* encounter."

PART II

The Rebirth

⌈ Chapter 1 ⌋

DURUELO was a tiny hamlet sitting unobtrusively on the green, rolling plain to the south of Medina del Campo. It was a quiet village, housing for the most part farmers who followed their simple agrarian routine day after day without variation; nor was there a desire on their part for any change: their fathers, and their fathers before them, had scratched away indefatigably at the brown earth. In their minds, no life could be more satisfying.

John, crouched on the narrow seat of the small cart he was driving, snapped the reins, urging his donkey through the single dirt street of Duruelo; he had no desire to pause in the village or become engaged in conversation with any of the inhabitants. The donkey responded to his proddings and clopped briskly past the weather-worn homes, continuing on through the village along the rocky road laced with ruts and crevices.

Squatted beside John on the swaying seat was Vincent Ramirez, fat, perspiring, and uncomfortable. Ramirez was a carpenter, engaged by Teresa to help John in repairing and adapting a small house she had acquired in Duruelo for the first foundation of the Discalced Carmelite friars. It was a slightly unusual task for which Ramirez had contracted: a fortnight of work on an old building near Duruelo. But he had been paid well by Teresa; and one could not afford to pass up good *ducats*, even if it did require two weeks' sojourn in this desolate, forsaken region.

John held the reins tightly in his right hand, pawing in his pocket with his free hand for the piece of paper on which Teresa had scratched the directions to the house donated to her by Don Velasquez. He spread the sheet on his knees, studying it furtively, while darting an occasional glance at the donkey. Teresa had etched a clumsy representation of the Almar river, indicating with a broad check a place where the river curved near Duruelo, the point at which the house would be found. John pushed his sombrero to the back of his head, squinting ahead at the shining Almar river, which twisted lazily before them. Taking his bearing from the river, he glanced to his left along the bank and saw for the first time a squat frame house sitting some three hundred yards back from the bank. This unpretentious building, he realized, with a flush of elation, must be the dwelling Teresa had obtained to serve as their first monastery. Excitedly, he jerked the reins, and the small cart, which was piled with ecclesiastical furnishings, blankets, books, lumber, and Ramirez' tools, creaked sharply, as the sweating donkey strained against its heavy burden.

Reining up before the house, John jumped to the ground, leaving the obese Ramirez to pull his frame laboriously from the cart. It took but one glance for John to see that the structure was perfect for the purpose intended.

It was a one-story, wooden house, containing a half-dozen rooms. The garret was high and full, and John thought immediately that the space in it could probably be put to some useful purpose. On the debit side, however, the house was in rather shabby condition: the paint was almost entirely peeled off the outside walls; and filmy cobwebs had been industriously woven at every conceivable place.

Ramirez did not seem to share John's enthusiasm for the building. He commented gruffly:

"What a mess! It'll take me six months to do anything with this."

The disgruntled remark brought John's attention back to Ramirez, whom he had forgotten in his excitement. "Don't be pessimistic. With your skill, you can make this place sparkle in two weeks."

Ramirez turned disgustedly back to the cart, where he began to rummage through the load for his tool kit.

John strode into the building, making a quick inspection of the floor plan and the general state of the house; the dilapidated appearance of the exterior was reflected on the inside. The walls were stained by water from the leaky roof. The garret was a long, low room, which could definitely be utilized. John immediately decided that they would employ the room as the choir, in which they would chant the Office and recite their prayers. Downstairs, they could have their living quarters and the refectory and kitchen.

His cursory survey completed, John walked jauntily out through the main door. He paused to watch, with some amusement, the muttering Ramirez, who was still tugging at his toolbox, which was lodged tightly under a heavy packing case. Despite the carpenter's pessimism, John felt that the man could make the building habitable in a short time.

John, standing there drawing in the fresh drafts of cool air, which rolled off the river, was relieved that at last the Reform was under way. The final year at the university had been a difficult one, one which found his mind frequently flitting away from his studies to plans for the Reform. Teresa and Anthony had pledged him to secrecy; and, therefore, there was no one in Salamanca — not even Peter — with whom he could discuss this thing which preoccupied him. Teresa sent him periodic bulletins, dashed off in her scrawling, almost illegible script, which informed him of her progress in obtaining a site for the friars' monastery; and Anthony had written him twice in precise, clipped phrases, which described his actions in the project.

It was in April — eight months after his return to Salamanca — that he finally received the letter from Teresa which informed him that one of her benefactors, a Don Raphael Velasquez, had given her a small house and a piece of property near Duruelo for the friars' foundation. Don Velasquez, Teresa wrote, had been apologetic about the neglected condition of the building, but was sure it could be rendered habitable with not too much labor.

In May, at the conclusion of the scholastic year, John once again made the tiring foot journey from Salamanca to Medina with Peter.

"You've got something up your sleeve, haven't you?" Peter had asked suspiciously.

John had been distressed at his inability to discuss the Reform
with Peter, in whom he had always confided, but Teresa was insistent that no word of the project leak out until the moment of
action arrived. Therefore, John could only reply:

"I'm sorry, Peter, that I have to be so secretive. When I'm free
to discuss my plans, you'll be one of the first to hear."

"Huh," Peter grunted at the evasive answer.

Back at Medina, John threw himself into the final preparations
for the trip to Duruelo. At Anthony's request he scoured the library
for duplicate books, and he carried a number of old musty volumes
down to a corner of the cellar of the monastery where they secreted
away equipment for the new house at Duruelo. During those weeks,
an alert observer at the monastery of St. Anne could have noticed
the prior and one of his young priests making frequent descents
to the cellar, furtively depositing some mysterious bundles and
scurrying rapidly away, only to return shortly again on the same
clandestine mission.

The original plan had been for Anthony and John to depart
together on the trip to Duruelo, but a late message from the Father
Provincial advised that the prior would not be permitted to relinquish his office until a substitute arrived — probably some time late
in November. John, therefore, requested permission from Anthony
to leave immediately for Duruelo so that he could attempt to
arrange the house in some semblance of order before Anthony
arrived. Anthony had no special relish for participating in the irk-
some, dirty business of reconditioning the dwelling, and so he
readily agreed to the revision of plans.

On the day of John's departure, near the end of October, he
searched out Peter to inform him of the new project. He found
Peter in the sacristy, where he was vigorously polishing a gold
candlestick.

"Who said we priests never work?" Peter laughed. He continued
his task, making no further comment to John, who stood uncomfortably beside him.

"I'd like to tell you something," John began.

"What have I done now? Is somebody complaining about me again?" A half-amused smile was on his face.

"It's not about you: it's about me."

"Oh, don't tell me you're finally going to tell me about this Reform business."

"What? . . . How did you know?"

"How did I know, he asks," Peter said, throwing his hands in the air in a gesture of mock despair. "I know *everything* that goes on in this monastery. You didn't really think that you could hide all that junk you've been storing in the basement from old Peter, did you?"

"But . . . but, the Reform itself; how did you learn about that?"

"Listen, I was born with a nose for news. I won't tell you where I got my information because if my spies hear that I've given them away, they might lose confidence in me."

"Peter, you're incorrigible!"

"That's what my mother always told me — but, then, she was prejudiced."

They both laughed in a merry violation of that sacred place in which they were standing.

"Well, you know all about the Reform. How do you feel about it?" John asked.

"I think it's wonderful, marvelous! It was made to order for you; it solves all your problems about Carmel and a more contemplative life."

"It certainly does. I couldn't have asked for a more perfect solution. The Blessed Virgin surely answered my prayer."

Peter nodded his head in agreement, and then a frown crossed his usually tranquil face.

"We're . . . we're . . . going to miss you here, you know," he stammered. "We've got rather used to you."

John was slightly embarrassed at Peter's sudden manifestation of sorrow at his departure, and he, too, felt a certain sadness over the fact that his entrance into the Reform would necessitate a separation from his mischievous, irrepressible companion. Peter, he reflected, represented the finest in the Catholic priesthood: he was zealous, kind, affable, and utterly devoted to his work. He would, of course, never join the Reform — his active, almost restless temperament precluded that — but he would continue to be a more than creditable member of the Carmelite Order.

"I'll never forget all the wonderful Carmelite friars, and the many things they've taught me," John said to Peter. "I'll miss all of you."

Once again John found himself in the uncomfortable position of leave-taking. Five years ago the same emotions of sadness and separation crowded around him when he left his mother and brother to enter the monastery. Must life always consist in leaving the persons and places one loves?

The two words — loss and gain — fluttered through his mind; they were, he concluded, an inescapable part of the service of Christ.

John promised Peter that he would pray for him, and extracted the promise in return that Peter would visit John whenever his work took him near the monastery of Duruelo, and on this friendly, sad note, John took his leave of Peter.

As John stood gazing happily at the dilapidated building in Duruelo, all these thoughts went swirling about in his head. He thought of Anthony holding the reins of the hastily loaded cart at the rear door of the monastery, while John climbed eagerly into the driver's seat; he recalled his quick visit to the nuns' convent at Medina where he accepted the new Carmelite habit which Teresa had designed herself; he remembered the austere ceremony at the convent when he invested himself with the habit, then took it off, stuffing it into his bag so that he could don it again when he arrived at Duruelo.

The thought of the habit sparked him into action, and he turned back to the wagon to join the grumbling Ramirez, who was still fumbling with his tools, some of which had spilled out of their box and were lying somewhere in the bottom of the cart. John spied the bundle which contained the habit and deftly withdrew it from the cart, while Ramirez eyed him suspiciously.

"What's that?" he asked.

"It's the new Carmelite habit we're going to wear here," John answered softly.

Ramirez returned to his task of gathering up his lost tools. John went into the house, untied the bundle, rolling out the rough serge habit, which the nuns at Medina had sewed for him. Removing the habit he was wearing, he slipped the tunic, scapular, and cowl of the new habit over his shoulders in excited movements. Then, in one final gesture of severance with the past, he unlaced his shoes, placing them with the discarded habit. He was now a Discalced Carmelite.

John fingered the scapular, pulling it into line, and gazed fondly, admiringly at the length of brown cloth. The new habit was, in its over-all aspects, very similar to the one from which he had just divested himself. It was, like the original habit it replaced, composed of three principal parts: tunic, scapular, and cowl, and, like the parent habit, had a large white cape for street wear and more formal occasions. However, the robes which John now wore typified the severity of life which was to characterize the Reform; all excess material and folds of cloth had been deleted, giving a neat, trim appearance to the habit. The most striking innovation, of course, was the absence of footwear; John stood barefooted in the house of Duruelo. He and Anthony had agreed that they, in their attempts to fulfill literally the title *discalced*, would eliminate even the use of sandals, imitating the unshod monks of old. It was a pious, dramatic idea, but one which would in time prove impracticable; it was unrealistic to expect the future preachers and apostolic workers of the Order to hike over the rough roads and highways without some type of footwear to protect their feet. But the Reform was a new venture, and it was necessary to test many ideas and discard many, too, before the most feasible procedures were conclusively adopted.

Not only did John adopt a new mode of dress, but he also adopted a new name, or at least part of one. Following the custom established by Teresa with her nuns, Anthony and John decided

to add the name of some saint or mystery to their own names —
therefore, Anthony became Anthony of Jesus, and John became
John of the Cross. John had selected "the Cross" as the suffix to
his name because it was a forceful reminder to him of Christ's love
for mankind, and also of the sacrifices entailed in following the
Saviour.

So, there he stood — John of the Cross — a Discalced Carmelite in
name, in dress, and in fact.

Chapter 2

ON THE twenty-seventh of November, Anthony arrived at Duruelo, excited, and bereft of his usual composure. He was accompanied by Brother Joseph — a thin young cleric from Medina, who had been selected to form the third member of the community. Anthony, like John before him, came riding on a lumbering cart crammed with supplies and furnishings. Brother Joseph had driven the cart from Medina, while the recently retired prior sat at his side, tall, uncomfortable, and ludicrous of appearance on the fragile seat. Ramirez had made his departure some days previously, mumbling something about how satisfied he would be to return to civilization, leaving John to await the appearance of his confreres in the Reform.

Ramirez, for all his grumbling, had done his work well, and the tired old house at Duruelo was now at least habitable. John followed his original inspiration in apportioning the space in the dwelling for monastic purposes, and Ramirez had faithfully and skillfully given shape to his plans.

The three men clasped hands in a warm salute, a gesture signifying their solidarity of purpose and their personal devotion to each other. John had met Brother Joseph a few months earlier at Medina when Anthony had introduced them at one of those secret conclaves they held in the prior's cell to discuss the plans for the Reform. It had been Anthony who selected Joseph as the third member of their trio, but John heartily concurred in the selection.

Immediately after their arrival, Anthony and Joseph garbed themselves in the habit of the Reform, as John had done on his first day at Duruelo; they appeared in the corridor after their exchange of robes looking slightly self-conscious in their new habits and bare feet.

"Now we've got a community of Discalced Carmelite friars," John said, his small face cracking into a wide grin.

"Not a very big one," Anthony said, "but it's a start." He turned to Brother Joseph. "How do you feel?"

"Fine," answered the young man.

"Any regrets that you decided to join us?" Anthony asked.

"None at all," Joseph said firmly.

Anthony took charge of the monastery immediately; he had, because of his age and experience, been appointed prior by the Carmelite provincial of Castile. John was nominated as subprior and novice master, although his only subject was the young Brother Joseph. Teresa had expressed satisfaction with the appointments; she felt that they were indicative of the roles the two men were to play in the Reform: Anthony would be the administrator and the legislator, and John would be charged with the interior development of the Reform.

It was Anthony who, after consulting John, drew up the schedule of the day which they followed rigidly. The horarium called for an interruption of sleep each evening shortly before midnight, at which time the Divine Office was chanted; this part of the Office consumed a little over an hour and was followed by a period of mental prayer before they again retired to bed. The three friars rose again early in the morning and chanted some more of the Office, assisted at Mass, and knelt in their garret chapel for the long morning period of mental prayer. Breakfast was a hasty, frugal exercise, at which the three men gulped down some coffee, and quickly withdrew from the cramped kitchen on the ground floor. For the remainder of the morning, Anthony's schedule prescribed that the friars remain in their cells, studying, reading, or praying — this, as Anthony and John had agreed, was a point of prime importance in the life of the Reform, for the characteristic feature of the life was to be solitude and retirement. They were to imitate, as far as possible, the ancient hermits who dwelt in caves among the rocks on Mount Carmel. Solitude, in addition, would distinguish them from the main branch of the Carmelite Order — retire-

ment was one of the elements which had been revised in the mitigation of the Carmelite rule. A return to the primitive rule, then,
must imply a return to solitude.

The noonday meal was one more striking demonstration of the
distinction between the Carmelite Order and its reformed branch:
the diet at Duruelo was entirely meatless. The original rule had
prescribed abstention from meat, but again this had been mitigated
to abstention on only three days of each week. The Reform, accepting the primitive rule in its entirety, forbade the eating of flesh
meat in the monastery at any time — the only exception would be
in favor of those who were ill.

After dinner, the three friars assembled for the single recreation
period of the day, an hour's time, which they used in walking along
the banks of the shimmering Almar river.

It was during one of these midday excursions, some weeks after
Anthony's arrival, that the prior casually remarked:

"I've received a number of letters from some of my old confreres
in the Order requesting admission to the Reform."

"The good news travels fast," John said.

"I don't think that we're ready to accept any more members as
yet." Anthony squinted at John. "Do you agree?"

"Yes," John answered. "We should get a little better established
before we add to the community."

"Yes," Anthony said. "I do think, though, that we could begin to
accept new members for the community some time around Easter."

In the late afternoon, Vespers was chanted in the choir they had
outfitted in the garret, and at five o'clock the friars assembled for
another hour of formal mental prayer. There was a light supper
about nine o'clock, then the chanting of Compline, after which the
three men retired to their stiff wooden beds for a few hours' sleep,
until the monastic day started again with the chanting of Matins
at midnight.

The schedule they followed was a rigid one, but yet it allowed
the three friars long hours of solitude and silence in their cells, time
in which they could search out a closer union with Christ.

It was, therefore, prayer, coupled with penance, which made up their life at Duruelo. And their way of life, they felt, was an important, critical movement in the Carmelite Order. Carmel, in the sixteenth century, had lost contact with the ancient tradition: there was too little penance and, most important of all, too little time for prayer in the Carmelite Order. The Reform would right all that: it would reassert the primacy of contemplation in the Carmelite life by offering men the opportunity to lead a life of intense prayer and mortification. Hence, the Reform would recover a lost tradition; and it would start doing it right here at Duruelo.

The recovery of the prayer-life was easily accomplished: long, formal hours of prayer were contained in the daily schedule, and, in addition to that, the day-long monastic silence, interrupted only during the hour of recreation, gave birth to an atmosphere of prayer and recollection which pervaded the little monastery by the Almar river. The penance came easily, too: the prescriptions of the primitive rule concerning fasting, abstinence, and rigid poverty were faithfully observed, and the very frugality of the house in which they lived — its cramped quarters, its stark simplicity — put the mark of sacrifice on their whole lives.

There was one aspect of penance in their life which John had not even considered before coming to Duruelo: the question of food and its preparation. Unlike the large monasteries in which he had been living, Duruelo had no cook and no regular supply of food. The first problem was solved almost immediately by Anthony, who decided that the three friars would alternate as cook, each doing the job for one week at a time. The second problem, the provision of food, presented a more serious difficulty, and although the initial lack of substantial food was somewhat solved, the basic problem of diet was resolved only in the supernatural realization that their life was to be one of severe penance.

Anthony had brought with him in his cart more of the same basic foods that John had been eating while Ramirez worked at Duruelo: cheese, bread, dried fruit, and wine. The new prior of Duruelo then purchased, out of the money he had collected from benefactors in Medina, some vegetables and fresh fruit from nearby farmers.

Thus, John, during his weeks in the cramped kitchen, was presented with no great culinary problem. For breakfast, he served a murky-black coffee and bread. Dinner, the principal meal, consisted of cooked vegetables, potatoes, fruit, and some wine. The evening meal, a simple collation, was a frugal thing of cheese, bread and wine. Admittedly, John was no cook, but at that he fared better than Anthony, who invariably boiled the vegetables until they were limp and tasteless.

To pay for the small amount of food they had to purchase, Anthony relied on the generosity of friends from Medina who sent him small, but regular contributions for the work of the Reform. And when the Reform grew, Anthony had said, they would meet more benefactors who wished to further the contemplative program of the Discalced Carmelite friars.

Actually, John thought, there was no need for any large financial income. They lived simply at Duruelo, and the only expenses were the few vegetables they purchased from the farmers. It didn't require much money, John felt, to support friars who followed the austere, primitive rule of Carmel.

So, then, prayer, penance, and a return to the Carmelite tradition was the program at Duruelo, a program which John found immensely satisfying, and which convinced him that he had discovered, finally and without any shadow of doubt, his vocation in the Church.

The news of the foundation soon reached the attention of the local clergy, and a number of requests arrived at Duruelo for a friar to preach or hear confessions in some of the adjacent parishes. Anthony collected these petitions (most of which had arrived by post), analyzed them, arranged them, and one day in late autumn spoke to John about them.

"I've got a number of requests here for apostolic work."

He had entered John's cell, finding him seated before a small wooden desk, on which lay open a bulky edition of the Scriptures. Anthony waved the sheaf of letters in his hand absently in the air.

"Do you think we should accept these offers?"

"What kind of apostolic work have we been asked to do?" John said.

"These are requests from some of the local pastors, and what they want us to do fits in perfectly, I think, with our purpose."

"Yes?"

"They want us to preach some sermons and hear the confessions of the people."

"That's certainly within the scope of our vocation," John said.

"I thought so, too. Therefore, I've decided to accept some of these invitations. Of course, we'll only take those parishes within walking distance for the present. In this way, we can walk over to the parish churches after our religious exercises and return again in the late afternoon in time for our evening exercises."

John made no comment, and Anthony continued: "Naturally, we won't go out on these apostolic expeditions everyday — just a few days a week for the present." He fingered a small note on the top of his pile of letters. "Here's a letter from Father Altimeria, the pastor at Nuevo Campo. Do you know where that is?"

"That's the small hamlet to the south of here, isn't it?"

"A small hamlet is right; I don't think it's much larger than Duruelo. However, Father Altimeria has a thriving little parish there, and he wants us to conduct his Vesper service on some Sunday afternoon — just sermon and confessions. It wouldn't take much time, and you could be back here quickly."

"It seems ideal," John said brightly.

"All right, then, you will go there this Sunday afternoon for the Vesper service. I thought that since you were the first Discalced Carmelite friar to arrive here at Duruelo, I'd give you the opportunity of doing the first apostolic work in the community."

"I'd better start to write a sermon for Sunday, then."

"I know you'll do well," Anthony said, moving toward the door.

Walking back to Duruelo the following Sunday afternoon, John moved rapidly over the picturesque Spanish countryside. The light was beginning to fade, and somber shadows cast themselves weirdly over the narrow road. It was far later than he had anticipated for his journey back to Duruelo; there had been an unusually long line of penitents after his sermon. Travel over the rude mountain roads at night was hazardous, and the prospect of such a dangerous trip quickened his steps.

He was pleased with the events of the afternoon at the parish church at Nuevo Campo, satisfied with the facile accomplishment of the first apostolic work in the Reform. Today's events, he thought, contributed another landmark in the life of the new organization. He felt that he had to run the full gamut of experiences in the Reform, he had touched both extremes of the mixed life. And he knew, in a rush of elation, that contemplation and action were not incompatible ideals.

There had been lurking in his mind a fear that perhaps a combination of prayer and action would be an impractical ideal. But now he examined his doubts and hesitations boldly; he knew that they were unfounded, that in the light of today's experience, the Reform was a practical, workable ideal.

All that had been done thus far — the monastic life at Duruelo and the new apostolate — had been in the nature of a test. That, perhaps, was the underlying reason why Anthony and John had decided to forestall the application of new candidates: they had been disinclined to develop the Reform until they definitely established in their own minds the feasibility of the philosophy upon which the new organization was built.

But now John was convinced that the Reform had proved itself to be sound in operation as well as philosophy. They could, therefore, proceed with confidence and hope to build and develop.

A welter of thoughts crowded in upon John. They were thoughts of growth, progress, development, recruitment of vocations; they were jubilant thoughts, the thoughts men have upon witnessing a new vista of progress opening before them, the thoughts saints have as they discover new avenues along which they can advance the work of God.

John was alone on the shadowy road, marching along with determined steps; and since no one could possibly see or hear him, he threw his head back and laughed aloud in the sheer felicity of his mood.

[Chapter 3]

SEATED in the cramped sanctuary of the small church at Mancera, John was still slightly bewildered at the rapid succession of events which had preceded the transfer of the community from Duruelo to this nearby village. Even he, who had no little respect for Teresa's ability to accomplish her projects with dispatch, was astonished at the swiftness with which this plan had been executed. These thoughts, swimming around in his head, made it difficult for him to follow the sermon Anthony was preaching from the wooden pulpit on the right of the sanctuary to the small congregation. Anthony — tall, erect, dignified — was an impressive figure in the pulpit; and, with his resonant voice and facile choice of words, he was delivering his usual fine address. John preoccupied with his own thoughts, caught only snatches of Anthony's sermon that day.

"This foundation is clearly the work of God," Anthony was saying. "The Reform of the Carmelite friars was but a dream, a hope, only a few years ago. And yet, today, in the summer of 1570, the dream is well along the road to accomplishment. The ceremony you are attending this morning marks the official transfer of the original Discalced Carmelite friars' monastery from its temporary site in Duruelo to its permanent home here in Mancera."

John wondered if Anthony, eighteen months ago at Duruelo, had any notion of just how temporary the site would be. He was sure that he had not.

"A year and a half ago we established the first monastery at Duruelo; then in the following summer, the second foundation was made at Pastrana, east of Madrid."

Teresa had written from Pastrana that she had obtained, by some inexplicable twist of good fortune, a magnificent building for

73

a new foundation; and what was even more astonishing, she had enlisted three men to staff the monastery, one, a Carmelite priest, who had requested a transfer to the Reform, and two other gentlemen with reputations for saintly lives. Everything had been arranged; all that remained was for Anthony to come and take formal, canonical possession of the building. John remembered Anthony's reaction to Teresa's note.

"This woman never ceases to amaze me," he had said. "She decides that it's time for us to obtain a second monastery, and in a few months she has the building — and the friars that go with it."

Anthony trudged off to Pastrana, wondering; but on his return, he seemed to have lost some of his diffidence over Teresa's ability to make quick, decisive moves. He was, he frankly admitted, impressed with the whole situation at Pastrana.

The transfer of the Duruelo community, however, was performed more leisurely; a full year passed before Teresa was able to locate a suitable site for a permanent monastery. She was finally introduced to Don Louis, a wealthy gentleman from Toledo, who had just constructed a new church near the village of Mancera and was seeking some priests to staff it. Teresa immediately pounced on the windfall, accepting the church — and the large adjacent building — for the friars.

Again she wrote a note to Anthony, telling him of the acquisition and urging him to transfer the community immediately. Therefore, Anthony wrote a tactful letter to Don Velasquez, who had given them the house at Duruelo, explaining that the community had now grown too large for the small building, and that they were about to move to Mancera. He thanked Don Velasquez for his invaluable assistance in launching the Reform, and returned the deed for the building to him.

Early this very day — the eleventh of June, 1570 — the community of Duruelo, now numbering eight members, hiked through the rolling countryside over the hills to Mancera. The weird file of friars, their white cloaks gently flapping in the morning breeze, marched resolutely along, followed by two wagons crammed full of their possessions. Upon their arrival at the new monastery, the friars went immediately into the church, clapping the dust off their white cloaks, and took their positions in the crowded sanctuary, while Anthony addressed the congregation which had already assembled.

Listening to Anthony wend his way through the overlong sermon, John hoped that the man would conclude, so that the friars could retire to their new monastery. Almost as if he had read John's thought, Anthony brought his talk to a rapid conclusion.

"And so," Anthony said, bringing the flat of his hand squarely down on the pulpit, "the foundation of the monastery here at Mancera is completed. With high hope and supreme confidence, we leave the future to God."

" — and to Mother Teresa," John muttered to himself.

After the ceremony was completed and the guests had departed, John stood outside the monastery, inspecting its clean, new walls, as they refracted the dull rays of the setting sun. Anthony walked along the side of the building to meet him.

"Are you tired, John?"

"I'd be deceitful if I said that I wasn't."

Anthony smiled. "Well, you have a good reason for your fatigue today."

"It has been a long day, hasn't it?" John said.

"And a profitable one, too. This morning we were housed in that makeshift building in Duruelo and tonight we occupy a building which is practically brand new."

"It doesn't seem fair," John said, almost truculently.

"What doesn't seem fair?"

"The fact of our possessing this immaculate new building."

"And what's unfair about that?"

"Oh, it's not that it's really unfair; it just seems too easy. We're beginning the Reform of a religious order, and here we walk into a beautiful new monastery, with no effort on our part."

"That's bad?" asked the puzzled Anthony.

"It seems, if you read back through the history of the Church, that all those men and women who instituted or reformed religious orders had to undergo so much in the way of hardship and deprivation before they obtained a building as elegant as this."

"I see," grinned Anthony. "You want some type of adversity, is that it?"

"It's not that I want it so much; it's, rather, that we don't seem to be following the usual pattern of those who did the same things we're doing here. The cross has always been Christ's seal of approval upon any work for Him."

"I admire your spiritual outlook, Father, but I'm disappointed that you believe Christ has forgotten us. It's true that we have had scarcely any real problems, but the cross of Christ will come."

Anthony was not often given to prognostication, nor did he imagine himself endowed with any prophetic powers. On this occasion, therefore, his statement to John was more in the nature of an educated guess, a conclusion arrived at from the consideration of the usual development of God's plan. He reasoned — as John himself had stated — that Christ ordinarily gives His cross to those who work for Him, and the work of the Reform must, of necessity, someday bear this divine imprint.

In this, Anthony could not have been more correct.

⌈ Chapter 4 ⌉

DURING the next two years, three additional monasteries had to be opened to accommodate the new men who were joining the Reform. The first of these new foundations was at Alcalá, midway between Madrid and Pastrana. It was an important foundation. for it was near the famed University of Alcalá, and the young Discalced Carmelites were able to attend classes there, just as John himself had attended classes at Salamanca ten years before. The other two monasteries, at Altomir and at La Roda, were in Castile, still farther east of Pastrana. John watched these new foundations spring up, and was filled with an intense satisfaction.

The greater number of the new candidates were already priests when they joined the Reform, and most of them had been recruited from the parent branch of the Order, from Carmelites who were attracted to the contemplative life of the Reform, from friars who found themselves with too little time to pray. However, there was a steady flow of young laymen seeking admission.

The rapid development of new monasteries only re-emphasized the peculiar position of the Reform: it was a reformed branch of an ancient religious order, but it was still under the jurisdiction of the Carmelite superiors. Anthony, as senior priest in the Reform, began to act as the principal superior within the Reform itself, making decisions for the five monasteries, serving as liaison between the Reform and the Carmelite provincial of Castile.

Teresa continued her efforts in behalf of the friars, finding new benefactors for them, and paving the way for new foundations. She, of course, had no official position in the friars' Reform; she had obtained permission for the original foundations, recruited the vocations, and secured the buildings which served as monasteries, but beyond that, her function was one of an advisor, a friend, and an influential intercessor with important ecclesiastics. John and Anthony were, naturally enough, delighted to have her genius and zeal at work in their behalf.

Soon both John and Anthony realized that the monastery at Mancera was not large enough to handle all the new applicants. Therefore, the large monastery at Pastrana, their second foundation, was made the novitiate house, and all new candidates reported there. However, with the novitiate at Pastrana, John found that he was losing contact with the new members of the Reform. At Mancera, many leagues from Pastrana, he received lists of the new novices, but they were mere names on a piece of paper to him. This situation made him fearful that these new Discalced Carmelites might not completely capture the spirit of the Reform as he and Anthony had inaugurated it at Duruelo.

In April of 1571, ten months after coming to Mancera, John was transferred to the monastery at Alcalá — to become its superior. His appointment as superior appalled him: it meant that he would have to govern a monastery of over thirty friars. He protested to Anthony, but the old man was insistent: he wanted John at Alcalá.

"I think that it's absolutely essential for you to go to Alcalá," Anthony said. "All of the original friars from Duruelo are here in the east and the new men are running things by themselves over in the west. We've *got* to make sure that there's a uniformity of spirit in the Reform."

Therefore, with some grave misgivings about his ability to govern, John made the long foot journey to the university city of Alcalá. But his fears of government were almost immediately dispelled: with practically no effort on his part, the monastery functioned smoothly and efficiently. The thirty-two friars at Alcalá — all of them new faces to John — were delighted to have the first friar of the Reform as their superior, and they followed his instructions with absolute fidelity. John, on his part, was equally satisfied with Alcalá. It was the first time he had lived in one of the large monasteries of the Reform, and the long rows of sandaled friars chanting office in the choir was a magnificent sight for him.

The year John spent at Alcalá was a quiet, tranquil one, despite the fact that the majority of the community left the monasery each day to attend classes at the university. And in that peaceful monastery, he could see the full flourishing of the contemplative life.

His superiorship at Alcalá came to an abrupt end in the spring of 1572 in the form of a terse note from Anthony: something was wrong at Pastrana, and John was commissioned to remedy things there immediately. The situation at Pastrana was a confirmation of John's fears about the failure of the new men to capture the spirit of the Reform. According to Anthony's letter, the novice master at Pastrana, Father Angelus (a friar John had never met, since he had entered the Reform when John was east at Mancera) was doing some strange things to the young novices. Angelus was making them participate in mortifications, and even public penances in the streets of Pastrana — to such an extent that the townspeople were becoming disturbed.

John was not to be superior at Pastrana, but Anthony gave him full power to correct the overzealous abuses. His successor at Alcalá, Father Gabriel, would arrive shortly; and after he had finished his task at Pastrana, Anthony would notify him of his new assignment.

And so John bundled together his few belongings for the trip to Pastrana — a dog-eared copy of the Bible, his breviary, and a few changes of undergarments — in a canvas sack. He drew a length of rope tightly around the bundle, and as he thought of of the situation in Pastrana, he gripped it fiercely in his hand until his knuckles turned white.

John was fortunate — at least from his point of view — in arriving at the monastery of Pastrana at a most critical moment. The entire community of thirty members was lined up outside the main door of the monastery in a single file, as if they were soon to march into the city; each friar held in his hand a grotesque leather whip, and a thin, white-faced friar stood at the head of the column addressing the group in high-pitched tones.

John, unobserved, stepped behind a convenient tree, where he could both observe the strange ritual and hear what was being said; a grim frown dug itself into his brow as he heard the speaker haranguing the friars.

"We are all sinners. We must do penance for our sins, and for the sins of the world." He pointed a thin finger toward Pastrana. "Down there are people who don't know the meaning of penance. We must show them what penance really is. When I give you the signal, you'll begin to whip the shoulders of the man ahead of you in the procession. Then we'll walk through the city this way, showing them what penance is. Now, let's begin."

However, the "penance" failed to begin, for John, stepping quickly from behind the tree, moved over adroitly to meet the leader of the weird pageant.

"Are you the superior of this house?" he asked the startled friar curtly.

"No, no . . . I'm Father Angelus, the master of novices. The prior, Father George, is away, and I'm in charge. Who are you?"

"I'm Father John of the Cross from Alcalá."

"Father John of the Cross!" The thin friar's face brightened, and he turned toward the column of friars repeating the name emphatically and respectfully. "This is the friar who, with Father Anthony, established the first monastery of the Reform," he explained, and there was pride and awe in his voice.

John's rancor against the man began to abate in the face of this honest admiration. Father Angelus was unknown to him; he had entered the Reform at Pastrana, and just recently was appointed master of novices. He was evidently a sincere religious, but an incompetent superior, who had been overcome by zeal and a misconception of the basic principles of religious life. John suddenly felt very weary and at odds with himself because of the task he must perform; he wished desperately that he were back at Alcalá or Mancera — any place but here.

"You'll be delighted to see what we're doing right now," the thin friar before him was saying.

"Will I?" John said tonelessly.

"Yes, yes. We're going to march through Pastrana doing penance. Do you want to join us?"

"No, Father, I prefer not to join you, and I'd like you to postpone the procession for a while. I want to have a little talk with you."

"Talk with me? Certainly. However, Father, this is the time for our daily public penance. We'll have plenty of time when we get back."

Father Angelus' eyes shifted nervously. John grimaced slightly, realizing that Father Angelus was determined to carry out his program. John sincerely hoped that he would not be compelled to reprimand the man publicly before the entire community. He thought, with a flash of relief, of the letter from Anthony in his pocket. He withdrew it, and shoved it into Father Angelus' hands.

Father Angelus read the letter, and then gave John a stricken look.

John felt genuinely grieved for him. "Could we have our talk now, Father Angelus?" he said.

"Yes, I guess we'd better."

After the procession had been disbanded, John joined Father Angelus in his cell.

"As you realize, Father Anthony's letter explains the nature of my business in coming here, Father," he began. "He's upset — as I am, too — about the reports on your activities at Pastrana. The exhibition I witnessed outside a few moments ago was a confirmation of all the reports."

John paused, giving Father Angelus an opportunity to say something — anything. He earnestly hoped that the friar would not sit there mutely, like a dumb beast receiving a beating. As much as he had been horrified at the abuses at Pastrana and desired to correct them, John had lost all enthusiasm for reprimanding the friar who sat uncomfortably across the desk from him.

Father Angelus moistened his lips. "But, Father John, I thought that you'd be pleased with what we've done here." His head jerked convulsively, and his thin, pensive face blanched even whiter than its usual ashen color.

"No, Father, I'm not pleased — how could I be pleased with these excesses, with your utter failure to comprehend the meaning of penance and mortification."

"But, but . . . penance and austerity — aren't they elements of the Carmelite life?"

"They are elements of our life, surely enough, but they're not the principal purpose of the Carmelite Order. And these . . . these absurdities you have sponsored here have no place in the Reform at all."

John could see that, because of Father Angelus' obtuseness, it was going to be more difficult than he had anticipated. Father Angelus would have been more easy to deal with if he were blatantly malicious or cruel in his treatment of the novices, but he was not malicious or cruel, he was simply — John hesitated to employ the word — stupid. He couldn't perceive that what he was doing was horribly wrong. And how do you deal with a stupid person? A strange, twisted desire that Father Angelus be malicious rather than stupid flashed into his mind (he could have coped with the problem then), but John closed his mind against it and settled down to the realistic problem of the issue at hand: the re-education of a fatuous mind.

"Didn't the saints exercise severe penances upon themselves?" Angelus was saying.

"The saints — some of them — did exercise severe penances," he said listlessly. "However, they did so under a special inspiration from God. They were special people, with a special inspiration; and their deeds are not to be interpreted as practical norms to be followed by every person in the spiritual life."

Father Angelus nodded his head in agreement, not, however, with the assent of one who believes, but rather with the assent of one who feels compelled by circumstances to offer no objection.

John was aware of Father Angelus' interior resistance; nevertheless, he continued to explain his position; he felt that at least he should go on record as stating the correct doctrine, despite his failure to penetrate Angelus' mind. What an invincible sanctuary a man's mind is, John thought, a stronghold resistant to any force of word or argument.

"Sanctity, you see, Father, consists fundamentally and basically in love for Christ; it's a union of friendship with the divine Saviour. In other words, sanctity is love. It's as simple as all that. . . . Now mortification plays a role, and a very important role in our love for Christ. However, the function of mortification is a negative one, it prepares the way for love by removing the obstacles to it — namely, love for other creatures."

John rubbed his hand along his perspiring forehead; this conversion was taxing him more than he liked. "As for the public penances which I saw this afternoon . . . they're over; we'll have no more of them."

"But . . . penance, Father John."

John stabbed his finger in the air at Father Angelus. "Penance has been, and always will be, one of the prime works of the Reform. But in the practice of penance, we shall not descend to the bizarre, to the unusual . . . to . . . to the idiotic."

John immediately regretted the violence of his admonition against Father Angelus' apparently sincere attempts to do what he thought was correct; he, therefore, smoothed out his voice, and said:

"Come now, Father, let's see if we can't do something about revising these penitential practices here at Pastrana."

"Revising" had been a kind, delicate word, prompted by John's desire to deal tactfully with Father Angelus; a more apt term would have been "eradicating," for, in the following weeks, radical changes were effected in the monastery. Gone were the strange public penances, the severe humiliations heaped upon the young novices, and the over-all atmosphere of repression and gloom which seemed to have pervaded the house. John delivered a number of talks to the community, stressing the point that sanctity consisted in love and not in Manichaean penances; and he attempted, with success he thought, to explain the proper concept of mortification. As a result of his talks and a series of private interviews with members of the community, he watched with satisfaction a spirit of buoyancy develop in the monastery; the whole tenor of the community swiftly changed until it began to resemble the other monasteries of the Reform.

Of particular concern to John was the morale and spirit of the new novices; he feared that the excessive, fanatic penances imposed by Father Angelus might have forever destroyed their proper outlook on the religious life, and he, therefore, invited each one of them to visit his cell so that he might determine the exact amount of damage done to their ideals. It was during the course of these interviews that he first met Father Jerome Gratian. In retrospect, John could remember with remarkable clarity almost all the details of that first uneventful meeting.

The young man had slipped gracefully into the chair across the desk from John and said, pleasantly: "I'm very, very happy to meet you, Father. I've heard so many wonderful things about you." He paused, as it he had made a serious omission, then added, "My name is Father Jerome of the Mother of God."

Something clicked in John's head, and he asked:

"What is your family name, Father?"

"Gratian, Jerome Gratian."

Of course, John thought, this is Father Jerome Gratian about whom the prioress of the Carmelite convent here at Pastrana had written him. He remembered the glowing terms which the nun had used to describe the young Spanish priest — "a man of magnificent promise . . . keen intellect . . . charming personality . . . great holiness." John had been amused at her description of Jerome Gratian, and had simply ascribed it to the bubbling enthusiasm a nun so often demonstrates over a bright young priest. However, the young man who sat before him, smiling, poised, and relaxed, certainly did make an excellent first impression.

The letter from the prioress had outlined at some length the course of events that had brought Jerome Gratian to the Reform. Nevertheless, John asked him:

"How did you come to join our Reform, Father?"

There was an ulterior purpose in requesting a review of Gratian's vocational biography, despite the fact that he was already familiar with it: he wanted the young priest to speak, and to speak at length.

And so Father Jerome described his background: the large manor residence in which he was born; his wealthy father; his studies at the better schools in Spain; the relentless prodding of divine grace which compelled him to accept ordination to the priesthood; and, finally, his indecision of the last year and a half about joining the Discalced Carmelites. All the while, John kept his eyes fastened on Father Jerome. The young novice, John concluded, handled himself well: he spoke easily, effortlessly, and with evident sincerity.

"I'm afraid," Father Jerome said, "that I must put the final blame for my vocation to Carmel on Mother Isabella. I visited her here at the convent in Pastrana to arrange for the acceptance of a young lady into the Order, and was told that she was going to pray that I, too, become a member of the Reform." He laughed pleasantly. "You can't resist the prayers of a determined nun, you know."

"That's true, Father," John said. "I imagine that Christ has a hard time of it when a nun makes up her mind that she wants something from Him."

They both chuckled in that suave urbanity of men who think they understand the feminine mind.

"Now that you've joined the Reform," John asked, "do you like it?"

"I do now," Jerome said meaningfully.

John wrinkled his face. "Yes, all of you must have had a rather bad time of it here with Father Angelus and his odd notions of penance. But that's all over now — at least I hope it is."

"I'm glad you came when you did, Father John. There's no way of knowing where these penances might have ended."

Father Jerome's smile showed white teeth glistening in a flattering contrast to his dark, bronzed skin. Jerome Gratian's face was handsome in his ordinary cast, but its attractiveness was enhanced immeasurably by his smile: friendly lines etched themselves at the corner of his eyes, giving the over-all impression of warmth, humaneness, and kindness.

"You didn't approve of Father Angelus' tactics, then?" John asked, toying with him.

"I thought they were barbarous — the man must have some sort of mental aberration."

John winced at the statement. There, he thought, was a defect in Gratian: a brash outspokenness. However, it was a defect common to young men. He was only too ready to disregard the impetuosity of the young priest's statement. . . . John was amused at himself: here he was mentally chastising Gratian for his youth, while he, himself, was only a few years older than the man.

"Be that as it may," he said to Gratian, "it's past history now. The only important thing is for you to concentrate on living the Carmelite rule, which, I trust, you will be able to do now without further interruption. The year of novitiate should be a tranquil year, a gentle period of your life when you can learn about Carmel — and, what's more important, put into practice the things you learn."

"Certainly, Father."

"You know, the Reform of the friars is only about three years old. All of us — professed and novices alike — are pioneers in this adventure, and all of us must work hard for its complete accomplishment."

"I think you've done very well so far," said Father Jerome graciously.

"We've only made a beginning, simply a beginning."

When the interview with the young priest was concluded, John felt a sudden elation over the fact of Jerome Gratian's presence in the Order. He would, John thought, be an incalculable asset to the Order; and what a splendid superior he would make someday! He seemed to possess all the necessary qualities for leadership.

A few minutes later, while chanting the Office in choir, John found himself casting furtive glances at the erect, dignified figure of Father Jerome, and he could not help hearing the young priest's rich, baritone voice boom out the ancient psalms of the Church. When the Office had been completed, while the community knelt in silent meditation, John thought about Father Anthony, his original partner at Duruelo, another man of poise and charm. But there was a decided difference between the charm of Father Anthony and Father Gratian. They were both men of intellectual and spiritual stature; they both possessed that gift of impressing people — but there was a difference. Anthony was the tall, quiet, conservative type, a religious who possessed an almost regal mien; and yet his kindly face and soft smile invited confidence and respect. On the other hand, Gratian appeared to be more animated: his smile quicker, his features more mobile. Gratian possessed a more aggressive charm.

John was afraid, in an honest appraisal of himself, that he fell far short of either Gratian or Anthony as regards personality or personal magnetism; he could never command attention or respect as they did. But he did not envy them for their gifts, rather he was delighted. It augured well for the future.

His prayer that day, therefore, was the prayer of gratitude, of gratitude to God for giving so many fine vocations to the nascent Reform.

⌠ Chapter 5 ⌡

THE following day brought another letter from Anthony, a lengthy, flowery epistle, the gist of which was that John was to report to the nuns' convent of the Incarnation in Avila where he would serve as chaplain to the community. John was, at first, shocked by the news. What could have possessed Anthony to make such an assignment? Chaplain for a convent of nuns, indeed!

Then, reading the letter more carefully and revolving the whole matter in his mind, he began to see the logic behind the appointment. There was another surprise appointment recounted in the note which was even more astonishing than John's. Mother Teresa had been commissioned by Father Fernandez, the apostolic visitor of the Carmelites, to return to her former convent of the Incarnation — which was not annexed to the Reform — where she was to serve a term as prioress. Father Fernandez had become so impressed with the Reform and Teresa's activities in it that he hoped to raise the Incarnation convent at Avila to a new pitch of sanctity by installing its former member as temporary prioress. John felt a sudden pang of disturbance for Teresa in her unenviable task. Imagine, he thought, Teresa, who had left the Incarnation convent to follow the ancient Carmelite rule more perfectly, is now sent back, some ten years later, to increase the spirituality of the convent. And — John had to smile to himself — she drags him into her awkward assignment as the chaplain of the convent.

However, as Anthony mentioned in the letter, it was not only because Teresa felt the need of some assistance in Avila that John was being assigned there. No, the move itself was advisable, independent of Teresa's problems. John's chaplaincy in that influential city would give the struggling Reform wide prestige, and it would serve to point out in a tangible way one of the principal apostolic works of the Reform: spiritual direction.

The chaplaincy at Avila would, of course, necessitate a residence outside one of the Discalced Carmelite monasteries (there was none as yet in Avila), but the more John considered the matter, the more disinclined he became to regret the situation, for he could see the importance of placing a man in a position of prestige at the outset of the movement. It was critical that it develop in the proper direction, that the members be convinced of the type of apostolic work in which Discalced Carmelites would engage. No more dramatic manner of conveying the truth could be found at the present time than appointing one of the first friars of the Reform to the office of spiritual director in one of the most important convents in all Spain.

John was to depart immediately for Avila, but before he could leave Pastrana, there was one final point of business at the monastery to which he must attend, the culmination of his six weeks of instruction and re-education here.

He searched out the novice master, Father Angelus, whom he found in the garden behind the monastery. John went through some conventional banalities about the weather and the prospects of a warm summer, to which Father Angelus responded with guarded phrases. Then John abruptly turned the conversation to the distasteful task he must perform.

"Do you enjoy being the novice master here, Father?" he asked.

"What . . . what do you mean?"

"Just what I said: do you enjoy the office of novice master?"

Father Angelus' eyes darted wildly to the left and right, as if seeking some avenue of escape. "It's a duty I've been given by my superiors . . . and . . . and . . . I do it."

"But do you enjoy this . . . this duty?"

"I've never really given much thought to whether or not I enjoy it. You're not supposed to consider that, are you?"

"That's true enough." John's eyes bored into the face of the uneasy novice master. "But, as a matter of fact, Father, you don't enjoy it at all; in fact, you dislike the office intensely. Isn't that so?"

"I . . . I don't know. I guess you could say that I find the office rather difficult."

"Of course you do," John said kindly. "You become tense in a position of authority like this, and the responsibility of training the novices produces a tremendous strain upon you."

These were the conclusions that John had drawn from his observance of Father Angelus during the past weeks; and a look of astonishment on Angelus' face, followed by one of relief in the realization that his interior anguish had been discovered and finally laid bare, convinced John that his conclusions were valid ones.

John talked slowly, picking his words carefully. "Yes, Father, you tighten up in a position of responsibility, and this makes everything most difficult for you and the men in your charge."

"What can I do about it?" he asked frankly.

"Don't you think you'd be happier if you resigned the office?"

"Resign?"

"There's nothing dishonorable in resigning. Father Anthony resigned his priorship at Medina so he could join the Reform. He simply wanted more opportunity to pray and draw closer to Christ. If you resigned, it would be for the same basic reason: to enable yourself to serve God with more peace and tranquillity."

Father Angelus appeared stunned by the suggestion, and John noted petulantly that the novice master's left hand had begun to twitch convulsively again. John was not quite sure whether Father Angelus was fully aware of the web he was attempting to weave. He had decided some weeks ago that the novice master was completely inept for the office he now held, and he had written to Anthony for permission to install a new novice master in his place. It had not been John's original intention to seek the deposition of Father Angelus; he thought that, with some instruction and readjustment, affairs could be ameliorated at Pastrana. But as the weeks passed, John had become more and more convinced that poor Father Angelus was beyond reclamation; he paid only lip service to John's advice, and appeared to be in no way converted from his abnormal ideas about penance and mortification. He made all the changes in the schedule that John had suggested, and abolished the penitential orgies that had become the order of the day at Pastrana, but John knew too well that not long after his visitation was ended, the situation would revert to its former intolerable state.

John had decided to install Father Benjamin, one of the older priests of the community, as novice master, and Anthony had concurred with his decision. Father Benjamin was not a particularly prepossessing person, but he was well equipped with that priceless ingredient, common sense. John felt that he would qualify as an excellent replacement for Father Angelus, that he was precisely what was needed at the monastery of Pastrana. However, the problem of Father Angelus still remained: how to dislodge him from his position without causing embitterment? It would be too cruel, John had thought, to inform him peremptorily of his dismissal from office. John took the delicate problem before the tabernacle, asking the hidden Christ for advice, for encouragement, and, above all, for tact. And the answer came: he would attempt to convince Father Angelus of his dissatisfaction with the office, and gently suggest that he resign for his own greater peace of mind. It was this procedure that John was pursuing, and he waited, hopefully, for a favorable reaction from Angelus. He was not disappointed.

"Maybe you're right," Father Angelus said. "Maybe I would be happier if I didn't have to worry about the discipline of the novices constantly."

"Certainly I'm right," John answered. "Listen, I received permission from Father Anthony to appoint a new novice master if I want. Shall I tell Father Anthony that you'd like to resign your position so that you could devote more time to prayer and reading?"

A faint streak of suspicion worked its way across Father Angelus' face, but quickly disappeared, and John wondered if he were aware of the stratagem being worked upon him.

"All right, tell Father Anthony that I tender my resignation — because I want more time for prayer," Angelus said.

"I'll tell him just that," John said.

So it was done, and John was finished with the distressing misadventure at Pastrana; he had completed the work he had been sent to accomplish.

John was convinced that the removal of Father Angelus had been a critical necessity for the success of the foundation at Pastrana; he would have been uneasy had he departed knowing that a return to former excesses was a constant possibility. A novice master could exercise what was, at times, frightening influence over the young men in his charge; this was even more true at Pastrana, where the superior of the monastery, Father George, who could ordinarily have done much to control the situation, was absent from the house for extended periods on preaching tours. This, too, caused John a pang of dissatisfaction: the prior of the house should be at home in the monastery for the greater majority of the time. John remembered having mentioned this to Father George.

"You do a lot of preaching, don't you, Father?"

"I do. There are a lot of invitations for Discalced Carmelites to give sermons, instructions, and lectures," Father George said rather truculently. He was an obese friar, with a deep, bass voice.

"That's all very good, Father," John said gently, "but don't you feel it's also important for you to remain in the monastery and insure its proper administration?"

"But it's also important, Father John, that we broadcast the work of the Reform. All the preaching that I've been doing is an invaluable way to build up a good reputation for the friars."

"Don't forget, though, Father," John had said, "that we're primarily men of prayer and our principal occupation is the monastic life. The apostolic work in which we engage — preaching, administration of the sacraments, whatever it might be — should be entirely subordinated to the life of prayer."

John had let it go at that; he felt that he was making no progress with Father George and, after all, he had only been sent to Pastrana to correct the abuses of the novice master.

But as John prepared to depart for Avila, he felt uncomfortable about the incidents at Pastrana: he had, for the first time, seen a disagreement in the ranks. Both Angelus and George had failed to comprehend the precise work of the Reform, both had resisted John's efforts to instruct them about it.

He was afraid that this was a foretaste of future difficulties within the Reform itself. And this was something he didn't want. The Reform *had* to prosper, he thought. The contemplative life of the friars was something too valuable for the Church to lose. And he now realized something else about the Reform, too: he had, in his own mind, personally identified himself with the movement. He had become a part of it; it was his cause. Years ago he had thought about joining the Carthusians, but that was over now. The Blessed Virgin had brought him to the Reform, she had given him this cause to work for as a life project. In working for the Reform, then, he would find his sanctity and his way to God.

$\left[\text{ Chapter 6 }\right]$

AVILA!

The sprawling, walled city of Avila was set on a gentle slope, which humped to its greatest height in almost the direct center of the town. Avila was in one of the most advantageous physical positions of any city in Spain: Salamanca, with its world-famed university, lay to the north; Madrid lay to the east; and Toledo to the south. Sitting almost equidistant from these other important cities, it possessed the unique advantage of being practically at the hub of the great wheel of cities through which the political, cultural, and economic life of Spain throbbed.

Avila, consequently, always appeared to be in a frenetic state of activity. An unending chain of heavily loaded wagons moved in and out through the city's stone gates. Foreign visitors, in strange and colorful costumes, walked the streets. And there was the constant presence of soldiers and colonists home from the distant points of the Spanish Empire — from Peru, Mexico, the Philippines, and the West Indies. Excitement filled the air of Avila.

And, in the late spring of 1572, that excitement was intense: the report of the Spanish victory at Lepanto had reached Avila, and the city was still reveling in the smashing defeat of the Turks.

As John strolled leisurely into the city to take up his duties as confessor of the nuns at the Incarnation convent, he was immediately struck by the mood of jubilee and triumph. An old man, whom he passed in the street, cried out to him: "Lepanto, Father. *Lepanto!*" John smiled and said: "Yes, Lepanto." He had, of course, heard the news while he was in Pastrana. King Philip's half brother, Don John of Austria, had crushed the Turkish fleet in the Gulf of Lepanto, ending Islam's threat to Europe. Spain was now in a position of unequaled power, and there was reason for rejoicing in Avila.

John walked past the northern rampart, out to the suburbs of the city, where the Incarnation convent was located. The convent itself was large and spacious, as well it had to be, for it housed nearly one hundred and fifty Carmelite nuns. The white brick walls of the building reached to a height of three stories, topped on one end by a square cupola and on the other by a bell tower.

It was with no slight trepidation that John knocked on the arched door of the convent. Teresa's position here was — to say the least — peculiar and John, as the confessor she had elected, would share her discomfiture.

"Lord forgive me for what I've got you into," were Teresa's first words to him, after he had been ushered into the convent parlor.

John smiled. "Why, what sinister trap have you drawn me into?" he asked.

"This strange situation here at the Incarnation, of course."

"I'm rather confused about the whole affair. Suppose you tell me all about it."

Teresa lifted her shoulders in a tiny shrug. "There's not much to tell, actually. The Pope's visitator, Father Fernandez, wanted some changes made here — the finances were in bad shape, and the discipline in the convent was far from what it should be. So he decided to install a new prioress. And since I'm a Carmelite, even though I belong to the Reform, he selected me — and here I am."

"But how can a Discalced Carmelite nun be the superior of a group of regular Carmelite nuns?" he asked.

"That's a very good question," she said laughing. "Really, though, I must say that the nuns have been very nice to me. I know it's been hard for them to accept me back here. After all, I left here ten years ago to become a *Discalced* Carmelite, and now I get pushed back on them as their prioress."

"It's only a temporary assignment, though, isn't it?" John asked.

"Well — I haven't been assigned here for life. But I do have to stay until Father Fernandez thinks I've done the job — or until he becomes convinced that I can't do it."

"You'll do well. I'm sure of that," John said.

"I do feel better now that you're here to help me," she said.

He felt slightly embarrassed at the frank compliment Teresa had paid him, and he immediately turned the conversation in another direction. "Did you hear about Pastrana and Father Angelus?" he asked. Teresa said that she had not, so John proceeded to give her an account of his work in Pastrana the past few weeks.

Teresa, her face in a frown, said:

"That doesn't sound good at all, does it. And I've got more bad news for you, too."

"You have?"

"It seems that some of the Calced are not too happy about the progress the Reform is making," she said.

"The Calced? What are the Calced?"

"Oh, haven't you heard that expression yet? People here in Avila — and all over, in fact — are beginning to call the Carmelites 'Calced.' It makes sense, because if we are 'Discalced' — without shoes — they must, of course, be 'Calced' — with shoes. The only thing is that the Calced themselves don't like the expression *at all*."

"I can see why they wouldn't like it," John said dryly. "They've been known as the Carmelite Order for centuries, and now because a Reform branch develops, they suddenly become Calced Carmelites. . . . And you say that they're not too happy with our progress, either?"

"Not all of them, but a number of them. They think that the Reform should be a very small, specialized thing, consisting perhaps of one or two monasteries. They don't like the idea of our opening up a lot of monasteries, and getting bigger and bigger. They say that pretty soon there'll be two Carmelite Orders."

"That's what is going to happen eventually," John said. "It's got to happen. But are you sure that the — uh, Calced — really feel this way about it?"

"I'm sure, all right," Teresa said grimly. "Some of them have even visited me here and thundered away at me that we're trying to destroy the Order."

John sat in silence for a minute, then he said: "What we need is a formal separation into two separate Orders. Until that happens, there'll be all kinds of difficulties like this."

"Why don't you friars petition Rome for a separation, then?" Teresa asked.

"We're not that big yet. Rome would laugh at us if we asked for independence now."

"Well, it will all work out in time," Teresa said.

"I'm afraid, Mother, that problems like this just don't work themselves out in time."

"You mean you expect some kind of trouble with the Calced? What do you think will happen?"

"I don't know, Mother. I don't know."

"Anyway," Teresa said, rising to her feet, "that's not an immediate problem. My immediate problem is to get this convent back in good shape."

"As I said before, Mother, you'll do all right."

She laughed. "I'll do all right as long as you're here to help me."

Leaving the convent after his conversation with Teresa, John again felt uneasy: for the second time this month, he had noticed danger signals that trouble was fermenting for the Reform. His stay at Pastrana had shown him that there were some fundamental misunderstandings among the members of the Reform themselves. And today he had learned that the Carmelites, their religious superiors, were becoming disenchanted with the Reform. The Discalced Carmelite friars, he thought, had come a long way from that little house at Duruelo, but they still had a long way to go.

$\left[\text{ Chapter 7}\right]$

NEITHER Teresa's nor John's confidence in each other was misplaced: the convent of the Incarnation soon took on a new, vibrant tone. Teresa insisted on a more faithful attendance at the choral exercises of the community, limited the number of visitors the nuns were permitted to receive in the convent parlor, and placed the finances of the community on a firmer basis. John, on his part, spent long hours in the confessional each week hearing the sins and imperfections of the nuns, and exhorting them to a more profound holiness. In addition to this, he was frequently summoned to the convent parlor, where he offered spiritual direction and advice to some nun who needed direction or guidance on any one of the hundreds of minor problems which harass nuns.

Surprisingly enough, the nuns of the Incarnation neither resented nor resisted Teresa and her chosen chaplain; instead, they responded enthusiastically to the new administration. Nor was this rapid change in the convent of the Incarnation unnoticed by the priests and townspeople of Avila.

Soon the comment: "Those two Discalced Carmelites are making saints out of the nuns at the Incarnation," was heard throughout the city.

John was housed in the chaplain's quarters, a small one-story, wooden building directly across the street from the main door of the convent; and shortly after his arrival, Anthony sent another Discalced Carmelite priest, Father Germain of St. Mathias, to live with him. Father Germain assisted John whenever he required aid in caring for the nuns of the Incarnation, but his main duty was as chaplain for two other convents of nuns — fortunately, both much smaller than the Incarnation — which had petitioned for a Discalced Carmelite confessor after learning of John's appointment.

John was to live with Germain for a number of years in the closest association: they dwelt in the same building, ate together, and often recited their prayers together. Yet, John could never really say that he ever knew Germain or arrived at any point of close friendship with him. This did not result from any fundamental disagreement between them, but rather from the fact that Germain built an impassible wall of reserve around himself. In fact, John doubted if any living person had ever reached anything approaching friendship with the man.

Father Germain was a tall, thin friar, with deep-set eyes and heavily bearded jowls. He moved in swift, lithe movements, and appeared to be in constant activity. While at home in the chaplain quarters, he was either busily engaged in sweeping out the house with a reed broom, or hammering up a loose board somewhere on the wall, or in any one of the interminable projects which he seemed to find in the building. He departed early each morning, striding hastily down the street, and returned from his chaplaincy duties late in the afternoon, only to pick up a broom or hammer and begin his program of cleaning and repairing again.

Conversation in the chaplain's house was at a minimum; Father Germain preferred it that way, and John certainly had no objections to it. John had always imagined himself to be rather reserved, which he was, but he was forcefully made aware of the distinction between a reserved person and a taciturn one by the presence of Germain. John was quiet, recollected, and preferred to live in an atmosphere of silence, but when the occasion presented itself, he enjoyed a lively, spirited conversation. Germain, on the other hand, was totally incapable of any extended conversation, and would confine his discussions to short phrases on pertinent business or practical problems.

As far as John was concerned, the situation in the chaplain's quarters was ideal. He could foresee what would have occurred if some loquacious friar had been assigned to live with him: there would have been an endless succession of chatter and small talk which would have proved most distasteful to John.

Teresa had been correct, too, in asserting that John would now be in a position to observe intimately the struggle in the Reform for survival and growth. Strangely enough, the period of John's chaplaincy at Avila was the only extended time in his entire religious life in which he dwelt outside the monastery, and yet at no time in his life would he be more acutely aware of the internal affairs of the Reform and more irretrievably caught up in them. He had frequent conferences in the convent parlor with Teresa about business pertinent to the Reform; they exchanged the numerous letters they received from Discalced Carmelites in the five monasteries, discussed their contents, and often collaborated on replies. In addition, the chaplain's cottage witnessed a steady stream of Discalced Carmelite friars, who made it a resting point on their journeys from monastery to monastery. John warmly welcomed the dust-begrimed friars, offering them the hospitality of his quarters; he cordially invited them to spend a few days with the taciturn Germain and himself; and he eagerly listened to the latest accounts of the Reform, its friars, and its monasteries. Even Anthony made an occasional appearance in Avila, and John looked forward to visits from the senior Discalced Carmelite, who occupied the dubious position of quasi major superior of the Reform.

On Anthony's first visit he said to John: "You didn't think we were trying to get you out of circulation by assigning you here, did you?"

"I'm hardly what you could call out of circulation," John answered. "I'm very much in contact with everything that's going on."

"Splendid," said Anthony. This was his favorite epithet, employed in his conversations as an indication of any degree of approval, from reluctant acceptance to wild enthusiasm; its constant use in his talk caused some mild annoyance to many of the friars, and John had even heard Teresa mimic Anthony's stentorian mouthing of the word. For his own part, John was amused at Anthony's verbal mannerism.

During Anthony's first appearance at the chaplain's cottage, however, John indulged in a bit of wry humor in replying to the elderly priest.

"It is *splendid*, isn't it?" John said.

The subtle jibe apparently escaped Anthony; he merely smiled serenely, and continued talking. "You can gain a lot of prestige for us by a retired life in your little hermitage here, and by your availability for confessions and spiritual direction. I know that when people discover your competence in spiritual matters, they'll be vastly impressed with you — and consequently with the Order you represent."

Anthony's statement was prophetic, because within six months of John's arrival in Avila, he was in constant demand by the many religious houses in the city for spiritual services of one kind or another.

John responded to these requests by accepting an additional chaplaincy at the Augustinian convent, and by serving as auxiliary chaplain at a number of the other religious houses; also, he was called upon to deliver frequent lectures in churches and religious houses. He, therefore, discovered himself caught up in the same vortex of active work about which he had upbraided the prior of Pastrana a few months previously; however, he carefully regulated his work, donating the major part of his time to prayer and study in the chaplain's cottage.

One new aspect of the apostolate presented itself to John after his reputation had begun to swell in Avila: he found himself presented with a variety of "special cases," problems of people who had intricate difficulties in spiritual matters. The parish priests of the city, when consulted by people whom they felt unable to assist because of the involved nature of the case or the amount of careful attention required to solve it, often sent them off to some religious order priest. John was gradually included in the classification of priests who handled these "special cases," and consequently had new demands made upon his time.

Sometimes by post, other times by messenger, and again by direct contact, he would be requested to see different people about any one of a wide variety of problems. John was forced, therefore, to establish some sort of office hours in which to receive these people. He selected a small room off the spacious lobby in the convent of the Incarnation in which he could deal with the cases. He expressly forbade any callers at the chaplain's cottage itself: he knew that Germain would resent the intrusion of outsiders upon their domain. Furthermore, many of the callers were women, and it would be indiscreet to have ladies paying visits at the chaplain's quarters. And so John insisted that anyone who wished to see him arrange for an interview across the street at the Incarnation.

It was as a result of his immersion in the apostolate of special cases that he encountered Maria Ortega, and was led through the strange sequence of events produced by her case. One day some eight months after his arrival in Avila John was summoned across the street by the ragged young boy who ran errands for the nuns.

Entering the room which Teresa had placed at his disposal for these interviews, John saw the girl, who, he imagined, must be about eighteen or nineteen.

"Don't waste no time on me," the girl said petulantly by way of greeting. "You can't do nothing with me."

"Oh, you never know about that," John responded, trying to ignore the hostility in her voice.

Groping for a seat, he studied the girl who sat glaring defiantly at him — she had not risen when he entered the room, a common courtesy extended to priests. He saw a large dark-haired girl with an oval face. She definitely could be classified as attractive . . . and perhaps, yes . . . sensuous, he thought. She had full, red lips, which she now kept slightly parted, showing a row of even white teeth.

"If you don't think I can do anything for you, why did you come to see me?" John asked.

"My mother made me, and I promised I'd at least see you."

"Oh," he said softly.

"But you can't do nothing for me," she insisted again.

"You said that before."

John noticed, on closer observation, that the girl's hostility was not spontaneous, rather it seemed to be a disguise used to mask her fear. Her lower lip trembled slightly as John gazed at her. He took up the challenge of this mysterious woman.

"Do you know what I think?" he said.

"What?"

"I think you're afraid that I might be able to help you — and you don't really want me to."

She looked at him mutely, and John knew that he had made a telling point.

"Suppose you tell me all about your problem, and then I'll tell you whether it's as hopeless as you seem to think," he said.

She took a deep breath, and bowed her head, avoiding John's eyes. "It's . . . well . . . I'm in love with a man who's already married."

"You're in love with him — that's all?"

"I'm sort of . . . living with him, too."

"Here in Avila?" he asked.

"Yes."

"And where is this man's wife?"

"She's down in Toledo. Carlos — that's his name — he don't want to live with her no more."

She looked at him fiercely again. "But I love him, terribly; and I'm going to keep living with him."

"If you're so determined about this, how did your mother get you to come here?"

"Oh, Mamma, she's been crying and screaming about this for months, but when I told her that Carlos was going to move up to Burgos — he's a merchant — and I was going with him, she carried on something awful. She said that after all she'd done for me, and all that, I had no right to disgrace her by becoming a . . . you know what."

John nodded his head, signifying he knew what.

The girl was talking more freely now, and John observed tears forming in the corners of her eyes. "Mamma said that the least, the very least, I owed her was to talk with some priest. She'd heard about you somewhere, and made me promise to see you before I go away with Carlos."

"When do you plan to go away with him?"

"Not for a couple of weeks yet."

That was something, John thought. It allowed him some time to work on the case, some time to disabuse this girl from ruining her life and her soul. There was one major factor which John had in his favor: it would be impossible — here in Catholic Spain — for her paramour to obtain a divorce and marry the girl legally.

She started to rise from her chair. "I've told you what my problem is, but there's nothing you can do about it. I've kept my promise to Mamma — I'm going to go now."

"No, no," John said quickly. "Sit down there."

Wonderingly, the girl obeyed him and dropped back into the chair. As she did so, her long dark hair bounced lightly on her shoulders, and a pair of metal earrings, from which tiny figurettes dangled, clinked melodiously. Those earrings were probably gifts from friend Carlos, John thought absently. The young lady — who later identified herself as Maria Ortega — was rather well dressed; her gown was made of soft green velvet, material usually worn by women in the upper middle class. However, like Peter in the courtyard of the high priests, her speech betrayed her, and John judged her to have come from one of the working-class families in the city; her new-found opulence, no doubt, resulted from her adulterous relationship with the merchant.

"What are you going to do to me?" she whimpered.

"I'm not going to do anything to you. I'm only going to try to help you."

"You can't help me. I told you that you can't. I love him. I love him. I love him." Her voice rose in a semihysterical wail, and the tears which had formed in her eyes now ran down her face.

John breathed a quick prayer, and started in again:

"Look, little one, let me tell you something. No one will deny that you love this man, and no one will deny that you love him very much. He's probably a very wonderful person." John had grave reservations about his last statement; the chap was probably an outright scoundrel, but in cases of this sort, it serves no purpose to deprecate the absent lover: it only alienates the soul from you. So, for the sake of some rapprochement with Maria Ortega, he was willing to concede the possibility that Carlos was a likable sort of fellow — which, as later events proved, he was not.

Maria looked at him through tear-laden eyes. "Why, then, if I love him is it so wrong to live with him?"

"Because that's the law of Christ. He forbids remarriage — or cohabitation — with a person who has already been lawfully married. Christ established the law of one marriage for the common good of the human race. If remarriage were allowed — and once it gets started, there's no stopping it — family life begins to break down. Now, it's entirely conceivable that this law promulgated by God for the general welfare of the human race is going to hurt certain individuals sometimes. But the law which provides for the common good must prevail over the private good. . . . But all that isn't much consolation to you now, is it?"

"No!"

"Perhaps the most forceful reason for discontinuing this affair is the sanction Christ has placed upon His law."

"The what?" she asked dispiritedly.

"The sanction, the penalty He will impose upon you if you disobey the law. Christ has clearly outlined in Scripture the punishment He has prepared for those who die in sin: the eternal fire of hell. You don't want to end up in hell, do you?"

"I don't care."

"Of course you care. No one could really be indifferent to an eternity of pain."

Maria Ortega buried her face in her hands, and her words came out muffled, choked, and piteous. "I know all that! I've tried to break away from him — but I can't. I love him too much. I even got as far as packing my things once to get out of there; but he began to make love to me again, and I couldn't go, I just couldn't."

The more that John presented cogent reasons for the ending of the adulterous affair, the more Maria Ortega protested her inability to do so, even though she reluctantly admitted that John was correct. After talking to her for almost two hours, he decided that it would be futile to prolong the discussion any further at the present time.

"Listen," he said, "will you promise me that you'll come back and see me again in a few days?"

"I'll come back. I don't know what you can do for me, but I'll come back. I feel better just for having talked with you. You're kind and understanding — and you don't shout at me like the others."

"I know that you *can* break away from your sin. And I'm going to pray very hard for you until we meet again."

He held her cloak while she pulled it over her shoulders. And as John walked to the front door of the convent with Maria Ortega, he was struck with the rhythmic gait of her tall, erect body. It was entirely comprehensible to him how the merchant had become enamored of this girl. Anyway, he thought resolutely, he would pray with a fierce intensity that he might be able to do something about the problem.

John spent the major part of that night in prayer, and practically all of the following night. Maria Ortega was faithful to her promise and returned to the convent of the Incarnation three days later, attired this time in a dress of bright red.

Maria Ortega had not only changed her attire, she had also changed her attitude: she was genuinely glad to see John, and said so. As they talked, John noticed an increased willingness on Maria's part to take some positive action about bringing her affair to an end; she still protested, though, her lack of moral strength to do so.

"If you leave Carlos," he told her, "it doesn't mean that you have to stop loving him — although you will in time. Many people fall in love with the wrong person, the person God doesn't want them to love. But the only thing that God demands then from these unfortunate people is that they don't do anything about the love they feel in their heart."

"Do you know," she said, "you must have been praying real hard for me. I couldn't get you out of my mind; and I couldn't forget the things you said about God's law and hell."

John felt that she was now ready for some positive action, and, therefore, began to insist — kindly, but firmly — that she move out of Carlos' house. In the end Maria promised to relinquish her paramour and return to her mother's house (her father was a soldier away on foreign duty: the reason, perhaps, that the young girl had been allowed to drift so far).

"I'll leave him, but there's one thing I'll tell you: I'll never stop loving him. Never!"

"All right," John answered soothingly. He knew that she would, but was disinclined to urge the point right now.

Before Maria Ortega left the convent, after her second visit, John heard her confession, quickly and deftly wiping away her sins with the gentle words of Christ's absolution. She departed with a promise to visit John again, especially whenever she felt the pressure of temptation to return to the man she loved.

That evening John prayed again, but his prayer this time was one of gratitude to the clement Christ who forgave the woman captured in adultery fifteen hundred years ago, and who had continued to exercise His compassion countless times since — from that first unnamed woman in Jerusalem, down to Maria Ortega in Avila.

John was pleased with himself, and for the next few days the pleasant memory of the soul restored to God's grace lingered in his mind; then he pushed it away from his consciousness, and had all but forgotten about it until two weeks later when he was picking his way through one of Avila's narrow alleyways on his return to the Incarnation. He was walking with lowered eyes, praying silently, and consequently did not see the thin, well-dressed gentleman waiting for him on the corner.

"You're Father John of the Cross?" the stranger asked defiantly.

John, surprised at the sudden salutation, stopped and looked at the speaker. He had thin features, accentuated by an aquiline nose; a line mustache, jet black and obviously highly greased, ran along his upper lip. (John had always possessed a vague, irrational distrust of men with carefully cultivated mustaches.) Then, suddenly — either by inspiration or intuition — John knew that he was looking at Carlos, the paramour of Maria Ortega.

"Yes, I am he."

"You're a pious meddler!"

"Indeed."

Carlos spread his feet apart and thrust his forefinger out at John, indifferent to the townspeople passing by, who gazed with some astonishment at the angry merchant glaring down at the short friar. "You got Maria to leave me. But it won't work, I tell you, it won't work: she's back with me again. . . . And this time she's going to stay with me, and go away with me, too." There was a triumphant gleam in his eyes, and his whole demeanor bespoke victory.

This was disastrous news for John; and he had no reason to disbelieve it. In fact, he was convinced that Carlos was telling the truth: Maria had returned to her illicit love. For the moment John was not particularly concerned with the strategy Carlos had employed to achieve this; his interest now lay in discovering some method of destroying the union again.

His only comment to the merchant was:

"That's too bad."

"That's your way of looking at it."

"Unfortunately, that's God's way of looking at it, too," John said grimly. "You know, my friend, that you're a married man in God's sight. Why don't you return to your wife and leave this poor child alone."

"Ha," Carlos sneered. "I don't want to hear any of your sermons. I just want to tell you one thing: leave Maria alone! If you bother her again with all the Church nonsense, I guarantee you that you'll regret it the rest of your life."

"Is that a threat?"

"You can interpret it any way you want. I'm just stating a simple fact: if you appreciate your good health, leave Maria alone." He extended his forefinger again and thumped it sternly against John's chest. "Understand!"

John made no comment, but returned the man's gaze until Carlos whirled about and strode angrily away.

The remainder of John's trip back to the convent was consumed in some serious thinking about the problem of Maria Ortega and her violent suitor. He was not overly surprised that the girl had returned to her lover: you can expect anything in cases of this nature, he thought, and a relapse is often quite usual. The immediate task, however, was to extricate Maria from Carlos' house, wherever that was. He knew practically nothing about the man, not even his family name, nor the location of his residence. His information about Maria was just as incomplete, except that he knew her family name, Ortega.

By the time he arrived back at the Incarnation, he had formulated a definite course of action. As the first step in his plan, he hurried into the convent, asked to see Teresa, and waited impatiently for her to appear. All nuns, he thought (somewhat uncharitably), have no appreciation of time. When finally the smiling Teresa made an appearance, he inquired whether she knew any of Avila's merchants, and if she did, whether there was one who would be willing to give her some assistance. He was fairly certain that Teresa, with her coterie of benefactors, would be sure to have some contacts among the city's many merchants. She did; and, in fact, she had made the acquaintance of Philip Balthasar, one of the more influential and respected businessmen, who had pledged his complete support to her for any project she selected.

"Good," exclaimed John. "Where can I get in contact with him?"

"He has a large store on the *Calle Domingo*. I'm sure he can be reached there."

"Thank you very much, Mother," he said tersely as he rose to leave.

"What are you up to?" she asked slyly.

John smiled mischievously. "Just a little apostolic business, Mother."

Philip Balthasar was a venerable gentleman with a full white beard. John liked him immediately, despite his lavish use of jewelry — several large rings and a golden amulet hanging from his thick neck.

"Certainly I'll help you, Father," the merchant said, seated behind his wide mahogany desk in the spacious office at the rear of his store. "I told Mother Teresa that she had only to ask me for a favor to get it. I'm glad she took me at my word by sending you here."

"I appreciate this, *Señor*," John said.

"Humph," Balthasar grunted, dismissing John's protestation of gratitude. "What can I do for you — money, property, goods?"

"First of all, I want some information, and then possibly some material assistance."

"All right."

"Do you know," John asked, "anything about a merchant who came here from Toledo and whose Christian name is Carlos?"

"Carlos Sanchez," the merchant said immediately, and then added: "He's a scoundrel."

"Wonderful! I thought you'd know something about him."

Balthasar toyed with the amulet, which lay indolently on his chest. "In my business, Father, I make it a point to know all the merchants in town, what they're doing, what they're selling, and what they're charging. This Sanchez person is an itinerant merchant: he moves into a town with a lot of inferior fabrics, sets up a temporary shop, sells his junk cheaply — underselling all of us — and moves out before his customers can return to complain. In fact, I understand that he's leaving here in a few days.

"Fine! Do you know where he lives?"

"No, but I can find out easily enough." Balthasar rang a small silver bell on the desk. Almost immediately, an obsequious employee appeared. Balthasar mumbled a few hushed sentences to him, and the man disappeared as rapidly as he had come.

"I'll have the address in a minute," Balthasar explained to John.

"Now," John said, "I need some information of a more delicate nature. I'd like to know when Carlos — Sanchez, you say — will definitely be absent from his house."

"There's a merchants' market in the city tomorrow. Sanchez is almost certain to be there now — he goes to buy all the cheaper fabrics, those rejected by the rest of us."

"This market is held in the morning?"

"It begins at eight o'clock, and will last at least until noon."

"Hmmm," John mused aloud. "That takes care of that. And now about the material help I need."

"Name it," Balthasar said, an air of graceful magnanimity in his voice.

"I don't know yet whether I'll really need it or not. But if I do — could you provide me with a carriage and driver tomorrow morning to take somebody up to Mancera?"

"Is that all you wanted? I'll have a carriage with four horses and one of my best drivers ready here tomorrow from . . . say, eight o'clock on." His eyes twinkled. "I presume all this has something to do with Sanchez' absence from his home?"

"You're a very clever merchant, *Señor* Balthasar."

A knock on the door interrupted them, and the employee entered again and deposited on Balthasar's desk a slip of paper. After glancing at the paper, Balthasar shoved it across the desk to John, who read it and placed it in the pocket under his scapular.

A sly smile played around Balthasar's lips. "That's where you'll find him — or better, perhaps, that's where you won't find him. . . . All right, you've got your carriage and your driver. What else do you need? Do you want some money?"

John rose to leave. "No, thank you, *Señor;* I have everything I need now for this little job of mine. I don't know how I can thank you for your help. I'm sure God will reward you."

Balthasar stroked his great white beard contentedly. "If you'll say a prayer for me sometime, Father, I'll feel amply repaid."

"I certainly will — and more than just one prayer. Good-by, *Señor,* and God bless you."

John glanced from the paper he held in his hand to the two-story, stucco building, and, satisfied that he had arrived at the proper place, approached an old woman who squatted in front of the house munching on a piece of fruit.

"I beg your pardon, *Señora:* is this the house of Carlos Sanchez?"

"He lives upstairs; but you won't find him home now. He's at the merchants' market," she said.

"That's too bad," John answered. "But I'll go up anyway and leave a message for him."

John ascended the steep stairway, which ran up the outside of the building to the upstairs apartment. I'll leave a message, indeed, he thought — a message that will hardly please him. On the upstairs porch he found a single door, and rapped loudly on it.

There was no response for a minute or so, and he was about to repeat his knock when a thin voice from inside inquired:

"Who's there?"

John recognized the voice of Maria Ortega. "A friend," he answered.

There was a slight gasp from inside, a momentary pause, and then the door was opened a few inches. "What do you want?"

"I want to see you."

"You do?" she asked unbelievingly. Maria Ortega appeared confused and bewildered by the sudden appearance of the little friar. Finally, she opened the door wide. "Come in, Father. Come in."

John followed her into the square sitting room. Two large trunks stood half open in the middle of the floor; they were in the process of being packed. John selected a chair while Maria perched herself nervously on the edge of a couch directly opposite him. Her hair, which fell loosely around her shoulders when John last saw her, was now piled in a neat roll over the crown of her head; she wore a sheen taffeta dress, which rustled noisily as she moved. Her eyes, however, were red-rimmed, undercast with shadowy black lines, and her face was drawn and sallow.

"How did you . . . where did you, . . ." she said in a rush of confused words.

"Never mind how I learned about you or found you. The important thing is that I'm here — and I want to get you out."

Tears began to well up in her eyes. "I was real determined to stay away from him after that last time you saw me — and I felt so good — but Carlos, he met me on the street and pleaded with me to come back."

Friend Carlos had been doing a lot of business on the streets recently, John thought grimly.

Maria clasped her hands, squeezing them until the knuckles turned white. "You've been very kind to me, but can't you see that I'm bad, real bad?"

"I don't think that you're irredeemable, though."

"What?"

"I mean that I feel you can get out of this, that down deep you really want to. Listen, Maria. Didn't you feel wonderful after you left Carlos, after you broke with your sin and returned to God's grace?"

"I did, yes, I did. I felt good and clean. Now, I feel dirty and rotten again," she said bitterly.

"Of course you do, Maria. That's what your conscience does to you. And this gnawing unrest will never leave you — even if you go to Toledo, or Paris, or anywhere."

Maria slid off the couch to her knees and grabbed at the end of John's brown habit. "Help me, Father, help me. I want to do what's right, but I know when he comes home and makes love to me, I'll go anywhere with him."

John gazed down at the girl kneeling at his feet, and in a whispered voice said:

"I've worked out a plan to get you out of this mess completely. I've made arrangements for a carriage to take you to Mancera

immediately. You'll stay there for a few weeks — until we make
sure that Carlos is gone for good — then you can return here to
Avila, to your mother's house."

She looked up at John through the film of tears in her eyes,
seeming not to comprehend his plan.

John talked rapidly. (He had already consumed a considerable
amount of time, and there was no way of knowing when Carlos
Sanchez might return.) "The time you spend in Mancera will give
you an opportunity to pray and get things straightened out in your
own mind. When you come back Carlos will be gone, and with
him your immediate problem. You'll probably never see him again;
or, at least, it will be years before you do. By that time, I'm sure,
you'll be happily married to some nice young chap from Avila.
You're living and acting now in the fire of your passion for this
man. Get away to Mancera, and you'll be able to extinguish that
fire."

He was uncertain as to whether he had made his point with
Maria, but he had no time for any further discussion, so he asked
her the question, the crucial question on which depended the success of his machinations for the past days:

"Will you accept my offer and go to Mancera?"

The suddenness with which she capitulated surprised him. "I'll
go," she answered limply.

"God bless you, Maria. You'll never regret this. But — come! Let's
move quickly. Do you know where the shop of Philip Balthasar is?"

She nodded her head listlessly.

"Good! That's where I have the carriage ready. You get some
clothes together — not too many — and meet me there as soon as
you can. But, Maria — rush!"

Standing in front of Balthasar's busy store, John began to regret
that he had not brought Maria with him, instead of leaving her in
Sanchez' apartment to follow later. It had been over an hour since
he had left her, and there was no sign of the girl yet. He was just
beginning to dispair of her arrival when suddenly she appeared at

the end of the street. John did not recognize her at first: gone was the lavish taffeta dress, and in its place Maria wore a simple black gown with a shawl pulled over her head. She carried a small carpet bag.

"Did you think I wasn't coming?" she asked. Maria appeared more composed now, but her eyes were still watery. "I changed my clothes. I left all the beautiful gowns he gave me back at the apartment — it's a break with the past."

"Good girl," John said, directing her attention to the waiting carriage. "There's your conveyance to Mancera." This was a delicate enterprise, and he wanted to complete it quickly.

As she climbed into the enclosed carriage, John handed her a note he had withdrawn from the pocket of his habit. "Here is a letter addressed to Father Anthony of Jesus at our monastery in Mancera. It will explain your situation to him. He'll arrange a place for you to board during these few weeks. When everything is all right here in Avila, I'll borrow another carriage to fetch you back."

Maria looked forlorn, lonesome, and somewhat frightened. "Three weeks ago I never thought I could have made this step. You must be very close to God — only a real holy person could have got me to do this."

"God sometimes chooses strange instruments to complete His designs," he said awkwardly.

John's hand was resting on the sill of the carriage window, and the girl bent her head, kissing the friar's hand lightly. "Thank you, Father — for everything."

He stepped back, motioning the driver to go, and the vehicle careened wildly away. John remained motionless for a minute, watching the carriage disappear; and as he turned away, he could still feel the moisture from Maria's warm lips on his hand.

John returned to the cottage that afternoon, basking in the silent satisfaction of a task well done. Arriving at the chaplain's quarters, he remembered, as an empty feeling stretched itself in his stomach, that he had eaten no dinner. If he were at home during the meal hour, the nuns would have sent food over from across the street for Germain and himself, or if he were at some other convent or church, he would be fed — and sumptuously, too — wherever he happened to be. As a provision against situations of this kind, Germain had built a small wooden food chest, and hung it out the rear window of the building; John found that it now contained some dried fruit, a loaf of bread, a heel of cheese, and a half-filled flagon of sour wine. From these provisions he fashioned himself a meal which served at least to numb his gnawing hunger.

Having completed his simple meal, he remembered — with a start of surprise — that he was expected to hear confessions at the convent of Augustinian nuns this afternoon. Throwing his white cape over his shoulders, he dashed down the street toward the convent.

The confessions at the Augustinian convent were routine: the usual round of petty failings in the constant struggle for religious perfection. One nun requested a private interview in the convent parlor after the confessions, and, her request granted, proceeded to launch into a dolorous account of her difficulties in the religious life.

"You have no idea, Father, how much I have to suffer. The noise that floats up into the convent from the street below is simply terrible. And our convent itself is so poorly constructed — it's full of drafts which chill me to the bone. And then there's the . . ."

John listened patiently as the old nun recounted her woes and grievances, and it seemed to him that her list was interminable. He was forced unconsciously into a reluctant comparison between the problems of the nun, with her petty complaints, and those of Maria Ortega, who had to forsake the man she loved to remain in God's grace. He almost blurted out: "Sister, you have no problems at all; if you only knew of the real difficulties some of the people in the world experience." But he restrained himself, and said:

"The way to heaven, Sister, is the way of the cross, and we must all bear our difficulties with peace and equanimity."

When John finally succeeded in extricating himself from the nun, who was apparently prepared to talk for the remainder of the afternoon, he started on the tiring walk back through the city to the cottage. The darkness of the late fall afternoon had begun to shroud the city in eerie shadows, and a stinging wind whipped around the corners of the buildings. He pulled his cape snugly about his shoulders, bowed his head, and trudged along the almost deserted streets.

He was not far from home when he heard the clap of a footstep on the stones behind him. He disregarded it and continued to work his way against the brisk breeze. But when the footsteps were immediately behind him, he whirled about. John had only an instant to see the irate face of Carlos Sanchez, the paramour of Maria Ortega, but that one flash of a face twisted in fury and desire for revenge would be stamped into his memory for many years to come. Sanchez held a knotty piece of wood in his upraised hand, and as John turned to face him, brought it swinging toward the friar's head. It caught him on the side of his neck, sending him sprawling to the ground.

"I warned you not to meddle in my business," Sanchez cried. "Now, I'll give you what you deserve."

John, lying on the ground, was struck again and again in the stomach. The last thing John remembered before he lost consciousness was the figure of Sanchez standing over him, swinging the weapon down upon him.

Father Germain was an efficient housekeeper, but John never fully appreciated his effectiveness in that department as much as he did in those three weeks he was confined to bed after the brutal beating he received in the streets of Avila. Germain canceled his expeditions around the city during that period, remaining almost constantly at John's bedside, feeding him and otherwise caring for him. John protested this continual vigilance at his bedside, claiming that all he needed was rest. But Germain insisted, and he remained, ministering faithfully and expertly to his fallen friend.

Naturally enough, the strange episode of the attacked friar received wide notice and was the principal topic of conversation in

Avila for days. The whole incident, however, seemed to be cloaked in incomprehensible mystery: the only fact known was that John had been discovered lying in the street, beaten and bloody.

No one knew the identity of John's assailant, and John himself did nothing to enlighten anybody on the matter.

"Oh, I don't know," he said when questioned in bed by one of the local constabulary, "it may have been a brigand. Forget all about it, officer. No permanent damage has been done."

Not long afterward John received a letter from Philip Balthasar, the merchant, near the end of his stay in bed. John read the note with wonder and amusement:

My dear Father John of the Cross,

How horrified we all were to learn of the unprovoked attack upon your person a few weeks ago. My only consolation now is that reports tell me you are rapidly improving, and should be able to resume your invaluable work for God in a short time.

I hope you will forgive me, but, after the news of your misfortune reached me, I undertook a little investigation of the incident myself. However, the men employed by me could find no proof to the identity of your assailant — at least, no proof that the police would accept.

By the way, another mysterious attack has been reported to me. It seems that a certain itinerant merchant by the name of Carlos Sanchez — did we discuss him at some time? — was set upon by an unidentified group of ruffians as he was journeying between here and Burgos. The merchant was given a severe beating, and is now recuperating in a hospital somewhere north of here. My informants tell me that they feel Señor Sanchez is so displeased with the hospitality of our fair city that he is extremely reluctant to ever return again. Oh, the times of violence in which we live!

> Believe me,
> Your friend and benefactor,
> Philip Balthasar

⌈ Chapter 8 ⌉

ALMOST before John realized it, a year of his chaplaincy at the Incarnation had slipped away. The constant suction drawing him into apostolic work did not in the least diminish his preoccupation with the development of the Reform, and it was with genuine pleasure that he learned of the foundation of yet another Discalced Carmelite monastery. Unfortunately, he found himself powerless to thwart in any way the growing resentment of the Calced toward the development of the Reform. (John discovered himself employing the term "Calced" with a casualness that surprised him; Teresa had been correct in saying that the term would soon become common usage — a fact which caused no small annoyance to the Calced themselves.)

John even made it a point to visit the Calced monastery in Avila, but received a reception that was anything but warm and cordial. He was hard-pressed to analyze for himself the mounting hostility of the Calced toward the Reform. It was, he supposed, something akin to what a mother experiences when her child decides to leave the family residence at an early age to seek a place in the world. Again, there was the inevitable feeling among the Calced that the Reform constituted a constant, tangible rebuke to their way of life.

The situation was rapidly coming to an impasse, and John was uncertain, and somewhat afraid, of the manner in which the problem would be resolved. He did receive some indication of the direction in which events would move after a long conversation with Teresa at the Incarnation in the late summer of 1573.

The errand boy had dashed breathlessly across the street from the convent, bursting in upon John:

119

"Mother Teresa says to come right away. She wants to see you."

John threw aside the book he had been reading and stepped across the street to find Teresa waiting for him in the parlor.

"Who, pray tell, is Father Jerome Gratian?" she asked peevishly.

It had been well over a year since John had seen — or even heard of — Jerome Gratian, the promising young novice he had met at Pastrana. The intrusion of his name here at Avila struck him as a pleasant memory from the past, a delightful remembrance of a talented new Carmelite. But why was Teresa so obviously upset about him?

John told her all he knew of Jerome Gratian, of his charm, his talents, his promise; then he asked her the reason for her inquiry.

"It's unbelievable," Teresa said, "but I've just received a letter from Father Anthony informing me that this young man, Father Jerome Gratian, has been given the office of apostolic visitator to the Carmelites in Andalusia."

"What!" John exclaimed.

"Your reaction is the same as mine, Father. It seems that Father Francis Vargas has delegated all the permissions and faculties he had received from the Pope to Father Jerome."

"I wonder if Vargas can do that — if it's permissible, according to the laws of the Church."

"Permissible or not, he's done it," Teresa said bitterly.

John shook his head in bewilderment; he wanted to get all this clear in his own mind, to disentangle the web of jurisdictional confusion this new appointment had woven. The general, Father Rossi, was legally the highest superior of all the Carmelites — both Calced and Discalced. Yet, the Pope, who is actually the head of all religious orders (although he does not often actively employ his authority, but permits the orders to function by themselves under his supervision) had appointed two apostolic visitators for the Carmelite provinces in Spain. These men — Peter Fernandez in Castile and Francis Vargas in Andalusia — were technically in higher positions of authority than the Carmelite provincials or even the general himself, because they were the Pope's personal representatives. This alone produced a confused state of affairs; but now Vargas had passed on his authority to the young Gratian, placing him in the impossible situation of being, for all practical purposes, the superior of all Carmelites in the province of Andalusia.

"Wait until the news of this reaches the Calced," Teresa said. "This will really stir them up!" She tugged violently at her wimple, as the thought of what had happened asserted itself with a renewed fury in her mind. "But how could it happen? How could Vargas give his faculties to a young man just out of the novitiate?"

John smiled indulgently. "You don't know Father Jerome Gratian, Mother, or else you'd never ask that question. The man is fascinating; he's a . . . well, a charmer, one of those rare men who can impress you that they're competent at doing anything. I know just how all this happened: Vargas was dissatisfied with the position given him by Rome — he hasn't done one positive thing in Andalusia, has he? — and then he meets this brilliant, eloquent Carmelite. Gratian, for Vargas, is the solution to all his problems; he can pass his office along to the man, confident that Gratian will do a brilliant job. In one swift stroke, he has discharged himself of this unpleasant position and transmitted it, he thinks, to an eminently competent successor. That's precisely what happened — you can be sure of that."

"He should have refused the office," she said flatly. "No good can come of it."

John lifted his hands in a gesture of mock despair. "As you yourself said, Mother: right or wrong, he has the office. We can only hope now that he uses his new position wisely. In fact, it would be better for everybody — Calced and Discalced — if he didn't use it at all, if he just retained the title as did his predecessor."

"Do you think a young man would really do that?"

John laughed. "No, I guess he wouldn't. I guess he'll sail right into action with all the idealism of youth."

"Action? What kind?"

"Ah, there's the rub," John said gravely. "If he's the apostolic visitor in Andalusia — as he, unfortunately, is — he has full authority to make as many foundations of the Reform in Andalusia as he wants — without consulting anybody."

"Oh, no," Teresa groaned. "That's the one thing the superior-general didn't want. He expressly limited the growth of the Reform to our own province of Castile."

"Now, now, Mother, it hasn't happened yet," John said soothingly. "Let's just pray it doesn't happen."

But John's worst fears were realized: not only did the youthful Father Jerome make a foundation in Andalusia, but within the space of the next two years, he made *five* of them. Father Jerome Gratian acted temerariously, rashly, and with complete disregard for tact or propriety. Gratian failed to advise the Calced superiors of his new position — which common prudence would at least suggest; and, what was even more incomprehensible, he also acted independently of the Discalced superiors in Castile. Consequently, John and Teresa learned of the new apostolic visitator's activities second-hand, sometimes long after they were accomplished.

There was, John rationalized, a second side to the coin, though: the Reform was definitely growing — perhaps in a way that would not have been possible without Gratian's foundations in Andalusia. New candidates were applying for admission every day; the houses of studies were full; the priests were in constant demand; and all over Spain the clergy and laity alike were becoming aware of this new Reform. However, as John had expected, the Calced did not share this general enthusiasm; they regarded Gratian as an upstart bent on furthering his own ends; and, with a more serious charge, they branded him a disobedient friar acting outside the limits of the faculties granted the Reform by the general of the Order. This, John was forced to admit, was a complaint they could make in all good faith, for they had received no official notice of the faculties under which Gratian was acting. The situation was, John concluded, an uncomfortable one.

[Chapter 9]

IN THE spring of 1575, John was involved in an episode which jarred him completely.

The principal figure in that episode was one Doña Helena Cortez, a fairly affluent widow who occupied a stolid mansion near the southern wall of the city. John had first met the widow, a petite, dark-eyed, immaculately groomed woman, about a year and a half earlier, while preaching a course of Lenten sermons in St. Michael's, the church almost adjacent to her house.

He remembered their first meeting well: Doña Cortez had entered the sacristy and politely inquired if it would be possible to discuss a problem with him sometime. John arranged an appointment with her for the following afternoon in the office of the parish priest's house at St. Michael's.

Doña Cortez arrived promptly at the hour John had selected for the appointment, and was ushered into the parish office by a plump, wheezing housekeeper. John joined her almost immediately.

"I've been listening to your sermons during Lent, and I felt — that is, I know — you could help me."

"I hope so," John said.

Helena Cortez had launched into a narration of her difficulties. She explained that twelve years ago she had married the late Don Ferdinand Cortez, a wealthy landowner in Avila. Their childless marriage, while not an intensely romantic one, had nevertheless been reasonably happy. But two years ago, Don Cortez was thrown from his horse on a trip through the Sierras and was killed.

However, Helena Cortez explained, the sorrow of her loss was still with her. In all frankness, the young widow admitted that it was not Cortez himself that she missed so much as the state of being married — if Father John could understand that. John nodded his head, and then listened intently while she described her complete dissatisfaction with a widow's life and her frank desire for remarriage. This was, for all practical purposes, now impossible, for by the present standards of Spain she was considered above marriageable age — she admitted to being "slightly over thirty," but John judged her to be about thirty-five. Of course, Helena said, she could always marry one of the innumerable fortune seekers, who were only too happy to marry a wealthy widow; but she prudently realized that a union with one of these fortune hunters would be no real marriage at all.

John felt sorry for Helena Cortez. She was still an exceedingly attractive woman, very much in the prime of life. Her complexion was chalk-white (John was sure she used pale powders to heighten the transparent look her sallow skin gave), and her dark eyes and finely chiseled features added to the general impression of a fragile, delicate beauty. Doña Cortez' hair was jet black, tied in a tight knot on the nape of her neck; not one strand was misplaced, not one wisp out of line. She was slight of stature, about John's height.

As John looked at the petite widow perched delicately on the edge of her chair, he was reminded of a fragile, exquisitely executed china doll. He smiled at his own mundane comparison, and asked her:

"What have you been doing with your time since your husband's death?"

"That's the source of my problem, I guess. I haven't been doing much of anything." Her voice was soft and velvety.

"We've got to get you busy, then, doing something positive with your life." He outlined for her a program of charitable works in which she could expend some of her rather sizable fortune, and in which — most important of all — she could occupy her time.

"As far as your loneliness is concerned," he told her, "I can suggest no better friend than Christ Himself."

"Christ — my friend," she said slowly, enunciating the words carefully, as if hearing them for the first time.

"Yes, indeed: Christ wants to be your friend, and He can use the void in your heart as a new opportunity for occupying it." And so John launched into an appeal for a vigorous spiritual life for the young widow; he plotted out a definite program of prayer, meditation, and a conscious awareness of the constant presence of Christ.

John met Doña Cortez a number of times after that, occasionally at the various churches in which he preached, but most often in the small office placed at his disposal in the convent of the Incarnation. He sensed that the program of spirituality and charitable works he had outlined for her was successful, since Helena Cortez exhibited a new buoyancy, a new zest for living. Finally, he was satisfied that he had done all he could for her, that he had laid the foundation of a useful, well-integrated life, and, after a time, was somewhat annoyed with her importunate demands to see him.

"I've told you what you should do with your life," he said to her one day, somewhat peevishly. "There's nothing more I can do for you."

John, embarrassed, glanced at the pale face of Doña Cortez. Her lips were quivering slightly, and there was a hint of tears in her eyes, which were staring eagerly at him. A dull thought struck somewhere deep in his mind, but he dismissed it as impossible.

On the Christmas following his introduction to Doña Cortez, John was presented with five expensive leather-tooled volumes of St. Augustine's writings. When they were delivered he immediately demanded the identity of his benefactor from the carriage driver who had brought the books.

"They're from Doña Cortez," the uniformed carriage man said. "With the best of good wishes for Christmas."

John shook his head, examining the books; they were exquisite and fantastically expensive.

The next time he met Helena Cortez he protested the lavish gift, saying that he would be unable to accept her present.

Helena flashed a pert smile. "Certainly you can accept them.

I want you to have the books — I had them made especially for you."

"But they're so expensive," John said.

"Of course they're expensive. I wanted to give you something costly to show you how I feel about you."

John frowned. "I'll send them to the library of our monastery at Alcalá."

"You can do whatever you want with the books," Helena answered softly. "I just wanted them to be a demonstration of my appreciation of all you've done for me."

In the months that followed, John began to notice that the immaculately clad Helena Cortez was present at most of his sermons and lectures in the city; she would turn her delicate face up toward the pulpit, and with shining eyes follow John's words and gestures. He paid scant attention to her frequent reappearance, and, in fact, began to devise methods to avoid the good widow.

The shocking climax came on the evening of July 16. It was the feast of Our Lady of Mount Carmel, an extremely busy day for John. In the morning he had sung the solemn Mass at the Incarnation, preached the sermon, and participated in the procession; in the afternoon he walked through the city to the Discalced Carmelite convent of St. Joseph, where he delivered another sermon, and assisted in yet another procession. The nuns insisted that he remain for supper and then spend some time talking with them during the recreation period, and John reluctantly agreed.

Finally he was on his way back to the cottage. John would have the house to himself tonight: Germain was up at Segovia preaching for the feast, and was not due to return for at least another day. John thought to himself how good it was to be freed of Germain and his constant puttering for a day anyway.

Wearily, he entered the cottage. After some fumbling in the darkness, he ignited a candle — and the yellow flame revealed Doña Helena Cortez sitting coquettishly on one of the straight-backed chairs.

"I've been waiting for you," she said softly.

John stood at the door, holding the candle in his hand, stunned that Helena should invade his private living quarters. He leveled a fierce look at her. "You know I don't give any spiritual direction here in the chaplain's house."

Helena rose from her chair. "I don't want spiritual direction." John's next remark stuck in his throat, but he had to say it. "What *do* you want?"

"I want you."

Helena stood there, lips slightly parted, breathing heavily. The flickering light from the candle played on her lithe figure in its sweeping black dress, sending dancing shadows over her pale face and neck.

"Oh, Helena, no," John exclaimed with weary disgust.

She lowered her head and averted her eyes from John's glaring face. "You must know by this time that I love you, that I can't get along without you," she said.

John was filled with a violent anger. He was uncertain, though, whether he was angry at the widow's proposition itself, or at her obvious belief that he might consent to it. Did she really think that he would accept her proposal?

The problem now, however, was to select a proper — and immediate — course of action with Helena Cortez. The most sensible thing, he supposed, was to fling open the door and order the woman out. He was immediately reminded of a similar incident which had occurred to St. Thomas Aquinas: a woman had been sent into the Dominican saint's room for the evident purpose of seducing him; St. Thomas, acting on the impulse of divine grace, had grasped a flaming log from the fireplace and chased the startled woman from his room with it. Should he follow St. Thomas' course of action?

No! Not with this woman. Helena was in a bad condition spiritually, as he now realized: she had arrived at that distraught state where she had actually hidden herself in a priest's room for the purpose of seducing him. If he summarily dismissed her now the poor woman would flee in such embarrassment that she would probably never speak to him again. And he did not want to lose this soul for Christ.

He would talk the thing out with Helena — and now. But wasn't this perilous for him? No, he could honestly say it wasn't: the problem of chastity was something he had solved a long time ago, a matter definitely settled with no possibility of revocation. John was not unaware of the attractiveness of Helena Cortez and countless other members of her sex, but he had deliberately chosen to stifle his native response to feminine loveliness that he might love Christ better. He could not deny the beauty of Doña Cortez, but neither would he be allured by it.

"Sit down, Helena," he said quietly.

A new eagerness spread across her wan face. She took the chair to which John's gesture directed her, while he carefully drew his own chair to the other side of the table so that they sat facing each other. Helena started out in a torrent of words.

"Human love can't be thwarted," she said. "My love for you is an undeniable thing which just has to be expressed. I think I'll go mad if I can't have you."

John scowled, attempting to find the right words. Helena pounced on the momentary silence.

"Come away with me. . . . I have money — lots of it — and we can go anywhere: to France, or England, or even to the New World. I can make you happy. . . ."

"Can you?" John asked dryly.

"Of course I can!" Helena said, reaching out for John's hand, which lay idly on the table.

John drew back his hand quickly. "I gave my heart to Christ years ago," he said, "and I have no intention of revoking that gift now." He tried to make his voice smooth, gentle, and consoling; but he was very much afraid that he failed to do so.

"You could learn to love me. I could teach you," the woman said.

"Helena, can't you understand: I don't want to learn, I don't want to be taught."

She tilted her head sideways, assuming the coquettish pose again. "Don't you think I'm attractive? I've always been told I am."

"Of course you're attractive — you're beautiful. But that's not the point."

"You do like me, don't you? You just said so."

John breathed heavily. If he couldn't do any better than this, he might as well follow St. Thomas' method of getting rid of his unwelcome visitor. Like a patient teacher, he tried again, slowly and carefully.

"Let me spell it out for you: I don't love you; and I have no intention of doing what you want."

"I don't believe you," she said curtly.

"Whether you believe it or not, that's the way I feel. The only reason I didn't throw you out when I found you here tonight was that I thought I could drive some sense into you. Your offer is absurd."

"You wouldn't think it was absurd if you could see into my heart."

John disregarded her remark. "I'm not so much concerned that you think you've fallen in love with me — "

"I don't think I've fallen in love; I *have* fallen in love," she interrupted fiercely.

"All right, what upsets me is your willingness to commit sin, to offend the good God, and hurt your own soul."

Helena remained silent. John, the priest, was speaking, and she could offer no argument to his priestly analysis of the strange situation.

"Don't you realize that what you've done tonight is wrong and sinful?" John asked.

She didn't answer, but bowed her head. John asked the question again, and she responded reluctantly in a tearful voice:

"Yes, I guess so."

"Good, I just wanted to be sure that you realized it. Now suppose we forget all about what happened here tonight."

She finally looked up at him through watery eyes. "You must think I'm terrible. . . ."

"Not at all — just mixed up."

That remark seemed to break the tension. John rose from his chair, and made an obvious move toward the door.

She followed John to the door. "Father, I'm very sorry for . . . this. Please excuse me — I don't know what came over me."

"Forget about it; it's a closed incident."

"I promise you that it won't happen again," she said, weeping softly. "You're good and holy; and the remembrance of your goodness will give me the strength to be good, too."

"You'll be all right, Helena," he said kindly.

"And, Father . . ."

"Yes?"

"Thanks for not treating me like I deserved when you found me here tonight."

Watching Helena Cortez slip silently down the street, John was astonished at his own lack of perception in the whole incident. He should have realized that the young widow was becoming romantically attached to him, that the guidance he was giving her created an emotional dependence, which Helena, in her loneliness, seized upon.

[Chapter 10]

It was at this time that John's fears for the success of the Reform reached their zenith.

He was stationed at the Incarnation, and therefore removed from the area of conflict, but he watched and fretted over the sequence of painful events which brought the Reform to the crisis of its young existence.

The Calced held their general elections at Piacenza, Italy, in the late spring of 1575. Completely disgusted with Gratian, who still had not yet informed them of his faculties, the Calced Fathers made a violent decision to restrict the Reform to three or four monasteries in the province of Castile which were to be under the immediate supervision of the Castilian provincial.

Gratian then sprung into action. He approached the apostolic nuncio in Madrid, and obtained from him the rather dubious title of "provincial superior of all Discalced Carmelites." This new office made Gratian responsible, in the affairs of the Reform, only to the nuncio, and to the Pope above him, of course. Gratian's first official act as provincial superior was to declare the Piacenza decrees invalid and therefore not binding on the Reform.

Thus, the Calced demanded that the Reform comply with Piacenza decrees, and the Reform — following the orders of Gratian — refused to comply. It was a complete impasse.

Gratian was advised by the Fathers of the Reform (John among them) to petition directly to Rome for a formal separation from the Calced, which would give the Reform a juridical independence from the main branch of the Order. Gratian promised to do this, but for some unfathomable reason, procrastinated in making the formal appeal to Rome.

By the fall of 1577, John was fearful of the action the Calced might take to implement the execution of the Piacenza decrees. He feared for Gratian and what the Calced might do to him, but he had no suspicion that he himself was in any danger until late in October, when he received an unexpected visitor.

He had been alone in the chaplain's house, awaiting Germain's return from downtown Avila, when he heard a sharp rap on the door.

"Any contemplative friars in here?" a voice shouted from outside.

John was on his knees, praying, but that familiar voice pulled him immediately to his feet. He yanked open the door, and there stood the smiling, welcome figure of Father Peter Orozco, his Calced confrere from his student days at Medina and Salamanca.

"Peter! What are you doing here?" John fairly shouted back at him.

"Just passing through, but I thought I'd drop in and see how the hermit was doing."

"How long has it been since I last saw you?" John asked, pulling the grinning Peter into the house.

"Eight years, you rascal, eight long years."

John studied his friend's face: it was a more mature, more lined face than the one he had seen so often during their novitiate days and through the years at Salamanca. Eight years of hearing confessions, of listening to the problems of countless people, of giving advice had left their indelible mark on the young priest's countenance.

"Come in. Sit down," John bubbled. "Can I give you a drink of wine?"

"I don't want any of your abominable wine," Peter said, but nonetheless accepted the small cup John handed him.

There was much to talk about, much to discuss: eight years' worth. Peter seemed to have followed John's career closely. And he had, he told John when they seated themselves, spent most of the eight years in vigorous apostolic work, acquiring a modest reputation as a preacher; he was now on his way to Madrid, where he was to give a series of sermons.

When Peter had delivered himself of the account of his work and the news of men whom John had known before his entrance into the Reform, he leaned across the table to his old friend. "But what's all this trouble you Discalced are brewing up?"

John screwed up his face in mock anger. "That's right; I forgot: we're enemies now. You're a Calced, and I'm a Discalced."

Peter winced. "Oh, that name — Calced!"

"I knew that'd bother you."

"If you think it bothers me, you should hear what some of the other Carmelites say about it."

John sobered. "Seriously, Peter, is the situation bad?"

"Bad? It's terrible. . . . What's all the fighting about?"

Calmly, and with intense precision, John described the jurisdictional muddle which was a result of the offices bestowed on Gratian; he carefully outlined the confusion resulting from the dual authority which operated in the Reform — the Calced superiors on the one hand, and the extraordinary faculties of the apostolic nuncio on the other.

"In other words," Peter asked, "you fellows feel that you're acting under legitimate authority?"

"We not only feel we are, Peter — we *are*. The difficulty lies in the fact that Gratian has refused to inform your superiors officially about the new faculties he's acting under."

"Is he afraid to tell them?"

John threw his hands helplessly into the air. "To tell you the truth, I don't know whether he's afraid, or ignorant, or what."

"Who's right then, the Calced or the Discalced?"

"That's the rub, Peter. We're both right."

"Now, now, little John, you must be forgetting your logic from Salamanca. Two opposites can't be the same."

"That's what the book said. But in this case, the book is wrong. The Discalced are right because they're operating under the legitimate faculties given to Gratian; and the Calced are right because they officially know nothing of these faculties. Although, I must admit — even if it makes me a traitor to my cause — that Gratian is wrong in not at least advising the Calced of his new faculties."

"Hmm," Peter said, "so that's the way the situation stands. . . . What are you fellows going to do now?"

"The friars of the Reform requested Gratian — and he agreed — to make a formal petition to Rome, asking for a separation from the Calced. But . . . there's been some inexplicable delay in sending the petition."

"You'd better hurry up and get separated then," Peter said ominously.

"Why?"

Peter leaned back in his chair, "I'll tell you, and it's the main reason I came out of my way to see you today. Our superiors feel that the Reform is still under their complete jurisdiction, and they also feel that the Reform has been completely disobedient to our commands and directives. Therefore, they intend to crack down on it."

"In what way?" John asked.

"This is unpleasant, but I've got to tell you. They've appointed a Father Jerome Tostado — a Portuguese, no less — to execute the decrees of the Piacenza elections. He's in Toledo right now preparing to suppress all the houses of the Reform which were not founded with the express permission of the general."

"Oh, my!"

"You haven't heard the worst of it yet. What I've just mentioned is Tostado's ostensible mission; in reality, what he's been appointed to do is suppress the Discalced Reform completely."

"Suppress the whole Reform?" John cried, a look of anguish on his face. "Why?"

"You know how it is. We're still living in the wake of what that so-called reformer, Luther, did up in Germany. The superiors are afraid that you people are getting out of hand, like Luther.

The very word 'Reform' makes them shudder. Seventy-five years ago this whole thing would have been handled differently, but because of the Protestant Reformation, the superiors intend to act rigorously and decisively."

John rose from his chair, shuffled over to the window, and gazed out into the street. "The only thing we can do now is to pray to the good Lady of Mount Carmel."

"All right, pray for the Reform if you want; but you, John, you've got to do more than just pray."

"What do you mean?"

"Father Jerome Tostado has you as number one on his list."

"His list of what?"

"His list of Discalced friars he wants to lure away from the Reform," Peter said dryly.

"What are you talking about, Peter?"

"You always were a dull fellow; let me explain." Peter smiled pleasantly at him. "Tostado feels that he can best destroy the Reform by getting its key man back into the Calced — as you call us. He believes — and rightly so — that you are the foundation of the Reform."

"That's absurd," John said peevishly.

"No, it's not. You were the first Discalced Carmelite friar; you trained the first novices; and by your work here in Avila, you've put the Reform on the map. If Father Tostado can get you to abandon the Reform, I assure you that the whole thing will collapse."

"It will not collapse; I'm just another friar in the Reform."

Peter slapped his hands on his thighs, and rose to join John at the window. "Whether you believe it or not is of little importance right now. What is important is that Tostado believes it, and that he is going to act on it."

"So?"

"So, plenty! This Tostado is a tough customer. He always gets his way."

"What can he do to me? I'm not going to abandon the Reform."

"May I remind you, my little man, that as far as Tostado is concerned, you are a recalcitrant, disobedient Carmelite. In all honesty of conscience he can apply the punishments provided in our constitutions for recalcitrant religious. And may I further remind you that said constitutions provide such choice punishments as incarceration and scourging."

John continued to gaze out the window for a moment. A horseman was trotting down the street, and John's eyes followed him until he was out of sight. "That's what I like about you, Peter: you're always so cheerful and optimistic."

John's jibe broke the serious mood of their conversation, and Peter spent the remainder of his visit recounting a series of humorous incidents that had happened to him in the past years.

But when Peter departed, John returned to his thoughts of Tostado and his plan to suppress the Reform. He could very well understand the reason for the position the Calced were taking: they felt that the Reform was attempting to separate itself from ecclesiastic authority. But, he thought, the Calced were only looking at one side of the picture; they could only see the confused administration under which the Reform was operating. And a confused one it was, he thought: the Reform was growing like a weed, without plan or without an over-all program. This was, of course, caused by Gratian's government, and most of all by the tremendous number of unexpected new vocations.

However, John thought, there was the other side of the picture: the contemplative life the Reform was giving to the Church. And it was this that made the Reform a vitally important thing, it was this that made all the struggle worth while. John was willing to grant that the Reform, in its external administration, in its dealings with the Calced, was far from perfect; but in its internal life, in its program of prayer and contemplation, it was sound and strong. The external administration would catch up with the interior development of the Reform, John thought, but the Calced would have to give them time, they would have to remind themselves of the tremendous service the Reform was doing for the Church by establishing a vast organization of contemplatives.

But, as he sadly reminded himself, that seemed out of the question. The Calced were preparing to suppress the Reform. He wondered how it would all end.

Peter's dire warning had so unnerved John that he composed a detailed letter of their conversation, and sent it off to Gratian, who was then in Madrid. In the letter, he politely inquired of the reason for the failure to send delegates to Rome with the petition for separation, and he asked Gratian what course of action he should take in regard to the determined Tostado, only a few leagues away in Toledo.

The post was, as usual, wretchedly slow. Perhaps, John thought, he should have hired a special messenger to carry the note on horseback. At any rate — either because of the slow post or Gratian's procrastination in replying — it was a full five weeks before he received an answer. It arrived on a brisk, biting day in the first week of December. John tore open the letter and read it while the faithful Germain peered over his shoulder.

"That's it," John said.

"He says we're to leave Avila, eh?" Germain asked.

"That's right. Father Gratian paints an even worse picture of Tostado than Peter. He says we're to leave here immediately for the monastery at Mancera — that's one of the monasteries founded with the permission of the general, and, according to the decree of Piacenza, we're safe in living there."

"And we're not safe here?"

"Not according to Gratian. He thinks that Tostado could apprehend us here and charge us with living outside one of the approved monasteries."

"Well," Germain said dryly, "a trip will be nice."

"Let's pack our things then."

Germain stood motionless, looking around the small chaplain's house he had labored so hard to work into livable shape. "It's a shame, though. I spent years working on this house, and now because some Portuguese villain wants to play at being a buccaneer, I have to run away and give it back to the termites."

John was busy pulling books off the shelf. "You'll have a chance to see firsthand what a buccaneer Father Tostado is if you don't hurry up and get ready."

They consumed the next hour in a rushed packing of their belongings; it was dusk before they completed their task.

John, a smudge of dirt on his cheek, surveyed their work. "Let's just take what we need right away. We can send a wagon for the rest of the things."

Germain nodded his head. "Do you think I should take — "

But he never completed the sentence, for just then the door was flung open, and John had his first view of Father Jerome Tostado.

⸢ Chapter 11 ⸥

John never enjoyed traveling over the Spanish highways in those wooden, horse-drawn wagons: the vehicle constantly lurched to and fro, and exhibited an amazing penchant for discovering ruts and crevices in the road. He found that mode of journey no less satisfactory on the cruel journey from Avila to Toledo after Father Tostado had taken him captive. John's hands were bound tightly behind his back with a rope that stretched down to a similar binding around his feet; a rough gag had been bound over his mouth; and he lay helpless, face down, in the bottom of the wagon.

It was incredible, John thought bitterly, that Tostado had to bring constables from Toledo to apprehend Germain and himself — and a number of them, too, perhaps ten or twelve, dressed in their black uniforms and brilliant gold braid. Tostado had played the scene to the hilt, reading a formal document in a rasping voice, while the constables pinned his and Germain's arms behind their backs. Snatches of the proclamation Tostado had read still rang in John's ears:

". . . that whereas the friars dwelling outside of those monasteries duly founded with the permission of the Most Reverend Father General are judged to be recalcitrant, rebellious, and contumacious, they are to be punished with the full severity of the measures outlined in our holy constitutions. . . ."

John had no delusion about the disciplinary measures contained in the constitutions: he had studied them as a novice at Medina, and he knew them to be severe. The main thing that troubled him now — aside from the floor boards of the wagon beneath his face — was his concern over the whereabouts of Germain. His fellow Discalced Carmelite had been separated from him and was being taken somewhere else. John had heard the driver of his own wagon mention their destination as the Calced monastery in Toledo, but he was certain that Germain was being taken to some other monastery.

The secrecy of the abduction from Avila, John reasoned, must have been due to Tostado's fear of resistance by the local citizens if they had seen the two friars being forcibly removed. No fear of that now, John mused; for no passer-by would ever realize that the chaplain of the Incarnation lay, trussed up, in the bottom of the unpretentious wagon that lumbered out of Avila.

The Calced Carmelite monastery in Toledo was huge, massive, and formidable, with exterior walls of enormous gray stones, giving the building the general appearance of a fortress.

On his arrival at Toledo, he was thrust into the narrow damp room, whose every crack and crevice was to become so familiar to him. The room — a small enclosure of ten feet by five feet — was located somewhere on the second or third floor of the monastery, and was situated at the rear of the building. Apart from the thick wooden door, there was only one aperture in the room, a tiny window about a foot square up close to the ceiling.

Before he was put into the room, the habit of the Reform had been stripped from him, and he was roughly garbed in the Calced habit once again — a dirty and tattered one. Thus, when the lock on the door clicked behind him, he found himself surrounded with strangeness: a strange habit, a strange room, and, above all, a strange situation.

He groped about in the semidarkness, touching the wet walls of his tiny cell. He found a small, crude stool and sat down on it. When his eyes adjusted to the gloom he saw only one more object: a wooden plank bed covered with one torn blanket. He was receiving the full severity of the punishments, all right.

He threw himself down on the narrow bed, drawing the ragged blanket tightly around him. The damp room, the frosty night, and the inadequate coverlet all conspired to make his teeth chatter.

He lay there, cold, alone, and uncertain of the future; and he prayed, talking to Christ, offering Him the sufferings of this present situation as his contribution to the ultimate success of the Reform. John's conscience was clear: he had done no wrong, he had acted in complete accordance with what he felt was right. He was being punished — yet he had perpetrated no conscious malicious act. But, then, hadn't Christ Himself been falsely accused, falsely punished; and what had Christ said? — ". . . the servant is no greater than the master."

This thought afforded John no small consolation in the dampness and the stricture of his new home.

Father Jerome Tostado was a swarthy, dark-jowled man of average proportions; his nose was sharp and pointed — a feature emphasized somewhat, perhaps, by his quick piercing eyes. John, viewing his captor in the morning light, had the impression of looking at a raven in quest of prey.

"You've heard the charges levied against you," Tostado was saying. "Do you deny them?"

John surveyed the scene here in the Calced monastery at Toledo on the morning after his abduction. Tostado, flanked by a Carmelite on each side, was seated behind a table in one of the monastery offices, while John, still garbed in the tattered habit, stood on the opposite side of the table facing them. His feet were untied, but his hands were again bound behind his back.

"I admit," John said evenly, "to all that you have stated about my living at the chaplain's house at the Incarnation, and my refusal to comply with the decrees of Piacenza, but I deny that there was any disobedience implied in my doing so. I was simply following the directives of my superior, Father Jerome Gratian, who is acting under the special faculties bestowed on him by the papal nuncio."

"We know of no such faculties," Tostado rasped.

"Nevertheless, Father," John answered, "these faculties do exist, and they are valid."

Tostado, apparently disinclined to argue the matter, pointed a finger at John. "Do you know that we can impose the penalties of our constitutions on you?"

"I do; and I am quite willing to accept your punishments."

John's forthright declaration caught Tostado by surprise, and he consumed the next few minutes rifling through some papers that lay before him. Then he worked his face into what he felt was a pleasant smile.

"Come now, Father John, let's not bicker about mere legalities. We're intelligent men, and I'm sure we can come to an intelligent agreement." He gazed at John, and then, as if noticing for the first time the cords binding his wrists, turned to a thin priest standing on the other side of the room. "Father, are his hands tied? Unbind them! We don't need that: Father John of the Cross and I are going to have an intelligent discussion."

John was suddenly very weary of Father Jerome Tostado and the whole proceedings.

Tostado waited until John's hands were loosened before he spoke again. "Father John, I can tell you confidentially that the Discalced Reform is a failure; it will be completely suppressed in a few months. I know that you and many of our good priests were beguiled by that . . . that ambitious woman, Teresa. But we're willing to overlook all that in the case of a few of the more talented members of the Reform."

John almost laughed aloud. Tostado was ridiculous, ludicrous: his flattery was patently obvious.

Tostado moved his hand in a gesture of condescension. "Why don't you just rejoin the main branch of the Order — no formalities would be necessary, only your rejection of the Reform. Then we could forget all these charges levied against you. . . . We think so highly of you, Father John, that we're prepared to offer you the priorship in one of our larger monasteries. Think of it: you could be freed from these charges and be superior in a large monastery. All you have to do is renounce the Reform."

There was silence as Tostado's sharp eyes bored into his captive.

John shrugged his shoulders; he supposed that he was expected to say something; he took a deep breath, and began:

"I appreciate your offer. But I have made my profession in the Reform, and I intend to die in the Reform."

Tostado jumped to his feet, pushing the chair violently away, his face twisted into a menacing scowl. "There might be a lot more truth in what you say than you now realize. . . . All right then, we'll see how cocky you are after you receive the punishments of the constitutions."

John very shortly experienced the force of Tostado's threat: that evening he was marched into the spacious community refectory and shoved to his knees in the middle of the floor. His habit was worked off him by a friar who stood silently behind him; and, stripped to the waist, John knelt patiently, waiting for what he knew was to come.

The first crack of the lash was followed almost instantly by the second. He heard the movement of the friars behind him: they were walking in a slow circle, each friar swinging a lash at John's white back. In a few minutes his back was covered with a criss-cross of welts.

The pain became excruciating as additional blows fell across the already burning skin. John felt his eyes begin to smart. He hoped that he could keep those tears in his eyes — that they wouldn't course down his cheeks. He so much wanted to show them how manfully a Discalced Carmelite could suffer.

The blows continued to fall on him, flicking at the bits of torn flesh that now hung on his back. He prayed, and in his prayers his thoughts mounted up over Toledo and drifted back to a similar scene some fifteen hundred years before when another Man had been scourged, when another Man suffered those searing stings on His back.

John had joined the Reform to find solitude and more time for prayer; if nothing else, his incarceration at Toledo gave him just that. He was closeted in the narrow room for the entire day, and was removed only in the evening to receive his daily flagellation in the refectory. He made ample use of the opportunity by devoting long, unhurried hours to his prayers. His only reading matter was a worn Breviary the Calced had given him; and since there was no candle in the room, he had to read the prayer book standing on the stool, so as to capture the thin shaft of light from the small window near the ceiling.

The daily scourgings took their severe toll on his back, which was kept so sore that when he lay down to sleep he had to roll over on his stomach or his side.

This was his hour of darkness, and his only consolation lay in the conviction that he was attaining new intimacies at prayer with Christ. Toledo was his crucible, but it was also the refining place for a new flame of love for God which burned brightly and bravely in his soul.

Alone in the prison cell, freed from the mounting work at Avila, John had ample time for a calm appraisal of the whole situation: of his imprisonment, of the struggle with the Calced, of the Reform's value.

He, first of all, subjected the Reform to a searching inquiry, and his conclusion was that the Reform — despite all the recent difficulties — had vindicated the optimistic hopes which he had for it nine years ago, that it was very much of a success. The Reform was accomplishing precisely what he and Teresa had hoped it would. The success of the Reform was proved not only by the number of monasteries which had been established and by the many applications for admission which were received, but by the manner in which the members of the Reform themselves were enthusiastically adopting the spirit of the new organization. The Discalced Carmelite monasteries were houses of prayer, of contemplation, of penance; and from them, came forth friars, alive with the love of God, to preach, to hear confessions to win souls for heaven. And in this, John concluded, the Reform was fulfilling its mission in the Church.

The problems the Reform was experiencing were, he supposed,

to be expected. Didn't Mother Teresa warn him that it would be an "encounter"? And could he expect anything else but initial struggle for the infant Reform, when the Church itself was begun on a blood-splattered hill outside Jerusalem?

However, as resigned as he was to the fact of struggle, it was when he turned his consideration to the Calced that he became upset. It was tragic that the Reform should be in conflict with the Calced. It was more than tragic, he thought, that good men had to waste their time fighting each other, when there was so much evil in the world to fight. But this had always been — and always would be, he thought, somewhat grimly — one of the paradoxes of Christianity: that good men would so often wrangle among themselves as to the best means for accomplishing God's work. It had started back in the time of the Apostles; it had occurred frequently in the lives of the saints for the past sixteen hundred years; and now it was happening again.

He had to admit that, because of the muddled jurisdiction and Gratian's imprudence, the Calced were not to be condemned for the position they were taking. They were certainly in good faith in their attempts to suppress the Reform, which they sincerely believed to be now operating outside the limits of religious authority. Nor could the Calced be criticized for the harsh punishments they were inflicting on him: they were simply applying the sanctions contained in ecclesiastical legislation. All of the modern, sixteenth-century orders possessed such legislation, and they used it frequently in dealing with recalcitrant friars. John realized, of course, that personal pique and some overenthusiasm was contained in the application of these penalties to him; but, nonetheless, the Calced felt they were completely justified in employing those punishments, and in fact, they probably would have felt negligent in their duty had they failed to do so. These were the days of the Inquisition, the days of the Protestant Revolt, and religious disobedience had to be dealt with sternly.

As for his own position in the whole affair, John was resigned to whatever happened to him at Toledo. All of his sufferings could

be offered to God for the ultimate triumph of the Reform. He was still amazed, though, that the Calced had singled him out, that they were attempting to get *him* to abandon the Reform. Was Peter right? Did they regard him as the foundation of the Reform? He thought that improbable. Turning the situation over in his mind, he concluded that it would have been practically impossible for the Calced to incarcerate Gratian — or even Anthony, for that matter. They both lived in large monasteries, and it would have been too difficult for the Calced to march in and abduct one of the friars — to say nothing of the public disturbance it would cause. No, he felt that he had been taken prisoner because of his accessibility, because of the ease with which he could be captured. Of that he was sure.

However, the only fact of importance for John now was that he was imprisoned. It was in God's plan, he thought, that he should be here, that he should suffer for the Reform. And so he prayed — to God and to the Blessed Virgin — not for his release, only for strength to bear the hardships of his imprisonment. There was no sense, he thought, in asking the Blessed Virgin to free him, when it was evidently the will of God that he be here. "Just give me courage, Mother of God, give me courage," he prayed.

John met Tostado once more — the last time he was ever to see him — and his captor attempted again to force his renunciation of the Reform. John, as before, of course refused. After that, Tostado disappeared, off somewhere, John supposed, to continue his efforts to suppress the Reform. But John was not left without a jailer for Tostado's office was assumed immediately by the prior of the monastery, Father Ferdinand Maldonado. The prior of Toledo was no stranger to the case: he had accompanied Tostado to Avila when John was captured, and had, in fact, led Tostado to the chaplain's house at the Incarnation.

Maldonado, a thin man, with a pock-marked face, had complete confidence in Tostado's ability to stamp out the Reform, and saw no urgent necessity to spend any time in cajoling John back into the ranks of the Calced. As far as Maldonado was concerned, the sole reason for John's imprisonment was punishment. Therefore, after Tostado's departure, John received no more requests or inducements to abandon the Reform; he was simply held prisoner.

"Let him rot in there until he learns to obey," Maldonado said indifferently.

John had two special torments of soul during his months at Toledo: first he was refused permission to receive the sacraments, or even assist at Mass; second, he was gravely disturbed at the thought that no one of the Discalced knew the location of his imprisonment. He felt sure, and rightly so, that the Calced would not advertise the fact that Father John of the Cross was at Toledo. This uncertainty about his present whereabouts would, undoubtedly, be a source of distress to Gratian, Anthony, Teresa, and all the other members of the Reform. It was impossible to get a message out to them, for he was securely locked in his cell all day, meeting only a brother who brought food to him. The brother was apparently so confused and frightened at the entire situation that he would deposit the food and hastily leave.

The scourgings continued nightly for the first two months of his captivity; then they were reduced to once a week, and finally he was beaten only sporadically, whenever Maldonado felt in the mood for it. John wondered at the reason for the decrease in the amount of corporal punishment.

The vigilance placed over him, however, was not mitigated. One day, three months after his imprisonment, Maldonado himself visited John in his narrow room.

"Still here, are you?" Maldonado said.

John peered at his ecclesiastical captor. "Yes," he said simply.

"I'm glad you like it. And to make *sure* that you stay with us, I'm putting a stronger lock on your door." He held in his hands a lock of immense proportions.

John looked at it indifferently. "That big lock for me?"

"I've just received word that your friend, Father Germain, has escaped from our monastery at La Moraleja. I'm going to make sure that you don't escape us."

When Maldonado had left, clamping on the new lock with a loud click, John released his mood of glee that he had restrained in the prior's presence. Germain, good old Germain, had escaped! He didn't know how Germain had done it, but he should have known that no ecclesiastical prison could hold the practical, inventive friar. John's prayers that day were ones of thanksgiving for the deliverance of his friend.

But John himself was not delivered. Nor did he foresee any possibility of his liberation. And he felt sure that Gratian could not force his release because he was certain Gratian did not know where he was. All Gratian could have known was that he was taken from the chaplain's house at the Incarnation.

John, therefore, resigned himself to the impossibility of escape. This small, damp prison cell in Toledo was obviously the place where God wanted him to be.

While John sat in the cramped prison cell during the winter of 1578, another young man — exactly John's age, 33 — was gaining applause and fame for himself in the city of Toledo. Dominic Theotocopuli (known in Spain as El Greco) had just completed his painting, "The Assumption," in the Church of St. Dominic, and was now working on another art creation, "The Stripping of Christ." The young artist, with his oils and paints, was creating masterpieces which would survive the ages.

And yet John, in his prison cell not too far from the Church of St. Dominic, was doing the same thing as El Greco: he was creating masterpieces which, in their own field, would endure as long as the portraits of El Greco — he was writing poems about contemplation. He had obtained a quill, ink, and some paper from the brother who brought his food, and he sat, crouched on his bed, scratching away indefatigably on the rough paper.

In the past, Teresa had often urged him to do some sustained writing, to put on paper some of the things he had been preaching about over the years, but he had insisted that he was too busy at the Incarnation for any writing. He could remember one afternoon in Avila, after he had given a sermon to the Carmelite nuns: Teresa wanted to see him in the parlor immediately. She said to him, breathlessly:

"Father, that talk was *beautiful*. You simply must put some of those things down on paper."

John had demurred, but Teresa continued:

"The things you preach will last only as long as you have the breath to say them, but the written word can live on for centuries."

The excuse that he was too busy was not valid now, not in the solitude of the prison cell. And so he began to write. He wrote first, against the background of his present experience, about the abandonment to God necessary for sanctity:

> *On a dark night, enkindled with yearnings of love (oh, blessed occurrence),*
> *I departed without being noticed, since my house was now at rest.*
> *I was in peace, and oblivious to all things; I reclined my face upon my Beloved.*
> *All was quiet, and I abandoned myself, leaving all my preoccupations forgotten among the lilies.*

Then as he considered contemplative union with God, his poetry became more mystical and more lyrical. He wrote:

> *My soul has spent all it had, and all my possessions are in His service.*
> *I no longer watch over any flock, nor do I hold any office. My only occupation now is Love.*
> *If, then, I am no longer seen on the common ground,*
> *You may say that I was lost, and that, wandering love-stricken, I lost my way and have been found again.*

The poetry he wrote was the outline of a full treatise on the contemplative life. It demanded some type of prose commentary and explanation, and he could see that such a commentary would require a number of volumes. But, holding the quill in his hands, he felt that he wanted to write those books. He now agreed with Teresa: writing was an important thing, and he resolved that, when he got out of his prison, he would make time for it.

The months dragged wearily on: winter turned into spring, and spring into summer. In the winter, John had shivered in the cold dampness of his cell, but in the summer, he nearly choked as the stagnant air tightened around him. It was not until August that he made a deliberate study of his own physical condition. He discovered himself alarmingly emaciated; there were great hollows in his face, and his ribs protruded sharply through his almost transparent skin. He had weighed somewhere around one hundred and forty pounds when taken captive, but he doubted if he weighed even a hundred pounds now. He could feel with his hand bald patches on his head, where whole hunks of hair had fallen out.

More disturbing even than those tangible evidences of failing health was the general lassitude and weakness he experienced continually. He spent the major part of the day lying on his taut bed; an erect, standing position had become a major effort for him. Furthermore, there was that persistent cough, which began to wrack his body, a cough which hit him in seizures, leaving him almost unconscious after a violent attack.

It was then, in August, that John came to the sudden conviction that if he remained captive in the monastery of Toledo much longer, he would surely die.

John was in no way afraid of death; rather, he looked forward to it, longed for it as the passageway to an indissoluble union with Christ. But the point now was: did Christ want him to die in the monastery of Toledo? It took John a long time to discover an answer to the question, but when he did, he was sure it was the right one.

His death at Toledo, he concluded finally, would severely hamper the work of the Reform. He had been abducted secretly, and imprisoned even more secretly: no one knew the location of his place of imprisonment. Perhaps there were some who felt that he had abandoned the Reform and was living quietly in some monastery far from Castile. If he died at Toledo, he would be buried secretly in an unmarked grave, and Father John of the Cross would never be heard from again. The sudden and complete disappearance of one of the original friars would shake the Reform, and might even cause an incalculable number to lose heart. His death now would serve no purpose; his reappearance would be a healthy thing for the Reform.

As he lay on his bed, staring at the ceiling through his hollow, red-rimmed eyes, revolving the whole problem in his mind he decided that he must live; he must escape from here. But how? Almost before he asked himself the question, he knew the answer: the Blessed Virgin! Mary somehow would liberate him. It was only a few days until the feast of the Assumption, and John spent those days in a private novena, beseeching Mary for her assistance in his escape.

On the fourteenth of August, the vigil of the feast, John received another visit from Maldonado. When the door creaked open, John was lying on his bed, breathing hard after a fit of coughing.

"Why don't you rise when the superior of the monastery enters?" Maldonado said to him.

John propped himself up precariously on his elbows. "I'm sorry, I can't: I'm too weak."

"Oh, you're too weak!" Maldonado said. "So this is the strong Discalced Father who was so bold in his refusal to obey."

"I'd like to ask a favor," John gasped. He looked up for some sign of response in Maldonado's face, but he could only see the dim outline of his figure. "Tomorrow is the feast of the Assumption. Could I have permission to say Mass on our Lady's feast?"

"Say Mass?" Maldonado repeated incredulously. "Not while I'm prior here will a recalcitrant friar say Mass." He wheeled around and stalked angrily out of the cell.

The following night — the feast of the Assumption itself — John received another visitor, one who was not constrained to use the heavy door as a means of entrance into the tiny room. John was sitting on the edge of his bed, humped over in a half crouch, praying to the Blessed Virgin, moving his lips in a staccato litany of invocations to the Mother of God. He had been sitting there for some time when a soft white light began to inundate the room. Thinking that someone had opened the door to his cell, he glanced at the wooden portal — but it was firmly closed. Still the brightness continued to mount until the small room was completely flooded with light.

He sat there foolishly, almost in giddiness, as the light illuminated him, bringing into sight his worn filthy habit and his blanched skin and the stringy beard — an eight months' growth — which hung matted on his chest. Then he saw her, coming into focus right before him — the Blessed Virgin dressed in a white gown of incandescent brilliance. She looked so beautiful, so clean in comparison to the grubby appearance of the little friar who sat transfixed.

"Have patience, my son, for your trials will soon come to an end. You will leave this prison, say Mass again, and be consoled." Her voice was soft and melodious, like the tinkling of a thousand tiny bells; her eyes were understanding, full of compassion for the beaten friar who had fallen to his knees before her.

John's lips trembled, and he had difficulty articulating the words. "How . . . how will I get out of here?"

"Watch," she said, pointing a finger downward.

John watched, and he saw a swift tableau of scenes appear at the feet of Mary: a lock, a rope improvised from a blanket, and a window.

He looked back into the smiling face of the Blessed Virgin. "When should I escape?"

"Tomorrow night after the friars have gone to sleep."

The Blessed Virgin continued to gaze at him for a minute in evident fondness until she began slowly to fade from sight.

"Mother of God: I dedicate myself completely to you and the work of your Order!" John cried out to her.

"I know . . . I know," she said softly.

She was gone, and the white light had disappeared.

[Chapter 12]

ON THE following day John was in a state of elation. Throughout the entire day he reviewed over and over again in his mind the details of the magnificent vision of the Blessed Virgin.

About six o'clock in the evening the heavy door swung open, revealing the figure of the brother who placed a bowl of some unidentifiable stew on the floor.

"Here's your meal. I'll be back in a few minutes with a jug of water."

During the early days of his captivity, the brother had always carefully locked the door again, while he departed to fetch the water; but lately John's weakened condition had made that unnecessary: he could barely walk, and if he did walk, he would surely meet any number of friars who were moving through the monastery at that time. So the brother shuffled off, leaving the door slightly ajar.

When he heard the footsteps fading away, John started the labored process of pulling himself wearily off the bed; finally, after an unbelievable expenditure of effort, he shakily rose to his feet. He picked up one of the flat loose pieces of stone from the floor, and, clutching it in his hand, staggered out through the door. His cell, fortunately, led out into a small vestibule which separated it from the main corridor. Consequently, he could stand in front of his cell with no fear of being seen by anyone who might be in the corridor.

He laid his hand on the lock — yes, it was the same lock Mary had shown him in the vision. However, it was not the lock itself that interested him, but the metal brace hanging on the wall which supported one of the rings through which the padlock passed. He put his fingers on the three large bolts, which fastened the brace to the wall, and then placed the flat stone into the wide cleft in the head of the bolt. John twisted the piece of stone, moving the bolt easily: the wall was old and the constant dampness had caused the stone around the bolt to pulverize.

Beads of perspiration formed on his forehead. He tried to work quickly; the brother would return in a few minutes. He unscrewed each of the three bolts to the point where a firm pull would tear them from the wall. He surveyed the completed job and felt that the brother would be unlikely to notice the protruding bolts because of the dimness in the small vestibule.

The brother was returning; John dragged himself back into the cell, his weakness forcing him to a maddening slow pace.

"You haven't eaten your stew," the brother said, arriving back at the open door. "Aren't you hungry?"

"No, not tonight. But thanks anyway for your kindness in bringing it to me."

"All right. Suit yourself."

John held his breath as he heard the door slam and the lock click back into place. It worked; for the brother walked unsuspiciously away.

He threw himself on his bed, exhausted from the nervous tension of the past few minutes. More than anything else he needed strength — the strength that had completely vanished during his imprisonment. He was sure, though, that Mary would give him the vitality he needed.

He lay there panting, emitting long hollow breaths for about fifteen minutes, then pulled himself painfully from the bed. He had one more preparation to make for the escape. Snatching the blanket from his bed, he began to tear it into long strips, which he eventually tied together, fashioning a tenuous cloth rope. He examined his product carefully and had grave misgivings of its ability to support the weight of his body; but this was the manner of escape Mary had shown him in the vision, and he would follow her plan implicitly.

He waited until he was sure everyone in the monastery had retired for the evening, sitting on the edge of the bed, his ear cocked to catch the last sounds of movement in the house. Finally, some time around midnight, he decided it was safe to proceed. As he started toward the door, he noticed instantly that his lassitude, his weakness, had vanished. Could this new energy derive from the excitement of the moment? No, he was sure that it was due to the direct intervention of the Blessed Virgin; and he exulted in this new power he felt welling up inside him.

Clenching his fingers into a tight fist, John delivered one sharp blow against the door on the side directly opposite the lock. There was a scraping of metal, and the loosened bolts thudded noisily to the floor, allowing the door to swing open. After a few moments' wait he pushed the door completely open and walked into the corridor.

At the end of the hallway he saw the window, the one the Blessed Virgin had shown him in the vision; it was a tall, doorlike window opening onto a fragile wooden balcony.

He stepped out onto the balcony. It was too dark to see much, but a few hundred yards away he could make out the Tagus River, rolling languidly along. It felt good to stand there, the breeze smiting his face.

The small balcony was attached to the wall by two thin beams. John knotted the end of his improvised rope around the juncture where one of the beams joined the balcony floor. With one final prayer to the Blessed Virgin, he climbed over the edge of the balcony and began to let himself down the rope, hand over hand.

Amazingly, the rope held — and even more amazingly, his strength held. Suddenly, he reached the end of the rope and glancing anxiously down he saw that he had some twenty feet to go. He hung there swinging gently back and forth. The drop might mean a broken leg — but that would be better than death in the prison cell, and he could perhaps drag himself along the ground after he fell. So, gritting his teeth, he relinquished his grasp on the rope and instead of plummeting to the ground as he had expected, he floated slowly down, landing uninjured on his feet.

As he stood on the ground, looking up at the dangling rope swaying in the breeze above him, a wild, intemperate joy took possession of him, and he chuckled audibly: the Blessed Mother had given him an air-borne ride!

He started walking rapidly away from the building, but stopped abruptly after a few paces: He had landed behind the high monastery wall and was still on the Calced property. He laid his hand against the wall, attempting to discover some way of climbing it. It was a formidable barrier; for the wall was at least twelve feet high. Then suddenly, as a few moments ago, Mary gave her friar some additional air-borne assistance: John was snatched up into the air, carried over the wall, and deposited gently on the other side.

There could now be no reasonable doubt of Mary's determination to free him: she had shown him the means of escape, and miraculously helped him to execute it.

Briskly John fled away from his prison. He continued walking until he had placed what he considered a comfortable distance between him and the monastery; then he lay down against the wall of a building to await the dawn.

He fell into a deep sleep, and was awakened at five o'clock by a grimy little dog, which stood in front of him barking furiously.

"Be quiet, little pup. You'll bring the Calced chasing after me," he scolded.

His entreaty had no effect, so he scooped up a small stone and flicked it at the dog, sending it scampering away.

There was a convent of Discalced Carmelite nuns somewhere in Toledo, and he decided to seek assistance there in his flight. A man — a laborer, no doubt, on his way to work — was walking sleepily down the street. John approached him, and asked for directions to the convent.

The laborer surveyed him critically, and for the first time John realized what a weird sight he must make in his tattered habit, and unkempt beard and hair.

"It's down that street," the laborer said, waving a chubby hand indolently toward a narrow avenue. "Just keep walking: you can't miss it . . . but they won't give any food to beggars this early in the morning."

John laughed. "I'll try, anyway."

He found the convent easily, and, after finally convincing the perplexed nuns that he was really Father John of the Cross, received an enthusiastic reception.

"We're so glad you're safe! We thought you were dead," they said.

"I thought I was about dead," John answered grimly.

"Imagine, you were here in Toledo all the time, and we didn't even know it!"

"I was in Toledo, all right, but I didn't see much of the city."

John laughed with the Sisters: it was good to hear laughing voices again. He had one urgent request to make of them, though: he wanted to say Mass again. His request was readily granted, and for the first time in eight months, John held the consecrated Host in his hands. He placed the unleavened Wafer that was Christ into his mouth, closing his eyes in an effort to crowd out of his vision the altar and the chapel, while he offered his gratitude to Christ and His good Mother for his escape.

John remained at the convent for the entire day, talking to the nuns and eating the wholesome food they took such delight in serving him. As the result of some frantic sewing and ripping, they were able to fashion a friar's habit that was a passable reproduction of the one worn by the Discalced Carmelite friars. It was with a sense of unrealness, of almost unbelief that he donned the habit of the Reform again.

"Mother, how can I get out of Toledo without being seen?" he asked the prioress late in the afternoon.

She was a wizened old woman with wrinkled skin whose eyes were clear and innocent, like those of a child. "Don't you worry about that, Father. I've been making plans for you. Father Henry

Mendoza, one of the local parish priests, is coming in his wagon tonight to drive you out of the city."

Father Henry Mendoza, a hulking, jolly cleric, arrived after supper, and invited John to occupy his wagon as a vehicle of escape.

"It's not the royal carriage, but it goes." Father Mendoza thought his own remark delightfully amusing, for he broke into a spasm of laughter.

John was in no position to deny the offer of Mendoza's antiquated wagon, nor to be critical of the man's humor. He forced a laugh, therefore, in return, saying:

"That's all right; I hadn't expected the king to send his carriage to fetch me from jail."

The stout, good-natured priest suggested that John ride back in the covered part of the wagon instead of up on the seat with him.

"You'd better lie back there and pull that blanket over your head until we get out of town. I understand that the Calced Carmelites have alerted the constables to be on the watch for you."

Thus it was that John departed from Toledo in almost the same manner as he had arrived: lying in the bottom of a wagon. However, on his departure trip, he was not compelled to suffer the inconvenience of bound hands and feet, and Mendoza had lined the floor of the wagon with some rugs for his greater comfort.

It was a fortuitous thing, too, that John had hidden himself in the rear of the wagon, for as they were drawing near the city limits, they were halted by a constable. John listened tensely to the exchange between Mendoza and the constable from his place of hiding under the blanket.

"Hey, there, Father!"

"Yes?" Mendoza answered condescendingly from the wagon seat.

"We're out here looking for a rebel friar who's run away from the Carmelite monastery. Have you seen anything of him?"

"No, officer, I've seen nothing of any *rebel* friar," Mendoza answered.

"Well, if you see him, let us know."

Mendoza did not answer, but clicked the reins, sending the ancient wagon back into its jolting, swaying motion.

John stretched out to his full length enjoying his new freedom. He was exultantly happy in the consideration of his liberation from prison; but he was even more delighted with the implications of that liberation. The Calced had attempted to break him, to force him to renounce the Reform, but they had failed; and their failure was significant. His escape would be to them, he was sure, a tangible rebuke to their efforts to suppress the Reform, a stinging reminder that it could not be stamped out.

But of even more importance, he now realized, was the fact that the Blessed Virgin wanted him to escape, that *she* wished the Reform to prosper. The Blessed Mother had given him positive, irrefutable evidence of her approbation of the work: and with Mary on its side, the Reform could not fail.

The dull, monotonous clack of the wheels made John drowsy. As his eyes began to close in sleep he pleasantly recalled the magnificent scene he had witnessed two nights ago: the Blessed Virgin standing in that dirty prison cell at Toledo.

PART III

The Storm Within

Chapter 1

JOHN stirred uneasily on his hard chair. It was difficult for him to sit in one position for any length of time since his escape from the prison in Toledo three years ago. The chair creaked under the shift of his weight, and Anthony, who sat beside him, flashed him a quick glance.

"Sorry for all this racket," John whispered to him. "My back hasn't been the same since Toledo."

Anthony leaned close to him. "It's all right, you're not bothering me . . . this will be over in a minute, and we'll have a recess."

Physically, John longed for the recess, but emotionally, he was reveling in the present scene, exulting in the accomplishment it marked. He let his eyes roam around the hall, fascinated with the entire panorama. On the platform at the front of the great room sat the Bishop of Alcalá, a monarchical figure in his billowing red robes. At the bishop's right was Gratian, ruddy and smiling, but demonstrating almost perceptibly some of the weariness resulting from the long years of struggle for independence. A portable rostrum had been placed on the edge of the platform, and at it a young friar, unknown to John, was seriously reading aloud a Latin rescript.

The rescript from Rome was wordy, the phrases tedious, but the context was magnificent: it solemnly proclaimed that the Discalced Carmelites were to be separated from the Calced, and were to be organized into a separate province under their duly elected provincial. It had taken a long time to accomplish this, and it had cost John much, but it was now done and they were engaging in their first official elections in the main hall of the University of Alcalá.

The friar completed his reading of the rescript, and a short recess was declared. "That's that," Anthony said, rising to his feet. "Let's step out into the corridor for a minute."

"Gladly," John said. He had to walk quickly to keep up with the long strides of his companion. "This is a big day, Anthony. We've been waiting thirteen years for this."

"Thirteen years," Anthony said reflectively. "It's hard to believe that it's been thirteen years since we first went to Duruelo."

"A lot happened in those years. That's what made them go so quickly."

"You mean a lot happened to *you*," Anthony said looking pointedly at John. There was a momentary pause, and then Anthony said: "You know, John, you never really explained to me just how you escaped three years ago."

"It's a long story, Anthony. Maybe I'll tell it to you some day when we have a lot of time."

But John knew that it would be a long time before he told Anthony, or anyone else for that matter, the whole story of Toledo: the brutality of his imprisonment, and especially the role that the Blessed Virgin played in his escape. When he had reached the Discalced monastery at Alcalá after his escape, he gave the friars only a fragmentary account of the episode, telling them that the Calced had held him prisoner and that he had managed to escape somehow one night when his captors were asleep. However, even that partial account of his incarceration was enough to shock the whole Reform. It was a stinging reminder to the friars of the crucial need of independence, and it was the starting point of a series of appeals to Rome for separation.

For John, however, the imprisonment at Toledo was a closed issue, and he preferred not to think about it. The only recollection he preserved of Toledo was the haunting memory of the Blessed Virgin standing in the dirty prison cell; and this was one memory he didn't want to share with anyone else — at least, not as yet.

After his escape, Anthony immediately appointed him superior of the monastery at Mount Calvary in Southern Andalusia. The appointment had a twofold purpose: it removed him from the immediate scene of conflict in Castile; and the warm, languid climate of the south afforded him a better opportunity for recuperation. The three years John had spent as superior in Andalusia were uneventful ones, but he enjoyed this tranquil period of his life immensely. And it was a source of special consolation for him to follow the full monastic schedule again. Together with the other friars, he rose at midnight to chant the Office, he knelt in the choir for the long periods of mental prayer, and he sat on the hard benches in the refectory, eating the plain, meatless meals of the Reform. It was wonderful, he thought, to be living the community life again. And as he reintegrated himself with this contemplative life, he became more profoundly aware of the fact that his trials at Toledo had been for a vitally important cause.

During the three-year period in Andalusia, he continued the writing he had started in prison. He wrote sections of two books: the first, *The Ascent of Mount Carmel,* was a detailed treatment of the mortification necessary for contemplative union with God; the second, *The Spiritual Canticle,* was a master synthesis of the mystical life. Because he was discussing the rather complex field of mysticism, his progress was slow and labored, and he was unable to complete either book during his stay in Andalusia. But he was determined to complete the two books — and to write some more, too.

Thus in the serenity of Andalusia, John was able to write and also to rebuild his health (although he soon realized that he would never completely recover from the harsh treatment he had received in Toledo). Up in Castile, however, the argument about the separation had still been raging, but from the time of John's escape the outcome seemed to be clear. The Reform had burgeoned into a large, robust organization, and its independence could not be long denied. There were now eleven monasteries and almost three hundred friars in the Reform, and the contemplative life of the Discalced Carmelite friars had captured the imagination and enthusiasm of all Spain. Even the king, Philip II, had become impressed by the Reform, and — to the delight of the friars — had petitioned the Pope for the Reform's independence. Finally the Calced themselves, recognizing the uselessness of prolonging the disagreement any further, agreed to the separation, and in November of 1580 Pope Gregory XIII issued the rescript of independence for the friars, and also placed the nuns under their supervision.

John had remained peacefully apart from this whole final phase of development — his work for the cause of separation had been done in the prison cell of Toledo. However, two weeks ago he had been summoned here to Alcalá for the formal separation ceremonies and the first provincial election of the Reform. On his journey north, he passed through Madrid, and he found the Spanish capital clamoring for war with England. Queen Elizabeth had commissioned her sea captains — Raleigh, Drake, and Hawkins — to plunder Spanish shipping, and they had been extremely successful in "singeing the Spanish beard." John was appalled at the war fever.

Therefore, when he arrived in Alcalá for the elections, his mind was filled with prayers of petition. He prayed that Spain would not be thrust into war with England; and he prayed that the Reform, now freed from its difficulties with the Calced, might enter into a period of peaceful expansion.

John and Anthony walked into the corridor outside the election hall and found it crowded with brown-robed friars. The snatches of conversation John could hear were about candidates for the election of a provincial, which was to begin in a few minutes. Most of the friars were unknown to John, and Anthony led him from group to group, introducing them to him.

"Fathers, I'd like you to meet Father John of the Cross."

"It's a *real* pleasure to meet you, Father John. We've heard so much about you."

"Father Anthony, could I ask you a question?" The speaker was a stocky friar with dark skin and flat, heavy features. He was definitely not an Iberian.

"Certainly. . . . Oh, have you met Father John of the Cross?"

"I don't believe I have."

"Father John, this is Father Nicholas of Jesus and Mary. His family name is Doria."

"Doria?" John questioned. "Any relation to Andrew Doria, the naval hero?"

"He's part of the family," Doria said. His face was serious and unsmiling.

"Let me explain Father's background to you," Anthony said suavely to John. "Father Nicholas is an Italian; he comes from the well-known banking family of Genoa, the Dorias. He was in Spain helping the archbishop with a . . . a financial problem when he met the Discalced Carmelites and decided to join."

He turned to Doria. "How long ago was that?"

"Four years ago." The answer was short and clipped.

There was something about Doria that John did not like: the man was too stiff, too unbending.

"What was it you wanted to ask me about?" Anthony inquired.

"I wanted to know," Doria said, "about this separation from the Calced. The rescript states that we're a separate province — does that mean that we're still under the jurisdiction of the Calced?"

"In a very vague way it does. Technically, we are still under the Calced general, but the Calced want no part of us now. Eventually, we'll be established as a juridically separate order — a new order. But Rome doesn't move as quickly as that: they make us a separate province first, and after a number of years, a separate order."

"There's no danger of any more trouble with the Calced, then?" Doria asked.

"No, our only problems now will be among ourselves."

A bell rang, indicating that the sessions in the hall were to commence again.

Anthony smiled. "And here's the first problem we have: the election of our provincial."

Walking back into the hall, Anthony whispered to John:

"You watch that Doria in the years to come. He's going places in the Reform."

"He is?"

"The men have a very high regard for his business acumen. He's a brilliant man."

John studied the stocky Italian who walked briskly into the hall ahead of him. He was still unable to resist the vague dislike he felt for the man.

Each one of the twenty delegates was given an oblong strip of paper on which to write his vote. John fingered his thoughtfully for a moment, then wrote Anthony's name across it. He folded the ballot and held it tightly in his right hand.

It was no secret that the contest for the office of provincial was principally between Jerome Gratian and Anthony. Gratian should have been the logical selection (he had held the office on an appointed basis for the past six years, and at the first election should have been chosen as an act of appreciation for his work in the separation), but there was some strong reaction against him. Many felt, as John did, that he had acted imprudently and rashly, and they wanted to return to the original superior of Duruelo, Anthony of Jesus.

The names of the electors were called out, one by one, and they filed up to the platform, where they placed their folded ballots in a small basket. When all had voted, the tabulating began.

Gratian, as the superior pro tem, pulled the ballots from the basket, flattened them out, and read the individual votes; a secretary sat at a small table, quill in hand, to record the votes. Gratian announced the votes in a clear, resonant voice.

"One vote for Father Anthony."

"One vote for Father Jerome."

"One vote for Father Jerome."

"One vote for Father Anthony."

The balloting was going to be close. When the count reached five votes for each of the two principal contenders, Gratian announced:

"One vote for Father Nicholas."

So, John thought, Anthony had been correct about this newcomer to the Reform; he did have some support among the friars.

"One vote for Father Jerome."

"One vote for Father Anthony."

"One vote for Father Gabriel."

That was only the second vote which had not been cast for one of the two main candidates; but it was to be the last wasted vote. Gratian received the next four votes, making the tabulation ten to six in his favor, with only two more ballots to be counted. Gratian and Anthony split the remaining two votes, and the final count showed Gratian the victor, by a count of eleven to seven.

It was certainly not a resounding victory for Father Jerome Gratian, and he knew it, but he recovered himself quickly, making a short, gracious acceptance speech.

The next item on the agenda of business was the election of the four definitors, the members of the provincial council, who were to meet with him periodically for a discussion of the major business in the Reform. It was during these elections that John really discovered Nicholas Doria's strength. Much to John's surprise, Doria was elected the first definitor. None of the friars sitting near John in the hall seemed to share his surprise, and it was then that he knew that a new power had arrived on the scene.

Anthony was elected the second definitor, and after that the thunderbolt struck John: he was elected the third definitor. He had no desire at all for any position of authority, he definitely eschewed any office; his only consolation was that the office of definitor was not really an administrative one, it did not involve the issuance of any commands to subjects.

Finally, Father Gabriel, who received the other single vote in the election for provincial, was elected the fourth and final definitor.

The election of superiors continued through another day. There were a number of offices to be filled, principally the priorships of the various monasteries; and if John thought that the electors were to be satisfied with bestowing only a definitor's position on the "martyr of Toledo," he was much mistaken. On one of the first ballots in the morning, he was elected prior of the monastery at Granada.

John, visibly shaken, rose to his feet. "Father Provincial, I beg of you to release me from this position. I don't want to be a superior, only a plain friar."

Gratian, standing on the platform, glared at him in mock indignation, saying:

"Father John, you pledged your obedience to the Reform, and the Reform has given you an order: to be prior of Granada."

As John sat down in his seat again, he saw the smiling faces of the men around him. One face was not smiling, though: Nicholas Doria had his countenance set in a dark scowl.

Chapter 2

THE elections completed, John took the long trek south to Granada in Andalusia. He had no particular predilection for the southern country, nor for the clumsy, almost boorish manners of the inhabitants; yet, as Gratian had said at the elections, this was the place to which religious obedience had assigned him.

The monastery in Granada was a large one, housing some forty friars, but its administration required no great effort on John's part. The community was awed by their prior, the first Discalced Carmelite friar and the "martyr of Toledo," and obeyed his suggestions and commands implicitly. The alacrity with which he was obeyed and the quiet, lethargic atmosphere of Granada — in contrast to the years of rush in Avila — permitted John to continue his writing. During the long period he spent in Granada, he finished the manuscript of his *Ascent of Mount Carmel* and completed another prose work, *The Dark Night of the Soul.*

In his first term as prior, he made only one long journey away from Granada: to visit Teresa in Avila, at the command of Gratian. The trip seemed unnecessary to John, since the sole purpose of the journey was to consult Teresa about the foundation of a Discalced Carmelite convent in Granada. The whole matter could have been handled by mail, but Gratian, hearing of the negotiations, had ordered John north for a personal interview with Teresa.

John, at first, regretted the trip; but in later years he was delighted in his recollection of the visit to Avila, for it was the last time in his life he was to see Teresa.

He sat, for his final visit with Teresa, in the white-walled visitors' room at the convent of St. Joseph. Teresa appeared ill, and John realized, with a quick pang of sadness, that the sixty-six-year-old foundress was nearing the end of her earthly trail.

"You don't look too well, Mother. How do you feel?"

Teresa, her face an ashen gray, forced a weak smile. "As well as could be expected for an old woman."

"Now, you're not old. Your heart is as young as when we first met fifteen years ago."

"My heart may be young, but my body is old."

John deftly turned the conversation from her health to the business at hand: the nuns' convent in Granada. He explained the advisability of the new convent in the southern city. Teresa, despite her illness, had lost none of her shrewdness or business perspicacity: she inquired about the location of the convent, the possibility of financial support, the attitude of the Andalusians toward the Reform, and the sources of new vocations. Satisfied that the new project was feasible, she promised John to dispatch a small group of nuns to Granada as soon as possible.

"I'll send Sister Ann of Jesus as the prioress."

John knew Sister Ann well, having met her at the convent in Beas, when he was traveling south after his escape from Toledo, and he had remained in contact with her by letter.

Recognizing Teresa's failing health, he now began to assess Ann's position in a new light, for she was, after Teresa herself, the most articulate, and most highly respected Discalced Carmelite nun. When Teresa died it would be Ann who would surely occupy her unofficial position as spokesman for the nuns; he was appreciative of the fact that Ann would be stationed in Granada. John had no idea, then, of the importance that his contact with Ann of Jesus was to have in his life.

"And how is our good friend, Father Gratian?" Teresa asked, a twinkle in her eyes.

The wry implication in her question was not lost on John. "Now, Mother, I don't dislike Father Gratian. I've always said that he was an excellent priest. I only objected to the prudence of some of his actions."

"I know, I know. I can't disagree with you on that. He does act imprudently at times. But don't you think he's learned better by this time?"

"I do," John said earnestly. "His only serious defect was his youth. But I feel now that, with the experience the years have given him, he'll do all right."

"You really do think he'll do well, don't you?" Teresa said, delighted with John's statement. "There's one fear I have, though."

"What's that?" John asked.

"It's Father Nicholas Doria."

"What's Nicholas Doria got to do with Gratian?"

Teresa studied the back of her hand. "This Doria person is rising fast in the Reform — and rightly so, for he's a man of rare talent. But he's so unlike Father Gratian, and so opposed to him. I hear that he's quite open in his criticism of Gratian's administration."

John smiled kindly. "I was opposed to Gratian's manner of action, too."

"It was different, though, with you. You disagreed with Gratian, but you didn't make any public demonstration of your disapproval. Doria is going around talking to the friars, stirring up resentment against Gratian. . . . I feel that there's going to be a major conflict between them soon."

"Let's hope not," John said.

"Look, I'm wasting your valuable time," Teresa said, drawing herself to her feet with visible effort. "You've better things to do than listen to an old woman cluck away."

"I can think of nothing else I'd rather do, now, than listen to you . . . cluck away," he laughed, "but I do have to be going."

"Good-by, then, Father John. Will you give me your blessing?" She wearily worked her way to her knees while John blessed her.

Thus ended his final meeting with the woman who had had so profound an influence on his life. Six months later, in Granada, he received notice of her death; and with that he noted the close of a major epoch in his life.

Walking back to Andalusia after his visit with Teresa, John

thought of age and death, and the passing of all living things. He himself had just reached his fortieth birthday. Forty years old! How did he ever get to be forty? And Anthony, how old was he now? — seventy-two! The man was indestructible. Teresa was near the end of her busy and ofttimes perilous journey, and John wondered how much longer he would have to wait before he stepped from the life of labor into the life of paradise.

Right now, however, there was work at hand: he had received a note from Gratian while in Avila, asking him to stop at Almodovar on his way south for a meeting of the definitory — the provincial with his four definitors. This was the first time that John would have the opportunity of watching Gratian and Doria in close contact with each other. The prospect quickened his steps.

Gratian and the three other definitors had already arrived at the monastery of Almodovar when John reached there, tired and dirty. After he had bathed and refreshed himself, the meeting was called into immediate session.

"A number of matters have been presented to the provincial for his consideration," Gratian said to the four definitors, "and I'd like to discuss them with you."

Anthony nodded his head, fastening his eyes on Gratian's well-proportioned face. Doria sat motionless, his head slightly bowed, and his eyes tightly closed. The early business of the meeting was concerned with trivial matters of discipline and finance, and there was little discussion or objection on the part of the four definitors. It was only when Gratian arrived at the principal business that controversy broke out.

"And now I'd like to present, for your approval, a proposal that I feel very much in favor of — the inauguration of Discalced Carmelite foreign missions," Gratian said.

"Foreign missions! This is the first I've heard anything about it," Doria said.

"No," Gratian said, "you wouldn't have heard anything about it. I've just received an invitation to send some of our priests to the African Congo. Would there be any objection to this?"

"There most certainly would be," Doria said petulantly. "We're not a missionary order; our work is monastic life, the contemplative ideal."

"Yes, we're contemplatives," Gratian said, "but we also have an apostolic element in our life."

"However, my dear Father Jerome, that does not include the hyperactive work of the foreign missions."

Gratian glanced around for support from the three other definitors, but he saw that this was to be, for the present anyway, a controversy between Doria and himself. "But, Father Nicholas, the work of the Reform does not consist in multiplying monasteries in small Spanish towns and neglecting everything else."

The argument continued between Doria and Gratian. Neither would give ground: Gratian was in favor of the foreign missions, and Doria was bitterly opposed. Finally, in desperation, Gratian called the roll of the definitors, requesting their votes on the proposal.

Doria snorted fiercely:

"You know my opinion: I vote against the proposal."

Anthony was more conciliatory:

"Now, I don't see any reason for argument. After all, what harm will it do to send a few missionaries to the Congo? I vote in favor of the proposal."

John, a bit perplexed by the sudden proposal, proceeded cautiously:

"The primary work of the Reform is contemplation. However, there is no reason why we can't establish monasteries which follow the contemplative ideal in mission territories. So, theoretically, foreign missions could be compatible with the primary function of the Reform. But I feel, at the present time, that we should wait before getting into this work. First, I believe that the proposed missions in the Congo would be highly active ones which would not permit the establishment of a contemplative monastery. Second, I feel that it is too early in the Reform to think about expansion across the seas: we should wait until we have more men and are better established. Therefore, with deference to the opinions of Fathers Jerome and Anthony, I vote against the proposal."

Doria turned slightly in his seat, and looked at John with new respect.

Gabriel, the last definitor, was forthright and direct in his statement:

"I vote in favor of the proposal."

Gratian remained silent for a few moments, heightening the tension in the room. Finally, he said:

"And I, of course, vote in favor, too. That makes the final count, three in favor and two against. Therefore, I will prepare to dispatch a group to the Congo missions."

He glanced around the table. "All of this, I hope, with no hard feelings on the part of those who voted against the proposal."

Gratian was the suave provincial again, attempting to placate the men who had disagreed with him. John shrugged his shoulders humorously, but Doria's face was cast in a grim mask.

Later that day, John visited Gratian in his cell in an effort to convince the provincial that he was not opposed to the general administration. Gratian, who had been writing at his desk when John entered, was understanding, and apparently not at all disturbed by John's negative vote.

"Certainly, I'm not peeved," Gratian said. "Even St. Peter and St. Paul disagreed on ecclesiastical matters."

"I'm glad you feel that way about it," John said. "I just wanted to assure you that there were no hard feelings on my part."

"It's good to hear you say that. I only wish that your partner, Doria, had the same sentiments."

John noticed the worried frown on Gratian's face. "Mother Teresa said that Doria has been giving you a difficult time. Is that true?"

"It's too true," Gratian said. "He's bucking me at every turn. The man's getting to be a thorn in my side."

"What is he complaining about?"

"Everything. He criticizes me for my administration; he keeps throwing up the difficulty with the Calced; and if he finds out that I've been away from the monastery for any length of time, he goes out of his way to bring attention to it."

"That's too bad."

"It *is* too bad," Gratian agreed, "especially when you consider that he's such an able chap. He'll make an excellent provincial himself, someday."

"Have you any idea how you're going to placate Doria for the remaining time of your office?"

Gratian glanced about furtively, as if someone might overhear him, and leaned across the desk. "I have a plan which I think — if you'll pardon my lack of humility — has the touch of genius in it. I've been asked to make a foundation at Genoa, in Italy, a monastery of observance, not a mission foundation, mind you. Well, now, Doria is a native of Genoa, and he has many friends there. What would be more natural than to send him there — as superior, of course — where he'll be out of my hair?"

John could not help smiling at Gratian's almost juvenile plan. "I hope you know what you're doing."

"Of course I know what I'm doing: I'm ridding myself of my self-appointed inquisitor."

John returned to Granada; and Doria went off to Genoa in Italy. Doria's absence precluded any further wrangles within the province, and John was able to continue his writing and spiritual direction in Granada.

One special satisfaction for John in the otherwise uneventful life in Andalusia was the arrival of Sister Ann of Jesus and the band of nuns who were to staff the new convent in Granada. He paid a visit to the convent soon after its establishment.

"Welcome to the southland," he said to Ann in the improvised parlor of the new structure.

"We're very happy to be here," she said.

Ann of Jesus was a tall, regal woman, some three or four years

younger than John. She had a beautiful, well-formed face with
high cheekbones; and, occasionally, John could notice slight wisps
of golden hair protruding out from under her wimple. She was
poised, self-possessed, and yet warm of manner.

"I've been told," John said, "that now Mother Teresa is dead,
you'll be the major power in Carmelite convents."

"I wouldn't believe everything you hear," she said gracefully.
"But, if it were true, I'm delighted to have you close at hand for
advice. I know how highly Mother Teresa thought of you."

"I'll be happy to help you in any way I can," John answered.

And John did help her: he was a frequent visitor to the convent,
hearing her confession and those of the other nuns. He found
in Ann a worthy, intelligent, and entirely capable successor to
Mother Teresa. With Ann of Jesus on the scene, he had no fears
for the fortunes of the nuns.

Suddenly, it was 1585, and Gratian's four-year term of office
had expired.

Gratian's administration, John felt, had been a successful one,
despite Doria's criticisms of it. Gratian had founded a whole
series of new monasteries, and had even started to expand the
Reform outside of Spain. There was a foundation in Genoa (where
he had sent Doria); one in Lisbon, Portugal; and, of course, the
mission foundations, the latest one being a mission in Mexico
in the New World.

In the spring of 1585, when the Reform convoked its second
general elections, there was an air of tension and anxiety through
all of Spain: the war with England seemed imminent. John shared
in this national anxiety, but he also had a particular anxiety all
his own: he was afraid the wrong man might be elected Gratian's
successor. And the wrong man, as far as John was concerned,
was Father Nicholas Doria. John was willing to admit Doria's
cleverness, his astuteness, his brilliance; but he still felt that Doria
was the wrong man for that important office in this critical period
of the Reform's growth. Doria was, John felt, a man who lacked

any real feeling for people; he had a tendency to be ruthless and inflexible in dealing with the friars; and, worst of all, he had an unshakable conviction that he was always right.

John realized that the Reform had made a tremendous amount of progress since Duruelo, but he knew that it was still in its infant stage. The wrong provincial now, at this crucial time, could wreck the whole structure. But as John analyzed the election scene, he was forced to the unhappy conclusion that Doria would probably be elected easily. The only other contender for the office, Anthony, was ill, and therefore considered ineligible. And John knew that he himself would not be considered: he was too quiet, too retiring for the vigorous task of governing hundreds of friars. Doria, then, was the logical candidate.

As John feared, Doria was elected provincial of the Reform with practically no opposition. And to his dismay, John was re-elected to the office of definitor. As definitor, however, John was able to observe Doria's administration closely. And what he saw confirmed his worst fears. Doria lost no time in taking over the reins of government; he wanted it to be known that he would now supervise *every* operation in the Reform. To accomplish this, he nominated each of his definitors as vicar provincials, friars who would act as the arms of his authority in the various sections of the Reform. John, therefore, was named vicar provincial of Andalusia, Doria's representative in the southland.

Before the elections of 1585 were concluded, Doria made one final appointment, one aimed at demonstrating his power: he assigned Gratian to Lisbon in Portugal, thus removing him effectively from the scene of activity. Doria had, with one swift blow, rid himself of his opposition. It was a move that made John uncomfortable, and increased his fears as to what the uncompromising Doria would do during his years of office.

At the conclusion of the elections John returned to Granada, Gratian went off to Portugal, and Doria set up his new administration in Castile. John, in Granada, was quite content to be removed from the immediate vicinity of Doria's new administration.

He had no personal contact with Doria for some time; however, hardly a week went by that John didn't receive a letter from Doria, inquiring about some monastery or some friar, or ordering him to visit an area of difficulty or to investigate a complaint in his district.

John's office of vicar provincial was a particularly distasteful one to him: he abhorred acting as Doria's envoy of discipline in the various monasteries in Andalusia, and each new commission from the provincial to visit some monastery caused a shudder of repulsion within him. He had an innate detestation for correcting friars, for admonishing them that they were not living according to the full ideals of the contemplative vocation. Yet, each commission from the provincial was a command, a manifestation of God's will, and he went off promptly to perform the mission.

One such commission from the provincial brought him to the monastery of Seville in the early spring of 1586; he had been commanded to investigate the discipline of the monastery, correct any abuses, and send a full report to Doria's headquarters.

John found the Seville monastery in excellent condition, both spiritually and materially, except for one matter that needed correction. Two of the friars had gained wide reputations as preachers and were spending lengthy periods of time outside the monastery delivering sermons. John felt that the two friars had lost the proper perspective of the ratio between prayer and apostolic work, that they were failing to maintain the contemplative spirit so essential to the Reform.

It was during the afternoon of his third day in Seville that he decided to see the two friars, Father Francis and Father James, after Vespers. As he chanted Vespers with the community in the choir, he prayed that God would give him prudence in dealing with the two friars; and by the time the last psalm was completed, he started to feel a little more sanguine about the situation. (He always enjoyed chanting Office in one of the large monasteries of the Reform: the long rows of friars chanting the psalms were a vivid testimony of how much progress had been made since

Duruelo, when just three of them chanted Office together in their tiny choir.) He then sent one of the brothers to summon the two friars to the cell he was occupying on the ground floor of the monastery.

The two men were apparently aware of the reason for their summons, because they entered the room diffidently, cast nervous glances about, and perched themselves uncomfortably on the edges of the chairs facing the desk behind which John sat.

John decided to try the indirect approach.

"I've heard some glowing reports about the magnificent sermons both of you've been preaching. It's a blessing for the Reform that we have men of such ability in our ranks."

Neither of the men looked directly at John. Francis was a tall, spare man with thin features and a great hooked nose; his companion, James, was a small, portly man with a furtive look. Neither of them had spoken since entering the room, apart from a response to John's initial greeting.

"However," John continued undaunted, "apostolic work is the secondary, subordinated part of our Carmelite vocation — prayer is our chief business. I think, therefore, you'd be more pleasing to God by devoting a greater amount of time to prayer and less to work outside the monastery. . . . I've informed the superior of the house to limit your apostolic work so that you spend an equal amount of time in the monastery to that which you spend outside it."

"You can't do that!" Francis interrupted.

"No, you can't," his companion said. "We have commitments which will occupy almost all our time for the next six months."

"That's no problem. You can cancel them," John said.

Father Francis, the taller of the two, squinted over his hooked nose until his eyes became two thin slits. "Who do you think you are, anyway? What right do you have to tell us what to do? You're not the provincial." His voice grated with a strange bitterness.

John tried to keep his own voice calm and his manner gentle. This was much worse than he had expected. The two friars were going to fight him on the issue, and their belligerent attitude only convinced him of what he already suspected: that their intensive apostolic work was not the result of a driving zeal for souls, but rather an expression of their own restlessness, their own desire for acclaim.

"No, I'm not the provincial. But, unfortunately, I am the vicar provincial, acting in his name and with his authority. These orders — I'd rather like to call them 'suggestions' — that I give you are issued in Father Nicholas Doria's name."

"We'll appeal to the provincial himself," Francis snorted. "We'll present our case directly to him."

"You have every right to do that. But I can guarantee you that Father Doria will not be very responsive to your side of the case."

Francis quickly realized the inadvisability of calling upon Doria for support and changed his manner of attack. "This will humiliate us publicly if we have to cancel all our announced sermons. It's like being silenced."

"First of all, Father," John explained patiently, "you don't have to cancel all your sermons — just some of them. And, second, you won't be humiliated: rather, people will be impressed and edified by your life of prayer in the monastery."

Francis was seething with indignation, helplessly fighting the decision of the vicar provincial; James had left the argument of their case to his companion, but he was no less angry, no less bitter.

"Let's not get upset about this, Fathers," John said. "I've made a decision which I feel is for your own good and the good of the Reform. You can't go to pieces every time a superior makes an adverse decision."

Francis rose to his feet and pointed his finger menacingly at John. "You've not only made an adverse decision, you've made an idiotic one." He turned to his companion. "Come on, let's go. There's no point in arguing with a superior who can't see reason."

"And," James added by way of a parting volley, "you won't be superior forever."

"I hope not," John said quietly.

They stomped out, slamming the door behind them.

John was stunned by the hostility of their reaction. It was incredible that men dedicated to God, men who had left everything to work for Christ should act in such an infantile, irreligious manner. He sat at his desk, motionless, for almost twenty minutes until his musings were interrupted by a soft knock on the door.

It was one of the brothers with a letter for John, a letter from the Calced monastery in Medina del Campo. He tore it open and quickly read the unbelievable contents: a few brief sentences which stated that Father Peter Orozco had died of fever while attending the sick in a hospital during an epidemic.

John stared at the letter, then read it again. It couldn't be true that Peter, his companion at Medina and Salamanca, had passed away. It didn't seem possible that his voice had been stilled. But if Peter had to die — and John must surely accept the fact — there was certainly no more magnificent way to die than as a result of labor for souls.

John was caught in the snare of his reminiscences that afternoon: he reflected on his novitiate days with Peter, and the years they spent at Salamanca; he smiled as he recalled Peter's unexpected visit at Avila to warn him of the Calced persecution. Peter, he thought, was a thoroughly wonderful person and an excellent priest. The laughing Calced Carmelite, though, had no vocation to the Reform; it was too rigorous for him, too confining for his expansive spirit; yet, he was a credit to the Calced — and, now, a martyr of charity.

John fought against the inevitable comparison in his mind between Peter and the two friars who had just defied him. Peter, affable, pleasant, and mild-mannered, would never have rebelled as they had done; he would never have demonstrated such bitterness. And yet, Peter thought himself unworthy of the Reform, too weak to join it. It was strange.

And John was lost for some time in the consideration of that strangeness.

Chapter 3

PETER's death struck John forcefully, making him feel suddenly old and tired, although he was then only forty-four. But, as so often happens, a series of deaths around one almost automatically calls attention to the relentless process of aging and the inevitability of death. Before Peter, there had been Gabriel, John's co-definitor; and before him, Mother Teresa. Father Germain, his companion in the chaplain's house at Avila, had passed away shortly after his escape from Moreleca. People whom he had known and loved — now dead! It gave him a feeling of aloneness, and a sharp yearning to join his friends in the paradise of Christ.

He returned to Granada after his hapless experience at Seville in a mood clouded with these macabre thoughts of death and loneliness; however, he quickly dispersed his cheerless thoughts, recalling to mind the evident fact that he was still very much alive and still had work to perform for Christ. The first task presented itself shortly after his arrival home, when he was summoned to the Discalced Carmelite convent by Ann of Jesus, the prioress.

"Yes, Mother, what can I do for you?" he asked her in the convent parlor.

"I have some news to tell you — but that can wait. First, I want you to talk with one of the young novices. The girl seems to be having some problem about her vocation."

"Certainly. Send her in."

John waited in the plain, unadorned room, tapping his sandal idly on the floor, while Ann departed to dispatch the nun into the parlor. The young nun appeared almost immediately. (She *must* be new, John thought: nuns are supposed to keep you waiting.)

"Good morning, Sister," he said kindly.

"Good morning, Father John." The nun was a mere wisp of a girl, perhaps only seventeen or eighteen; she had a pert, button nose, and wide, childlike eyes, which stared innocently at John. "I've been having difficulties with my vocation, and Mother Ann thought you could help me."

"I will if I can. What seems to be the problem?"

"Oh, everything. I just don't seem to be happy here any more. When I first arrived everything was fine, but recently . . . I don't know, I feel so miserable all the time."

"How long have you been here?" John asked.

"About eight months."

"And you felt contented with your vocation when you first entered the convent?"

"Yes, very definitely."

"No homesickness?"

"A little bit, but nothing serious."

"But now you're not as satisfied with the life?"

"It's . . . it's just that I'm not happy here any more. The convent is wonderful, and the nuns have all been so sweet to me, but for some reason I find it all so hard, so difficult."

"How long have you been finding the life so difficult?"

"For about the last three months."

"Have you talked to any other priest about this?"

"I discussed it with two other priests — they weren't Carmelites — who visited here while you were away. Mother Ann did want me to talk with you about it, but you weren't in Granada."

"What did these priests tell you?"

They both said pretty much the same thing: that I was having temptations against my vocation, and that I should simply force myself to stay, even though I found it difficult."

"And did you force yourself?"

"Oh, yes. . . . It didn't do any good, though, I just became more miserable. I haven't been sleeping well, and my appetite is simply terrible."

John studied the earnest young face of the nun; on closer inspection he could discern thin dark lines under her eyes, lines which appeared so incongruous on her young face.

He continued his questions, which, unknown to the little nun, evoked a series of responses that presented him with a clear picture of the case. Finally, he asked:

"Do you think that you'd be happy as a wife and mother?"

"I know I'd be happy. But . . . the life of a nun is the more perfect vocation, isn't it?"

John smiled. "In the objective sense — that is, the theoretical sense — a religious vocation is the most perfect state in life; but in the subjective . . . er, the individual case, the most perfect state is the one to which the soul has been called by God."

"Oh, I see," the nun said.

John knew that she didn't see, so he continued to explain. "In other words, God wants all of us to be perfect in whatever state of life He calls us to — despite the fact that one state might be theoretically more perfect than the other."

"You mean I could be holy as a married woman?"

"Not only *could* you be holy in the married state, but I think you *should* be holy in the married state."

The nun's eyebrows arched. "What do you mean, Father?"

"I think, my dear, that the religious life is not your vocation. This despondency and unhappiness you are experiencing are evident signs that your vocation lies elsewhere."

"You don't think it's right to force myself to go on?"

"I don't think it's right — I think it's wrong. Oh, I know that the religious life is a constant sacrifice, that we have to cut ourselves off from everything, that we have to labor for the cause of Christ. But sacrifice and hardship should not deprive us of our joy and our happiness. In fact, your joy should be increased tremendously by living in the religious life. And, if after an initial period of adjustment, that joy is lacking, then something is wrong."

"I should leave the convent?"

"Yes, you should. There's no disgrace in that; rather, it's all to your credit that you gave such serious thought to God in planning your life. The Church has arranged the training period in religious orders in such a way that a new candidate may freely leave at any time during the first two years. This introductory period to the religious life is meant to be a time of decision — and I think your decision should be to return home."

The nun remained silent, her little face pensive in thought; finally, she smiled at him. It was the first time John had seen her smile; and it was a delightful smile, bright and frank. "Oh, I'm so glad to hear you say that," she said. "I've been fighting this thing for months, and it's been ruining me. . . . You know what, Father?"

"What?"

"I'm already beginning to feel happy again."

"Good! Now, do you want to make me happy too?"

"Certainly, Father."

"Tell Mother Ann that I'm still here, but that I have to go in a few minutes."

Waiting for Ann of Jesus to reappear, John reflected on his discussion with the young nun. In a few minutes' time, he thought, he had altered the whole course of her life. And how many of these cases involving all different types of situations does a priest handle in his life!

His reverie was interrupted by the reappearance of the tall, graceful Ann of Jesus.

"And what's this news you have to tell me, Mother?"

Mother Ann of Jesus was, as usual, composed and reserved, a definite contrast to her predecessor, the bubbling, effusive Mother Teresa. But while Ann possessed more of the grand manner than Teresa she nevertheless lacked her genius, her brilliance, and her limitless energy. Teresa was the engaging, lovable saint God had given to inaugurate the work of the Reform; Ann was her competent successor.

"We've been invited to start a new convent in the capital, Madrid," she said.

"That's good news. We've needed a convent there for some time now."

Ann clasped her hands neatly in her lap. "And I'm going there as the first prioress."

"Oh! When are you leaving?" There was surprise in his voice.

"Very shortly. In a few days, I think."

"This is a farewell, then?"

"Well, not a final one, I hope," Ann said. "You'll visit us when you come to Madrid?"

"Certainly I'll visit you whenever I'm there. But it's a long distance from Granada to Madrid, you know."

It *was* a long distance from Granada to Madrid, but John rather reveled in the many leagues that separated him from the feverish activity of Doria's new administration, now located in the Spanish capital. It was almost an identical situation to the one during the years he had been stationed at the Incarnation in Avila: during those years of his chaplaincy he had been removed from the immediate scene of the Reform's government. And, he was reluctantly forced to conclude, he disagreed with Doria's general program even more than he had with Gratian's. Gratian had been an inept bungler, a rashly imprudent superior in his dealings with the Calced; Doria was something worse than that: a ruthlessly efficient administrator, an almost fanatic rigorist, and an uncompromising exponent of his own ideas.

Letter after letter arrived at Granada informing John of Doria's roughshod method of dealing with the friars and of his constant attempt to control every possible situation that arose. Doria was the provincial; he would run the Reform; he would tolerate no resistance to his ideas.

It was a situation identical to the one in which Gratian had mishandled the Reform and which John had uncomfortably observed from afar; but in that situation, it was John who was forced to pay the price for Gratian's inepitude by being imprisoned at

Toledo. He wondered if history would repeat itself, if he would be the one chosen by God to suffer for Doria's errors.

John conducted himself in the same manner, too: he prayed; he did his work; he remained silent. However, Gratian — who was still exiled in Portugal — exhibited his usual spirit of imprudence, of brashness. Gratian would not suffer Doria's administration without official comment: he made biting public statements regarding Doria's dictatorial regime; he criticized his superior openly, calling Doria "the lion of Carmel." Gratian was so imprudent as to make these statements before gatherings of lay people, and even in sermons through veiled remarks. In addition, he had some pamphlets and tracts published which contained open attacks on Doria. The "lion of Carmel" could not fail to have received reports of the stinging criticism emanating from Portugal, but he continued undaunted in his program.

It was no secret that Doria had stationed a friar in Rome to guard the Reform's interests; and it was no secret either that this friar was working vigorously, under Doria's direction, for a final, definitive establishment of the Reform as a completely independent order. This was the step that Gratian predicted would occur in time, but Doria was impatient. He was unwilling to wait; he wanted complete sovereignty for the Reform now.

Doria's importunate efforts resulted in a decree from the Pope, Sixtus V, which established the Reform, not as an independent order, but as a congregation. This was not the definitive step Doria desired; however, it was a major achievement. The Reform, now elevated to the rank of a canonical congregation, would no longer be governed by a provincial, but instead by a general to be elected by the friars. The Pope's decree, which was received in Spain in the fall of 1587, was gratifying to Doria, not only because it placed the Reform on a new level of juridic independence, but also because it granted him permission to establish whatever form of government he wished to choose for the Reform.

John, in Granada, was informed of the decree, and he waited, somewhat apprehensively, for Doria to take action on it. Each day he thumbed quickly through the daily stack of incoming mail. Finally in the spring it came: an official notification from Doria that all superiors were to present themselves at Madrid in June for new elections and a meeting to study the provisions of the papal decree.

In early June, just before he started on his trip to Madrid, John heard the shocking news that Spain was declaring war on England. It was almost inevitable that it happen, for Philip II had been becoming more and more provoked over the years at the English pirates who were raiding his ships. And there was the religious issue too: Catholics in England were suffering violent persecution, and Philip wanted to reinstate Catholicism there. The final incident was the world-shocking news that Queen Elizabeth had executed Mary Queen of Scots, Philip's cousin by marriage. Philip decided to invade England. He announced the formation of a tremendous fleet, the greatest the world had ever known, to sail against Britain. His fleet, the Armada, would be invincible, he said, and Spain would soon rule England.

As John made the long foot journey north to Madrid, he saw a country in turmoil. Feverish preparations were being made in every city and village to equip the Armada. Long columns of soldiers were marching westward to Lisbon, the point of embarkation. And, again and again, he heard the exultant cry ringing in the air: "The invincible Armada, the invincible Armada!"

He arrived at the monastery in Madrid in the late morning, and immediately went to the choir, where the friars were chanting None of the Divine Office. The rhythmic chanting of the psalms was soothing to him, in contrast to the hysteria he had been seeing the past few days. After the Office, the first familiar face he encountered was that of Anthony.

"You look wonderful," John said to him. "How do you feel?"

"Splendid!"

John had to smile at his old friend. He did look "splendid," though. He had apparently thrown off all traces of his illness and, at seventy-eight, looked hale and sturdy; he had lost some weight, and there were deep lines worked into his brow and cheeks, but he carried himself straight and erect with an almost military bearing.

"What do you know about this new decree Doria received from Rome?" John asked him.

"Not much. It's all very secret. All I know is that Doria has engineered some new type of government, and that he's going to have a lot more power than he had before."

"I'll be interested in hearing what Gratian has to say about *that* at the meeting," John said.

Anthony looked sharply at John. "Haven't you heard about Gratian?"

"No," John said, surprised.

"Gratian won't be here."

"Why not?"

"Doria saw to that. You've heard, of course, that Gratian has been making unflattering statements about the provincial, and that he's even published some of these in pamphlets. Well, that was all Doria needed: last month he set up a tribunal and found Gratian guilty of insubordination. The penalty was that Gratian was made ineligible to hold any office, or even to vote at an election."

John shook his head slowly. "Doria must have realized that Gratian would oppose him on this new government business."

"Of course. Doria is a clever soldier: he eliminated his opposition before it attacked."

"I'm afraid," John said bitterly, "that the Reform doesn't need soldiers or statesmen. It only needs saints."

The meeting convened in the hall of the Madrid monastery, and the first order of business was the election of a general, the highest office in the newly formed congregation. The new status of the Reform provided for a general (supplanting the office of provincial) and four provincials (supplanting the old offices of vicar provincials). Doria, John thought, should have no trouble in receiving the office of general, for there seemed to be no candidate who could muster enough electoral strength to oppose him: Gratian had been removed; and Anthony himself, despite his return to health, was generally considered too old for that taxing, enervating position.

Once again the ballot slips were distributed and the friars began to vote. John wrote Anthony's name on his ballot — the man's age didn't bother him, but Doria's methods did. The tabulations were counted off by Doria in his flat, uninflected voice. As the ballots were announced, it was evident, after the first fifteen or twenty votes, that Doria would be the victor; but surprising to John, there was opposition: however, the votes cast against Doria were splintered among a number of friars. The final count gave Doria thirty-two votes out of the fifty cast. He was in power again — and this time for six years.

There was a lull in the proceedings after Doria's election, and Anthony turned to John, who was sitting beside him in the crowded election chamber.

"There it is: Doria again!"

"Why can't we get a simple ordinary friar as superior?" John said in a hushed voice. "Lord deliver us from these efficient geniuses — they'll be the ruination of us."

"I know what you mean," Anthony said. "Look! Your efficient genius is at the rostrum again."

Doria surveyed the assembly of friars before him: they were his friars again, and he would make something out of them no matter what the cost. "I don't know whether you are aware of all the details contained in the decree of the Holy See," he announced. "There is one item which I especially requested: the formation of a group which I call the 'Consulta.' "

John glanced at Anthony, who shrugged his shoulders.

"The Consulta," Doria continued, "is another project in my efforts to work out a more highly centralized administration. The Consulta is a board of six friars who will live in the provincial residence, and, with the provincial, run the affairs of the Reform."

John was confused as to the exact nature of the Consulta, or the precise function it would exercise; he, therefore, followed Doria's statements carefully, warily. As Doria explained the Consulta, picking his words carefully, a gradual awareness of the full implications of the project struck John. He was aghast! By establishing the Consulta, Doria was reserving to that group much of the authority formerly possessed by the vicar provincials and the priors of the monasteries. The Consulta, John discovered to his chagrin, was a device with which Doria could rule the entire Reform and its most trivial affairs directly from his own residence. Formerly, the prior of the monastery was the person who directed the house, made minor decisions, appointed the priests as confessors or preachers; the major superior was only approached on important issues. Now, the Consulta would take an active part in every detail of administrative business in the Reform. Nothing would escape Doria; nothing *could* escape Doria.

"And now," Doria said, "I'll announce the names of the six friars who are to serve in the Consulta. The first member — and therefore the man who will be second in command to the general — is Father John of the Cross."

John was stunned by his appointment; he scarcely paid any attention to the other five men nominated, although he did hear Anthony's name announced. Doria had appointed him a member of this oligarchical council, and the number one member, at that. This implied, of course, that Doria numbered John as one of his supporters; however, he was anything but that. John searched in his own mind for some explanation, some reason why Doria should consider him an adherent. There seemed to be no reason . . . except . . . yes, that must be it: John had sided with Doria against Gratian five years ago in the discussion about the foreign missions. Doria must have interpreted John's action as a personal rebuff to Gratian and an act of allegiance to him. But that wasn't the case: John had acted on principles and not on personalities.

Be that as it may, John thought dourly, he was now Doria's number one man.

At the conclusion of the meeting Doria announced that the six members of the Consulta, his supreme council, would reside with him at the monastery in Segovia, northeast of Madrid. Therefore, in August John arrived in Segovia to begin his duties as Doria's first councilor. From the very first, John didn't like the monastery in Segovia, a small house, with only eleven friars. The headquarters of the Consulta, John thought, was so unlike the other monasteries of the Reform: it was businesslike and bristled with cold efficiency. It lacked that quiet, gentle contemplative spirit which had characterized the Reform up to this time.

A few days after his arrival, John's mood of gloom and dejection was compounded. Unbelievable news was proclaimed in the city: the invincible Spanish Armada had been defeated! The small, maneuverable English ships had worked havoc on the ponderous Spanish vessels; and a furious storm had completed the wreck of the Armada. Philip II would be fortunate if one third of his ships were able to return. England now owned the seas.

Spain was in trouble, John thought grimly, and so was the Reform, too.

John's only consolation in Segovia was that he was living in the same monastery with Anthony for the first time in seventeen years. But it was small recompense for the sickness of heart that weighed on him. He watched Doria's Consulta swing into operation, and, to his dismay, it functioned efficiently — and ruthlessly. Doria, through his Consulta, was able to keep his fingers on every pulse beat in the Reform: the six members of that council were the channels through which he reached out to every member. Under Doria's orders weekly reports came flooding into Segovia from each monastery; and in the following mail, new decrees and new orders were sent out. And if any friar expressed disagreement with Doria's policies, he was immediately reprimanded and transferred to some remote monastery.

As the methodical machinery of Doria's administration began to operate, John could observe the disastrous effects immediately: a hostile discontent was growing among the friars, a servile fear began to oppress them, and they walked in constant fear of the "lion of Carmel." Doria had erected a police state in the Reform, John thought. It was wrong, all wrong.

Doria called the six-man Consulta into session almost every day, and thus John was brought into constant association with the man toward whom he had an uncomfortable aversion. Doria, his swarthy face worked into a grim frown, sat at the head of the long council table, a huge pile of papers in front of him. He listened intently to each of his councilors as the digested reports from the various monasteries for him, and then, in his flat voice, he issued curt orders and directives, which were to be executed by the councilors. John had to admit that this whole idea of a Consulta was clever: without it, Doria would never have been able to exercise the close surveillance he wanted over the expanding Reform.

Watching Doria in action, John began to wonder about the man. At first, he had thought that Doria was doing all this because he believed it was best for the Reform. But now John was afraid that the man wanted only power, that he wanted only to satisfy his own ambitions for supreme control of the Order. Perhaps, John thought, Doria was able to convince himself that he was only working for the best interests of the common good. perhaps he felt that a rigorous administration was what the Order needed. At least Doria had entered the Reform for the same reason he had: to lead the contemplative life. But now Doria's original ambitions had degenerated into this battle for power. And with such a man at its head, the Reform could easily split wide open and disintegrate.

It was this realization that Doria could unwittingly destroy the Reform which caused John the most concern. Admittedly, the Reform was *now* in good condition: there were over forty monasteries; there were almost five hundred friars in its ranks; and the friars themselves were faithfully following the contemplative life of prayer and penance, a life that they could never have found in the Calced. But Doria could destroy it all. It had happened before in the Church: a number of religious orders had started out well, but had then collapsed and been disbanded because of mismanagement. The Reform was only twenty years old; it did not yet possess the definitive approval of Rome as a religious order; and it was possible that Rome could call a halt to the whole thing.

Doria was certainly moving the Order in that direction, John thought. He was creating an almost tangible discontent among the friars. Soon there would be mass appeals to Rome for dispensations and transfers to other orders; soon prospective candidates would be warned not to join the Reform; soon Rome would be advised that the Reform was breaking asunder. And that would be the end of the dream Teresa had twenty years ago.

When John was thrown into the monastic prison at Toledo eleven years ago he had experienced serious fears for the Reform. But those fears were nothing like his present ones. The struggle with the Calced was one with people *outside* its own group, and it only served to strengthen the Reform itself. But this was a conflict within its own ranks. John was realistic enough to understand that the Reform would undoubtedly have in its ranks friars who fell far short of what could be expected of a contemplative friar. There had been Angelus, the warped novice master at Pastrana, and Francis and James, the two friars who fought him at Seville — to recall just a few. That was to be expected. But when one of these unfortunate friars rose to the highest office in the Reform — especially at this early stage of its development — then there would be serious trouble.

As all this confusion whirled around John — and thrashed about inside his soul, too — he maintained his silence about the distressing state of affairs which he deplored so much. He worked at the constant trivia of decisions which were referred to the Consulta; he executed Doria's interminable decrees; he traveled to the monasteries where Doria wanted some edict enforced. But he knew there would come a breaking point, that he could not long abide the situation.

The breaking point was the problem of the Discalced Carmelite nuns.

⌈ Chapter 4 ⌉

DORIA now had the friars in a position of rigid control, but the nuns were in a different arrangement entirely. Teresa had established the nuns in a loose union: each convent was governed by a prioress, who was an autonomous superior, and all the convents collectively were under the remote supervision of the friars. This meant that the superior-general of the friars would automatically be the major superior of the nuns; however, his authority was to be a remote, tenuous one, employed only in matters of seriousness or urgency. This situation was, of course, entirely opposed to Doria's concept of the function of authority in a religious order. Therefore, one day in the fall of 1588 at a meeting of the Consulta, Doria announced:

"I think we have to congratulate ourselves upon the smooth operation of the Consulta. We now have a highly efficient, centrally operated government. . . . However, we've not been as successful with the nuns. They are organized in a sloppy, inefficient organization. I propose, therefore, to do two things about it: first, make them refer all their business to the Consulta, as the friars do; and, second, try to revise their constitutions along the lines of a more centralized administration."

Doria looked around the table at which the seven men were grouped, searching for some sign of approval. John, as the first member of the Consulta, spoke first.

"Father General, why don't we leave the nuns alone? They've been doing all right so far without any close supervision."

Doria darted an unbelieving glance at John: could it be that his first councilor was disagreeing with him? "You don't think we should bring the nuns under our supervision?"

"I'm sorry, Father, but I don't."

"Do you disagree, then, with my ideas of government?"

"That's too long a discussion to enter into now, Father. But I do think that the nuns would be better off without our interference. Mother Teresa framed their constitutions, and I think they're perfectly satisfactory the way they now read."

Doria, his thick features immobile, said icily:

"We'll go into this some other time when Father John feels in a less rebellious mood."

The following day John received a report of Doria's reaction to their discussion at the Consulta meeting. Anthony came into John's cell, discovering him on his knees in prayer.

"Are you praying for the Reform?" Anthony asked drolly.

"Somebody had better pray for it," John answered.

"I think," Anthony said, "that you'd better pray for yourself, too. Doria is a little annoyed — to put it mildly — at your remarks yesterday. He has some suspicions now that his first councilor is no longer on his side."

"Was I ever?"

"He thinks you were."

John walked over to the window and looked down at the passing tide of Segovian life which ebbed slowly by. Some of the pedestrians tipped their caps while passing the monastery church; others glanced curiously at the somber walls.

"Doria has to be stopped somewhere," he said. "The Reform has no place in its ranks for a tyrant. . . . And I think this matter of the nuns is as good a place to start as any."

Anthony peered at him questioningly. "What are you going to do?"

"I think I'll pay a little visit to Mother Ann of Jesus and advise her of the danger to the nuns. She's an intelligent woman, she'll know what to do."

"You can't fight the general, John. He's entrenched in power; he'll destroy you."

"Maybe."

"Do you remember what Doria did to Gratian?"

"How can I forget?" John said softly.

A week later John was in Madrid, and his first business in the Spanish capital was a visit to the nuns' convent and Ann of Jesus. The former superioress of the convent at Granada received John with cordiality and an unusual animation.

"It's so good of you to drop in for a visit, Father."

"This is not a social visit, I'm afraid, Mother."

"No?"

"I'm not here officially, and I'd appreciate it if you wouldn't mention my visit."

"Of course not, Father."

John selected his words with painstaking precision. "Father Nicholas Doria has actuated a program for high centralization of authority in the Reform."

"I've heard of his work," Ann said acidulously.

"Good, then you know of his ideas and his manner of operation. Father Doria now intends to do the same thing to the nuns that he did to the friars: he wants to bring all the convents under the immediate jurisdiction of the Consulta."

"But," Ann protested, "he'd have to change our constitutions to do that successfully."

"Precisely. He intends to change your constitutions."

"Change our constitutions? The constitutions of Mother Teresa?"

"I know it sounds incredible; but it's entirely in character for Doria."

"But he can't. There's no reason for a change. Everything is going on smoothly." She knitted her brow in a deep frown. "What can I do to stop him?" she said grimly.

"I'm in a rather ambiguous position: I'm a member of Doria's Consulta, and it would be improper for me to advise you in operations against him. . . . However, I do feel that I can give you some general principles of good thinking."

"Yes?" Ann said, her face brightening.

"First, Doria will have to appeal to Rome for any change or revision of your constitutions: Teresa's legislation has papal approval. Second, Doria himself works on the principle that the best defense is an early attack."

Ann studied John's face for a moment, then said slowly:

"I see what you mean, Father."

"And that's all I have to say, Mother. Unfortunately, I'll be unable to give you any more help than that. But I'll be watching . . . with intense interest."

Ann of Jesus understood perfectly the implication in John's thinly veiled statement. Nor was she tardy in springing to action: she whirled her own machinery into operation, sending off a petition to Rome for an irrevocable confirmation of the Teresian constitutions. As an afterthought, she included in her petition a request that some friar of the Reform be named, what she termed a "Father Protector," a priest who would be charged with protecting the interests and welfare of the nuns; and she asked, in an undisguised rebuke of Doria, that the superior-general of the Reform be ineligible for that office. As a final rebuff to Doria, she requested that Father John of the Cross be assigned the office of Father Protector.

In June of 1590, the Pope, Sixtus V, issued a decree which forbade any alteration of the Teresian constitutions; he also agreed to Ann's request that the office of Father Protector be established, postponing, however, the announcement of the name of the friar who was to hold the office for a few months.

Doria was livid with rage: he suspected John of drafting the appeal to Rome, and he became more convinced of John's complicity when he learned the name Ann had proposed for the office of Father Protector. Actually, John had done nothing in the composition or presentation of the appeal; he remained sedulously removed from the entire operation.

The confusion was compounded when, in late August, the Pope suddenly died, causing a temporary halt to the entire proceedings. Doria utilized the interval between the Pope's death and the election of the new Pontiff as an opportunity to marshal his forces for a new attack. As soon as the new Pope, Gregory XIV, was installed in office, he was presented with a petition from Doria requesting a nullification of the previous decree which granted immunity to the nuns. Then Doria and Ann sat back to await the final verdict.

Doria, in his fervid operation to thwart Ann's victory, had no opportunity to take any punitive action against John, whom he now regarded as a hostile force which must be eradicated. An interterm election was due in June of that year, 1591, and Doria would settle John's account then.

By the time the June meeting convened in Madrid, no word had been received from Rome, and the electors assembled in a spirit of uncertainty as to Doria's success in bringing the nuns under his control. John, naturally, was present at the meeting, but he had no illusions about Doria's intentions to punish him.

There was much business to be performed: all the principal offices in the Reform were open for election — with the exception of Doria's, for he had been elected to a six-year term three years ago. However, before proceeding to the lengthy ballotings, Doria introduced a discussion about the present problem of the nuns. John wondered if Doria had opened the discussion to draw him out, to unmask him publicly as an opponent of the general.

"It's a source of deep grievance to me that the nuns are attempting to free themselves from my authority," Doria said, taking his customary stand at the rostrum in the front of the hall. "It's difficult to see why the nuns take this untenable position: the Consulta has proved itself throughout the last three years to be a magnificent method of obtaining maximum efficiency in the Reform."

Doria paused, then continued in his flat voice. "I presume that you all share my sentiments on this matter. . . . Does anyone disagree with me?" Doria's eyes searched the room, finally fastening themselves on John, who sat in the front row. It was an open challenge to him.

John had arrived at the moment of decision: should he respond to the challenge, publicly criticize Doria's actions? He had heartily disapproved of Gratian's outbursts against Doria some years ago; he thought that Gratian had acted imprudently, stirred up new discontent, and accomplished nothing apart from his own downfall. But this was different: this was an open discussion about business pertaining to the Reform. If these matters could not be discussed here — calmly, charitably, and objectively — where could they be discussed? And yet Doria really wanted no discussion — his challenge to John was in the nature of a dare: try to criticize these things, and you will see how I will crush you!

Doria was convinced that his decisions were beyond discussion. But John would not agree with that: Doria could make mistakes, and these matters must be open to review. Although John was unprepared for a public address, he decided, because of Doria's taunt and the entangled situation in the Reform, that he must criticize the superior-general's position.

John resolutely thrust his hand into the air, signaling for recognition.

"Ah, Father John of the Cross has something to say," Doria proclaimed sardonically.

John rose wearily to his feet, turned to face the group, and dug his hands into the leather belt that girded his habit. "I have always detested any insubordination or disobedience in religious organizations. It is for this reason that I have hesitated to make any remarks here. Yet, I feel that the criticisms which I make, which I *must* make, do not constitute a rebellion against legitimate authority, but are rather a calm discussion of matters which concern the common cause we have all embraced."

He spoke in a soft, deliberate voice, which caused those in the rear of the hall to lean forward slightly to hear him. Doria stood to one side, his face twisted in a tight scowl.

"I have not spoken publicly about these matters before because I felt any such action would have been useless. I am no less convinced now that my efforts here will be useless, but at least I will have satisfied my own conscience, I will have placed my views in the public record. . . . For the past six years I have witnessed the gradual tightening of authority to the point where every friar in the Reform is under close, constant surveillance, where personal initiative has been stifled, where servile fear reigns as the general atmosphere. This is a state of affairs entirely contrary to the concept of a religious order in the Church. An order should be a family where love, peace, and mutual trust abide; it should not be an impersonal machine.

"I take exception to three principal incidents of the past six years. First, I must object to the ruthless punishment meted out to Father Jerome Gratian, a former provincial, a friar who worked hard for the Reform before many of you here were even members. I certainly hold no brief for Gratian's method of procedure — I have criticized it strongly — but I do feel that the punishment given him was inconsistent with his offense, inconsistent with the amount of service he rendered the Reform."

Perspiration was breaking out on John's forehead and neck, and his back felt damp and moist under the wool habit. "Second, I object to the Consulta in its present form. I would object to any form of government which tends to treat men as dumb animals rather than dedicated servants of God; and the Consulta does just that. The Consulta is a weapon of tyranny, of which I cannot approve.

"Third, I object to the present proposal: the alteration of the nuns' constitutions. This is one more effort in the general program to erect a police administration. The nuns have operated success-fully and efficiently for these many years without the Consulta. I hope they continue to do so for many years to come — without the Consulta!

"I realize the seriousness of the charges I bring. But I have searched my soul for some justification for the general policies I have mentioned — however, I can find no justification or excuse for them. They are tyrannical devices which, if continued, will destroy the Reform from within. I can only pray that God will guide us through this period of inner disturbance to a new period of tran-quillity, of peace, of love."

John breathed deeply and set himself in his chair again. He stared at his hands: they were quivering slightly from excitement. He clenched them until the knuckles stood out taut and white. His face was creased in perspiration.

Doria walked slowly back to the rostrum in steady, deliberate strides. Arriving at the speaker's stand, he stared sullenly at John for almost a minute, then spoke:

"A very pretty speech. But one, unfortunately, that was as untrue as it was unwise." He looked up from John out to the group at large. "Do any more of you agree with these misguided sentiments? If so, please signify by raising your hand."

John lowered his eyes to the floor, unwilling to witness Doria's appeal for a vote of confidence. There were fifty-six friars in the room; only about fifteen hands were raised in support of John's position. Even Anthony, sitting rigidly beside John, refused to raise his hand. It was a triumph for Doria, a triumph of power and of fear.

Doria's face came as near to breaking into a smile as John could ever recall. The superior-general studied the men whose hands were raised in defiance to him, making a mental note of their opposition and their ultimate expendability.

"I imagine, Father John, that this demonstrates to you how much at variance your ideas are with the majority of friars." His dark face was flushed in the enjoyment of his victory.

The election of superiors followed, a session of special agony to John. It was then that Doria demonstrated tangibly the success of his police regime, then that he showed his absolute control of the friars. John had opposed Doria, and a vote for him would be a vote against Doria: it was as simple as that. And it worked exactly that way.

During the actual elections, there were a number of offices to be filled — priorships, provincialships, and many others — but it soon became evident that John was to receive no position at all. He was to be humiliated publicly, to be shown the foolishness of opposing Doria. John received a few votes here, a few votes there, but nothing in any way sufficient to elect him to a single office. He sat there stoically, patiently, in an anguish of soul.

When the session was completed, John wanted desperately to be by himself, free from the oppressiveness of the election chamber. He walked rapidly out into the monastic garden, almost colliding with two friars in his hasty exit. The tranquillity of the garden, its even grass and multicolored flowers, seemed to settle some of the disturbance thrashing about in his soul.

He had not been there long when he heard a footstep crunch on the gravel behind him; it was Doria.

"It seems, Father, that you are now without any office in the Reform," he said with unusual solicitude. "I don't think it proper that the first Discalced Carmelite friar should be without any position of authority at all."

John squinted uncertainly at Doria: the man was up to something, but he couldn't determine what.

"There's one position still vacant," Doria said. "I'm forced to send some more friars to Mexico to staff the unfortunate mission founded by your friend, Father Gratian. Since you feel so strongly about Gratian, I thought you'd be interested in furthering his project. The group leaves in a few months — you Father John, will head the group!"

Doria marched quickly away, leaving John to the garden and his thoughts. So Doria was going to exile him to Mexico, remove him from the scene just as effectively as he had removed Gratian. John could follow Doria's reasoning on the assignment to Mexico: it would serve to get him out of the way, but, even more important, it would render it impossible for him to accept the office of Father Protector for the nuns if the counterbrief to Rome failed. It would be especially distressing for Doria to have John wandering around Spain in the autonomous role of major superior for the nuns. Anticipating this unpleasant possibility, he determined to thwart it by sending John halfway around the world.

⌠ Chapter 5 ⌡

A COLUMN of Spanish soldiers, in gleaming breastplates and polished leather boots, marched across the road, blocking John's path. He waited until they had passed, then resumed his foot journey south.

John was hiking along the dusty road to La Penuela, a distant outpost of a monastery in southern Andalusia, because Doria had revoked the Mexican assignment. Doria canceled the appointment to Mexico for two reasons: first, he realized, after some careful thinking, that it would only serve to establish John as a martyr; second, the new Pope's decree for the nuns had made the assignment unnecessary. The decree had been a defeat for Doria — the nuns' constitutions were not to be altered — but it contained one concession to him: rejection of the appointment of a Father Protector. Therefore, despite his defeat, Doria had no fears now that John would be given that position. Instead of being sent to Mexico John could be sent to some out-of-the-way place in Spain. La Penuela, lost in the wastes of Andalusia, was selected.

The trip to La Penuela was a lengthy one, but John didn't mind it because the long hours he spent tramping along the road gave him an opportunity to think and pray for the Reform. He reviewed, with painstaking precision, the events of the recent elections: Doria's challenge, his own speech, the failure of the other friars to support him. He wasn't surprised that the friars at the election had sided with Doria against him. He knew, from his work on the Consulta, that Doria had called to the elections only those men he considered loyal to him. Also, he knew that Doria's policy of ruthlessly removing opposition had frightened them into submission. The whole thing was a supreme demonstration of how much fear Doria had driven into the hearts of the friars.

John's most painful thought, though, was Anthony's failure to stand up for him. The old man, thoroughly embarrassed, had tried to explain it to him after the elections:

"Now look, John, you know I disapprove of Doria as much as you."

"Then how could you side with him on that vote of confidence?" John asked.

"Let me put it this way: I didn't side *with* Doria, I just didn't think it wise to declare myself *against* him. I think you made a big mistake by giving that speech against Doria."

"Why? Don't you feel that error should be denounced — especially in an official meeting like the elections?"

"I do," Anthony said. "Of course I do. But only when there's hope of accomplishing something. Your denunciation of Doria didn't accomplish one thing. On the contrary, it gave Doria an excuse for getting rid of you. It would have been far better, I think, to have remained silent: then you could have stayed where you might have done some good for the Reform."

"And that's why *you* supported Doria on the vote of confidence?"

Anthony smiled. "Yes, I felt that one exiled friar was better than *two* exiled friars."

John felt better after talking with Anthony. At least now he knew the reason for his friend's lack of support. And maybe Anthony was right, maybe he should have tried to stay in Doria's good graces and thus have been in a better position to help the Reform. That's what Anthony had done, and he had been elected the provincial superior of Andalusia, the region in which John would be stationed.

His conversation with Anthony had convinced him of one other thing: the friars, as a group, were not hostile toward him: they were only terrified of Doria. The only friars who seemed to receive any satisfaction from John's rejection at the elections were James and Francis, the two men he had attempted to correct at Seville. Over the years, the two friars had allied themselves with Doria, and the recent elections was their moment of triumph in which they saw retribution for their reprimand of a few years ago. Their delight was intensified when they themselves were elected to offices, James as a member of the Consulta, and Francis as prior of Ubeda. But apart from those two, all the other friars had been disturbed and embarrassed at John's defeat.

The simple fact of John's removal from office was of no concern to him. Indeed, he rather enjoyed the prospect of being freed from the concerns of administration. What did trouble him, though, was that his removal demonstrated forcefully that no one could oppose Doria and survive, that the general had erected a complete police regime in the Reform. And, John thought, unless Doria could be stopped the Reform was finished.

During the journey to La Penuela, John churned the problem over and over again in his mind. He was oblivious to the people along the highway and to the carriages that clattered past him. Then suddenly, as he neared La Penuela, a gentle calm descended on him, and in that moment he knew how the problem would be solved. And he knew, too, that he had been wrong about many things.

Anthony had been right, he thought: he *did* act unwisely in speaking out against Doria. That wasn't the way the Blessed Virgin wanted him to serve the Reform; that was never the way he had served the Reform in the past. He had never acted as chief spokesman for the Reform, he had never been superior-general. And that was apparently the way the Blessed Virgin wanted it. But, he thought, there was one vitally important function Mary did want him to do: *she wanted him to suffer, to be a victim for the success of the Reform.* That was the role he had played at Toledo during the struggle with the Calced, and that — he was sure — was the role he was to play again in this hour of crisis for the Reform.

He was positive of it. And yet he was amazed at the certainty with which he believed it; the idea had clamped itself on his mind with a force that was almost physical. There were many unanswered questions in his mind: why had Mary chosen *him* to be a victim for the Reform? What would his sufferings be this time? But none of that was really important. The only important thing was that Mary *had* selected him for a victim, and that, in some way he didn't understand yet, his sufferings would be used to save the Reform.

Despite his certainty that there were painful hours ahead for him, John walked briskly up the path to the monastery at La Penuela, and there was a soft smile on his face when he reached for the knocker on the front door.

The monastery at La Penuela was an old frame building set back in the hills. It was removed from any main road of travel, and thus there were very few visitors at the monastery. An air of stillness and quiet pervaded the place. But John liked his place of exile: he liked the opportunity of following the monastic schedule without interruption, and he liked the six other friars who were stationed there. And the friars themselves were delighted to have the first friar of the Reform with them in their remote monastery. In fact, two of the friars were men Doria had sent in exile like John, and it was something they laughed and jested about. For John, the tranquil contemplative life at La Penuela was a refreshing change from the charged atmosphere at Madrid.

After Vespers in the afternoon, John often walked out through the sun-scorched fields and over the rocky hills, praying and wondering how the Blessed Virgin would use him as a victim again. He soon found out: a month after his arrival he started to get sick. First, a blotch of ugly red sores broke out on his feet and legs. He paid little attention to the annoying sores until they had persisted for about a week; then they began to suppurate. In addition to this, he was struck with an occasional dizziness which caused him to lurch violently. The prior of the monastery, a kindly man with white hair and piercing blue eyes, watched all this, and finally one day said to him:

"I think this has gone far enough, Father John. You're getting sicker and sicker."

In obedience to the prior, John showed him the ulcerating sores on his legs. The prior grimaced and sucked in his breath quickly.

"You've really got something there. You need medical attention, and you need it right away."

"All right," John said.

"It's not as simple as that. There's no doctor anywhere near here. We've got nothing in La Penuela."

John smiled faintly. "Father, you've got everything in Penuela."

The prior looked at him sharply for a second, and then relaxed his face into a comfortable grin. "Yes, I know what you mean. We do have everything, don't we? . . . However, you still need medical attention, and you can't get it here. I want you to go to one of our other monasteries where you can get adequate treatment."

"Which one?"

"The monasteries at Ubeda and Beas are fairly close, and you can receive good medical care at either of them. Which one would you prefer?"

Ubeda struck a familiar chord in John's mind: that monastery was where Father Francis, the friar he had reprimanded at Seville, was now prior. If he went to Ubeda his welcome would be anything but cordial; but it would be a magnificent opportunity for sacrifice, for making a complete oblation to the Blessed Virgin.

"I'd like to go to Ubeda," he said.

"Fine. You can leave first thing in the morning. I'll have one of the brothers accompany you."

The journey to Ubeda was a nightmare, a prolonged seizure of pain and discomfiture. The prior had insisted that John ride to Ubeda on a donkey, which a brother led along by a rope bridle. But as the beast heaved back and forth, John twitched perceptibly, while spasms of pain shot up his ulcerated legs. The fever grew within him, and John remembered little of the trip.

He did, however, remember one series of reflections: the pleasant realization that the Blessed Virgin was going to employ him as a victim, that it augured well for the success of the Reform. He knew, too, that he was very sick, and that Mary would not snatch him out of this difficulty as she had in the prison at Toledo. John realized that this was the beginning of the end.

⌈ Chapter 6 ⌉

DOCTOR MARTIN VILLAREAL held the tiny lancet firmly in his hand, paused a moment, then stabbed it into John's leg slightly above the ankle, opening a thin slit in the flesh. Villareal, still holding the blood-smeared lancet in his hand, watched the bleeding intently. There was nothing more effective for abating high fever, he thought, than a good bleeding.

John, stretched out on the board bed in his cell at the monastery in Ubeda, did not share Doctor Villareal's sanguine convictions. He knew that his sickness would allow no recovery; yet he cheerfully submitted to the doctor's ministrations. However, in all honesty, John could not claim that he had been indulged at Ubeda with needless or futile remedies; in fact, Father Francis had truculently decided that he was to be given the minimum of treatment.

John had expected a cold, perhaps unenthusiastic reception from the prior, Father Francis, but he was not prepared for the man's blatant hostility, his open lack of charity. Francis assigned him to one of the poorest cells in the monastery, a cramped room in the rear of the building, and forbade any of the community to visit him without express permission. Nor did Francis' hostility end there: he went out of his way to inform John that he was an unwelcome guest.

"You can have that cell at the rear of the house," he told John curtly. Francis, still chaffing under the remembrance of John's reprimand, treated him with none of the courtesy due an ill friar.

Villareal, the doctor, decided that he had drawn enough blood from John. He pressed a piece of cloth tightly over the new wound and held it firmly until the bleeding had stopped.

John, his face white from the loss of blood, managed to reply:

"Thanks a lot, Doctor. But you shouldn't bother with me. I think you're wasting your time."

"Nonsense! We'll have you on your feet in no time." But John noticed the ring of uncertainty in his voice.

Doctor Villareal was fighting a hopeless case here, John thought. His body had broken out in a complete pattern of tiny sores and festering wounds; the most serious of these were on his left leg. Added to this was the persistent fever which burned relentlessly within him, sapping his strength and his vitality. He had been in Ubeda for two months, and he was no better now than on the day or his arrival; rather, he was much worse. How long can the human body sustain its life in the face of this disease which raged uncontrollably on? How much longer, John wondered, would he live?

The door squeaked open, and a lanky young friar came stealthily into the cell, closing the door softly behind him.

"Brother Bernard! How nice to see you," John said weakly from his bed.

"Shh! Father Francis might hear me in here."

"What if he does? You're the infirmarian, and your job is to visit the sick."

"Yes, but Father Francis just told me I was only to enter your cell to bring you your meals. He doesn't want anybody to visit you. What is he trying to do to you, Father?"

"Nothing, Brother. He's only an instrument the Blessed Mother is using."

"What does that mean?"

John smiled wanly. "It's a long story."

"I'm going to do something about all this," the young Carmelite said sternly.

"Now, Brother, I'm perfectly all right."

"No you're not. The prior has you in this old hole of a room; you're given plain ordinary food; and nobody is allowed to visit you. It's the same as being in prison."

Yes, John thought, it was the same as being in prison, almost the same as fourteen years ago in Toledo.

"I'm going to do something about this, I tell you," Bernard repeated.

Bernard, in the fiery indignation of his youth, penned an immediate note to Anthony in Granada who was the provincial of Andulusia and, therefore, the superior with jurisdiction in that area. He explained John's illness and the merciless treatment he was receiving from Francis. Anthony, who had not supported John at Madrid, supported him now: he hired a fast carriage and came charging into Duruelo in a rage of anger.

"Where is the prior of this place?" he demanded loudly at the front door of the monastery.

Francis made a sudden appearance, frightened and perplexed. "Here I am, Father. What's wrong?"

"That's what I'd like to know! What's wrong with you? Are you insane?"

Francis peered uncertainly over his hooked nose. "I'm afraid I don't understand."

"I guess you don't," Anthony said bitterly. "You've got one of the holiest men in Spain practically locked up like a criminal. Now, listen to me. I want you to treat Father John of the Cross with all the courtesy any sick friar deserves." Anthony paused, turning his last statement over in his mind. "No, I want you to treat him with the courtesy the *first* friar of the Reform deserves. I'll spell it out in detail for you later, but right now I want to see Father John."

Anthony was quickly ushered into John's cell, where the emaciated friar greeted him with a surprised joy.

"Anthony! What are you doing in Ubeda?"

"I'm here to correct a major injustice, to see that you get the proper attention."

"Don't worry about me; I'm getting along famously."

"You are? In this little dungeon?"

"Look, Anthony, I've only got a little time left. Why don't you leave things as they are."

"Save your breath. From now on things are going to be different."

John was immediately moved into a spacious room, where the

sunlight flooded in through two large windows; he was given a special diet for the sick; and the friars, released from Francis' restrictions, paid frequent visits to his cell.

"Why didn't you let me know about this?" Anthony asked John after he was in his new room. "There was no reason for you to take all this nonsense from that vengeful Francis."

"There was a reason, all right," John answered cryptically. He looked thin and wan in the big bed, only an emaciated vestige of his former self.

Anthony studied the lined, drawn face of the man who had inaugurated the Reform with him at Duruelo twenty-three years ago. He noted the labored breath, the glazed eyes, and he suddenly realized that John was correct, that he would not recover from this illness. Then the injustice of the entire situation tore viciously at his heart.

He said angrily: "You spend your whole life for the Reform, and now when you should be enjoying the reward of your labor, this Doria person comes along and sends you off in disgrace."

"But — " John protested.

"And if that wasn't bad enough," Anthony interrupted, slumping wearily into the chair beside John's bed, "this other fellow, James — the friar you reprimanded along with your Francis here — is going around trying to collect information that he can use in an attempt to discredit you further." Anthony shook his head sadly. "What a muddled situation: Doria in complete control; Francis persecuting you here; and James trying to defame you. I don't know what's going to happen to the Reform. I'm afraid it's going to collapse."

John smiled thinly. "No, the Reform won't collapse. It's going to be all right."

"How can you say that? Doria is destroying everything that Teresa, you, and I started."

John looked up at the perturbed face of the kindly old friar with whom he had been associated for over two decades and, with a new awareness, realized his affection and his respect for the man. John wondered if he should tell Anthony the reason underlying his sanguine hopes for the Reform. It might appear boastful, but then Anthony was in such a state of discouragement. . . .

"Do you remember how bad things looked fifteen years ago when Gratian had so antagonized the Calced?" he asked.

"Indeed, I do," Anthony answered.

"And do you remember what happened?"

"Of course I do: you were thrown in jail."

"Yes, I was thrown in jail, but after I escaped, the Blessed Virgin took matters in her own hands. She solved all the problems, and the Reform was saved from any more exterior trouble."

"But that was fifteen years ago, and we have new problems now, internal ones."

"Wait a minute; let me finish," John said. He had propped himself up on his elbows, and was looking directly into Anthony's lined, old face. "When I was in jail, the Blessed Virgin appeared to me; and her appearance was the heralding of victory for the Reform. The same thing has happened here in Ubeda: the Blessed Virgin has appeared to me again; and again, I'm sure, that her presence is the sign of ultimate success for the Reform." He slumped back on the pillow, exhausted from the expenditure of energy.

Anthony stared at the drawn countenance of his friend. It was not at all surprising to Anthony that the Blessed Mother had appeared to John in Toledo, or Ubeda, or anywhere else, for that matter. But did Mary's new apparition really signify the happy conclusion of all the Reform's problems? Freeing John from prison was one thing; but this nasty business of a firmly entrenched superior was something entirely different. Anthony wondered; and he hoped that John was right.

"You really feel, then, that our problems are over?" he asked hesitatingly.

John nodded his head almost imperceptibly. "I not only feel that they're over; I *know* that they're over. We've passed our darkest hour."

Anthony appeared unconvinced. "And what about you? When

the Blessed Virgin appeared in the prison cell in Toledo it was a sign that you yourself were to be freed. Does this new vision mean that she'll free you now?"

"Oh, yes! Mary will free me now just as she did at Toledo."

"Splendid! That means she'll make you well again."

"No, she won't liberate me that way. . . . She'll free me from this whole encounter."

Anthony nodded his head sadly.

The first glimmering of the new dawn John had predicted for the Reform came about a week later. He was lying in bed, fingering the rosary beads he thumbed incessantly throughout his long day, when he heard a soft knock on the door. It was the prior, Father Francis.

"Are you awake, Father John?"

"Yes, Father. Come in."

Francis, an embarrassed look on his face, stood awkardly beside the bed. "I don't know how to say this. . . . I've treated you miserably. I've behaved like a child. I'm sorry for —"

"Please don't, Father," John interrupted. "It's all right, it's all right. We all make mistakes."

Francis slumped to his knees, laying his forehead on the edge of the bed; his voice came in sobs. "But not like this. You've done *nothing* to deserve the treatment I gave you. May God forgive me."

John stretched out his hand, and patted him gently on the shoulder.

When Francis had gone, John lay motionless in the bed, staring up at the ceiling. He was glad that Francis had apologized, for it meant that he had cut that blind hate out of his heart. It was peculiar, John thought, that a lack of charity was *the* vice of people who otherwise lead good lives.

But Francis' apology meant something else, too. John was sure that it was the first step the Blessed Virgin was taking to right things, that it was the beginning of a new promise for the Reform.

However, Francis' capitulation was the only sign of the readjustment John was to see. His disease — the fever and the spreading infection — continued its relentless conquest. His body became entirely covered with the festering sores, and Doctor Villareal was helpless to halt their progress. The friars at Ubeda were forced to the painful conclusion that Father John of the Cross had not long to live.

The first two weeks of December witnessed a rapid worsening in John's condition. On the night of December fourteenth, it became evident that the end was in sight, and at about eleven-thirty in the evening the entire community was summoned to the sick friar's cell, where they joined in the prayers for the dying.

John glanced around the room through his glazed eyes, seeing Anthony, Francis, Bernard, and the other friars. But he gave them only a passing look, closing his eyes again in prayer. This was the hour of his passing, the hour that every living creature had to endure, and he refused to spend it looking back on the people and the places he was leaving; rather, he looked forward to paradise, to meeting Christ, to meeting the Blessed Virgin. Gone was his preoccupation with the work of the Reform; gone was his concern over the damage Doria was wreaking on the work of his life. He had done all he could — the rest was in God's hands.

Soon he would be in the triumphant company of the saints, but now he was alone, moving helplessly toward the precipice. He imagined that this must have been how Christ felt hanging on the cross those last few minutes. The thought of Christ buoyed him up, and the words of the dying Saviour crashed vividly into his mind. He opened his phlegm-covered lips and spoke them:

"Into Thy hands, O Lord, I commend my spirit."

His body jerked convulsively, and his head twisted queerly to one side.

His encounter was over.

$\left[\text{ Epilogue }\right]$

(Incident at Granada, Spain: August 13, 1600)

ANTHONY began to squirm in his chair. The pillows that were stuffed in against his back had slipped down, and were now wedged in an uncomfortable lump at the base of his spine. He tugged at one of the pillows and threw it angrily on the floor. His helplessness infuriated him. Why did anyone ever live to be ninety years of age? A man felt like a useless relic from a past generation, something that had been left mistakenly behind.

From his immobile position in the chair, he squinted out through the open window with his feeble eyes. The endless tide of human life was surging by: women in their delicately spun *mantillas*, gentlemen wearing grandiose *chambergos* on their heads, peasants with richly colored blankets thrown over their shoulders, a few children in patched garments, and the ever present soldiers, magnificent and gleaming in their highly polished armor. Anthony looked at them — citizens of the seventeenth century, a new century, a century to which he didn't belong. And yet, they were the same people he had seen for the past ninety years in Spain — ah, their faces were different, but essentially they were the same people with the same human nature, the same weaknesses, the same strength.

He turned his head away from the window and swept a glance around the small room he occupied in the monastery. It was a splendid — how John had laughed when he had used that word — room, one quite suitable for an old friar to die in. He had no complaints: all the friars in the monastery at Granada were kind

218

and generous to him. They sent someone in the morning to get him up, someone to feed him, someone to visit him, someone to put him to bed again in the evening. They were kind, but their kindness incensed him — or rather, his need for their kindness incensed him. No, it wasn't right for a man to live so long.

A timid knock sounded on the door.

"Come in!"

Nothing happened, so Anthony repeated his invitation, but more truculently this time. "Come in, I'm not going to carry you in." There now, he shouldn't have said that. That was one of the difficulties of being an old man: he found himself becoming cantakerous.

A young friar entered the room hesitatingly. "Could I see you for a few minutes, Father Anthony?"

"Why, of course. Come in and sit down." He inserted a note of pleasantness in his voice. "What can I do for you?"

The young friar nervously seated himself on a chair close to Anthony. "My name is Brother Basil. I'm one of the new novices — "

"I can see that you're new, all right. How old are you?"

"Eighteen, Father."

"Eighteen!" Anthony boomed. "Why, you've just been born, you're hardly alive. Let's see . . . eighteen . . that means you were born in 1582. I was an old man *then* — seventy-two."

"Yes, Father," Basil said politely. This wasn't going too well; he had been told that Father Anthony talked a lot about his age, and if allowed to go on, could consume an hour discussing the difficulties of senectitude. "The novice master said I could ask you some questions about this book."

He held up an elaborate leather volume, which Anthony peered at uncertainly.

"What's that?"

It's a new copy of *Ascent of Mount Carmel,* by Father John of the Cross. The novice master said that you — "

"Bah! That book! It's causing the death of John all over again."

"I'm afraid I don't understand."

"Fetch that pillow on the floor and stuff it behind my back, and I'll tell you all about it."

The young friar scooped up the pillow and placed it gingerly behind the back of the hawk-faced old friar. Anthony wiggled his back, settling the pillow in place.

"That book — and the others John of the Cross wrote — are causing people to forget all about the man himself and what he did. People are saying: 'John of the Cross wrote this' or 'John of the Cross wrote that.' I'm very much afraid that John is going to be one of those unfortunate people who are completely hidden behind the books they wrote. . . . For instance, tell me what you know about John of the Cross."

Brother Basil wet his lips. "Well, he was the first friar to join the Reform, he lived a saintly life, spent much time writing treatises on the spiritual life, and died in Ubeda nine years ago."

"See, see!" Anthony exclaimed excitedly, pointing his long bony finger at the young novice, "That's what I mean: you don't know anything about John of the Cross, the real John of the Cross. Now you put your precious book down on the table, and I'll tell you about John of the Cross — the real story of the man."

Obediently, the friar placed his volume on a small dark table, and turned back to this strange, but fascinating old man.

"You see," Anthony began, "many years ago Mother Teresa had an idea to found an order of friars who would be, like the nuns, contemplatives, but who would also engage in some apostolic work. . . . You've heard of Mother Teresa?"

"Yes, yes, of course," Basil stammered.

"Splendid! At least they teach you something about the Order anyway," Anthony said dryly. "Well, Teresa got John and myself to start the first monastery in Duruelo. We did wonderfully: we received a lot of vocations, and we added a number of new monasteries. Things were going magnificently until Father Jerome Gratian — he was a young chap of exceptional ability — inveigled some vague assignment out of a few papal delegates which made him sort of superior-general of the new Reform. Then the trouble started: we were still under the jurisdiction of the Calced, but old Gratian, acting with his new faculties, began to operate without consulting the Calced superiors. He was probably technically correct, but that didn't help matters any — the Calced became infuriated and wanted to suppress the Reform."

"I never heard about that," Basil said.

"You haven't heard the best of it yet. The Calced wanted to suppress us — so they grabbed John of the Cross, charged him with being a recalcitrant friar, and locked him up in the monastery of Toledo. He suffered for eight months in their abominable jail until the Blessed Virgin came and got him out. Well, that did it: the opposition of the Calced was broken, and the continuance of the Reform was assured." Anthony beamed toward the young novice. "But it was John who was the scapegoat; it was he, by his prayers and suffering, who did the trick."

"That's wonderful," the young friar said enthusiastically. "John of the Cross was a real virile character, then?"

"He certainly was. But that's only part of the story. . . . You've heard of Father Nicholas Doria, haven't you?"

"He was the superior-general who died about seven years ago?"

"That's him, all right. After John got out of prison, this Doria person came on the scene and catapulted himself into power in the Reform. Everything was in good shape until he came along. He thought that the Reform was his own personal property and that he was God's gift to the Church. The man was an absolute rigorist, he destroyed all opposition to himself, and established a reign of fear in the Reform. Doria, by his ruthless handling of the men, almost destroyed the Reform from within. Then John of the Cross stepped into action again."

"What did he do?" Basil asked.

"The same thing he did in Toledo: he was a *victim* for the Reform again," Anthony said triumphantly. "He spoke out against Doria in our elections back in '91, and Doria exiled him to a distant monastery called La Penuela. Then the Blessed Virgin began to use him as a victim: he became critically ill with an ulcer which broke out all over his body; he was given cruel treatment by the prior of the monastery where he went for medical aid; and he died an obscure death in Ubeda."

"But . . . but what did that accomplish?"

"Oh, my," Anthony said in exasperation. "That accomplished everything! As soon as John of the Cross died, things began to happen. First, the Reform was given permanent status as an independent order with full rights in the Church, just like the Dominicans and Franciscans. That was the last step of the process which was begun back at the first elections in '81. *Then,* in 1594 Doria dropped dead while on his way to our elections; and James, a scoundrel of a friar who was trying to defame John, died the same year, as well as Francis, the prior of Ubeda. And they were all young men. Within three years after John's death, the Order was irrevocably established and all the troublemakers were dead. That's what John of the Cross did."

"It's an amazing story," Basil said wonderingly. "Is it all true?"

"Of course it's true," Anthony thundered. "And that's the real story of John of the Cross, the story that's being forgotten."

"Well, I won't forget it," Basil said, an intense look on his young face.

"I hope you don't. The Reform is a large healthy Order today, and we're able to lead the contemplative life in peace. But I doubt if we'd even be here except for John. You know," Anthony said, smiling, "some men work for a cause by administration or organizing and all that. But some work for a cause by suffering for it and praying for it. John of the Cross did that for the Reform: he suffered for it, he was a victim for it." Anthony leaned forward and tapped the young brother's knee. "And he did his work well."

"I certainly appreciate your telling me all this," Basil said. "It will help me a lot when I read John of the Cross's writings. Thanks for giving me all this time."

"Oh, don't thank me. We old fellows like to talk about the past. You did me a favor by listening. . . . And don't forget to take your book."

The young novice grasped the book, looking at it with a new admiration, and walked softly out of the room.

Anthony tugged the pillow out from behind his back — it had slipped down again — and threw it once more on the floor. How much longer was he going to endure this invalidism?

He glanced out the window: the tide of life — people, carriages, animals — still paraded on. Anthony stared vacantly through the window, but his thoughts were not on these citizens of the new century. He was thinking back through the years of the little friar with the large oval head, of the man who lived with him at Duruelo, of the prisoner at Toledo, of the dying friar at Ubeda.

They were an old man's thoughts, an old man's dreams. But they were comforting thoughts.

⌠ Historical Footnote ⌡

THE principal scenes in this book represent factual history, although a number of the minor scenes are purely fictional, contrived to bind together some of the main events, or demonstrate some facet of the protagonist's character. The principal characters in the book, too, are historical, but the author must admit to creating some of the minor characters from his own imagination — for example, Philip Balthasar, the merchant. Only one of the principal characters can be classified as fictional: Father Peter Orozco, the protagonist's Calced Carmelite companion. The chronicles of St. John's life inform us of a Carmelite priest named Peter Orozco, who was a fellow student with St. John at Salamanca, and made the return journey to Medina del Campo with him; but over and above that, the author has invented Peter's character traits, his activities, and his demise.

St. John of the Cross was beatified in 1675, canonized in 1726, and declared a Doctor of the Church in 1926.